The Music Master

Charles Klein

Contents

Chapter One 7

Chapter Two..16

Chapter Three 20

Chapter Four 24

Chapter Five 32

Chapter Six 39

Chapter Seven 46

Chapter Eight 51

Chapter Nine 59

Chapter Ten...66

Chapter Eleven...74

Chapter Twelve...84

Chapter Thirteen 97

Chapter Fourteen 106

Chapter Fifteen 116

Chapter Sixteen...124

Chapter Seventeen 135

Chapter Eighteen 143

Chapter Nineteen...151

Chapter Twenty 160

Chapter Twenty-one 174

Chapter Twenty-two 188

Chapter Twenty-three..201

Chapter Twenty-four...210

Chapter Twenty-five 221

THE MUSIC MASTER

BY

Charles Klein

THIS BOOK IS DEDICATED
TO
David Warfield, Artist
BY THE AUTHOR

Chapter One

Anton Von Barwig rapped on the conductor's desk for silence and laid down his baton. The hundred men constituting the Leipsic Philharmonic Orchestra stopped playing as if by magic, and those who looked up from their music saw in their leader's face, for the first time in their three years' experience under his direction, a pained expression of helplessness.

"Either I can't hear you this morning, or the first violins are late in attacking and the wood wind drags--drags--drags."

"What's the matter? We've played this a hundred times," growled Karlschmidt, the bass clarinet player, to Poons, the Dutch horn soloist, who sat at the desk next to him.

Karlschmidt was a socialist, a student of Karl Marx, and took more interest in communism than in his allotted share of the score of Isolde's **Liebestodt**. Indeed, nearly all the men were interested in something other than the occupation which afforded them a living. For them the pleasure of music had died in the business of attaining accuracy.

"What did he say?" asked Poons, losing Von Barwig's next remark in trying to hear what Karlschmidt was mumbling.

"He said it's his own fault," whispered the second flute.

"He's quite right," assented Karlschmidt.

"Hush, hush!" came from one or two others. Von Barwig was addressing the men again, and they wanted to hear.

"Let's play; cut the speeches out," growled Karlschmidt. "For God's sake, what's he saying now?"

"Damn it! How can we hear when you won't keep quiet?" blurted a Germanised Englishman who had an engagement at the old Rathaus and wanted to get away.

"We're dismissed," said Poons, who couldn't hear. But the men at the violin desks down front were rising and putting away their instruments, and the others were slowly following their example.

Karlschmidt's face expanded into a smile; the prospect of avoiding the unpleasant grind of rehearsal had restored him to good humour. The lines of men were now breaking up into knots; bows were being loosened, violins put into cases and brass instruments into bags, while laughing and chatting became general. Poons looked at Von Barwig, who still stood on the small dais, staring out into space, and he saw that something was the matter. He loved Von Barwig; for years before, when hard times had sent him over the border from Amsterdam toward the German music centres, Von Barwig had extended him a helping hand, indeed had almost kept him from starving until he got an engagement in one of the minor Dresden theatres; Poons was grateful; and gratitude is a form of love that lies deeper than mere sympathy.

"Can I do something for you, Anton?" he asked a few moments later, as he stood at the conductor's desk. Von Barwig did not answer; and with his round face, and smiling eyes glancing appealingly at his conductor, Poons stood waiting like a little dog that patiently wags his tall in hope of his master's recognition. Presently he shook his head gravely and sighed. Surely something was wrong, for Anton was not himself. Never before had he stopped rehearsal and dismissed his men on the morning preceding a concert night, and, moreover, the night of the first performance of a new symphony--Von Barwig's own work.

The men were rapidly disappearing, and the Gewandhaus concert platform was almost empty. Von Barwig seemed deeply interested in watching his men carry off their instruments, and yet, when Poons looked closely into his face, he knew that the leader did not see that which he was apparently watching so closely.

"Shall I wait for you, Anton?" ventured Poons finally. As if to remind Von Barwig of his presence, he touched him gently on the arm. Von Barwig started. A look of recognition came into his eye, and with it a smile that metamorphosed his homely, almost ugly face into something beyond mere beauty; a smile that transformed a somewhat commonplace personality into an appealing and compelling individuality. There is no need to describe the delicate, sensitive, rugged countenance, which, when he smiled, radiated love and sympathy for his fellow-beings and made him what is ordinarily described as magnetic.

Poons caught this smile, and his own broad grin deepened as he recognised his old friend again.

"Come, let's go," Von Barwig said briefly; and without another word they walked out of the Gewandhaus. They passed the statue of Mendelssohn erected in front of the building, walking down the August Platz as far as the University. Poons noticed that unusual things were happening that morning. First, his friend was walking rapidly, so rapidly that he himself almost had to trot to keep up with him; second, he was muttering to himself, a most unusual thing for Von Barwig to do; third, every now and then a look of intense hatred beclouded his face; and last, he was not talking over the events of the morning with his friend. Furthermore, so engrossed was Von Barwig in his own thoughts that he passed Schumann's monument without lifting his hat, and Bismarck's monument without shaking his fist; and these two things Von Barwig had done, day in and day out, ever since Poons had known him. Finally, when at the Thomas Kirche Poons ventured to ask, "Where are we going?" Von Barwig stopped short in the middle of the street he was crossing.

"That's it, that's it!" he said excitedly; "where am I going? Where am I going?" and he looked at Poons as if he expected that his frightened friend would answer his question.

Poons took his friend's arm and pushed him out of the road on to the pavement just in time to save him from being grazed by a cab which rapidly whisked by them. Then he stopped and laid his hand on Von Barwig's shoulder.

"What's the matter, Anton?" he said soothingly. "Can't you tell me? In God's name, what has happened?"

Anton looked at Poons. The unexpected had happened; his devoted follower had dared to question him. The shock almost awoke him to a sense of his surroundings, and the ghost of his old smile stole over his face as he shook his head slowly.

"That's it!" he gasped. "I don't know! I don't know! It's the uncertainty that is killing me. By God, August, I'll kill him! I'll kill him!" And then Poons understood.

They walked on in silence, whither neither of them knew. It was now Poons's turn to walk faster than his companion and to mutter to himself. His face had lost its grin, and he was no longer conscious of his immediate surroundings. After they had passed Auerbach's cellar he could contain himself no longer, and an explosion took place. He stopped Von Barwig in the middle of the pavement, grabbing him by the arm, and in a hoarse, gutteral voice, choked with emotion, shouted, "Anton! Anton!"

Von Barwig looked at his friend in mute surprise. Poons, oblivious of the by-standers--who were looking to see why a man should shout so unnecessarily--went on:

"By God, Anton, I kill him, too!"

This appealed to Von Barwig's sense of humour, and he burst Into laughter, a laughter perilously near to tears. It never occurred to him to ask Poons what he knew or what he had heard. The fact that what was preying on his mind, his care-fully guarded secret, was common property did not strike him at that moment. He merely thought that his friend was agreeing with him in the sentiment of killing "some one" as he agreed with him in all matters of music, philosophy and art. In Anton Von Barwig's condition of mind at that moment, had it occurred to him that Poons knew the awful fact that was confronting him, he would have taken him by the throat and then and there compelled him to confess what he knew or thought he knew; but he walked on in silence, followed by his devoted friend.

They turned up a small side street of the August Platz and stopped in front of the house where Anton Von Barwig lived. It was the centre of a row of large mod-ern apartment houses where lived for the most part the art world of Leipsic, and this world included beside the rich, professional element, the wealthy publishers, of whom in this important centre of Germany there were a large number. As Von Barwig stood waiting for Poons to enter with him, he noticed Poons's outstretched hand.

"Aren't you coming in?" he asked. Poons shook his head.

"I'd better not," he said simply.

"Why not?" asked Von Barwig.

"Because," Poons faltered. He did not want to tell his friend that at such times as these it is better for a man to be alone with his thoughts.

"Why not?" cried Von Barwig; but Poons did not speak. He stood like some dumb animal awaiting his master's lash; and then Von Barwig knew that Poons knew.

"Come!" said Von Barwig in a low, hard voice, with such firmness and determination that Poons, in spite of himself, was compelled to go forward. Silently they walked up three flights, neither of them noticing the salute of the porter as they passed him. Anton took out his keys and opened a door which led into a magnificently furnished musical studio, the largest apartment in Koenigs Strasse. It was here that he and Madam Elene Von Barwig, his wife, held their musical receptions and entertained the great German and foreign artists that came to Leipsic. These receptions were famous affairs, and invitations were eagerly sought, not only by musical celebrities, but by such of the nobility as happened to be in town. Members of the royal family had been known to grace more than one of these affairs; for though a conductor of the Leipsic Philharmonic is not necessarily a rich man, his social position is unquestioned.

Perhaps some such fleeting thoughts as these--glimpses into the past like those of a drowning man--came into Anton Von Barwig's consciousness as he stepped quietly to the door leading from the reception-room and studio and passed into the corridor toward the living apartments. He listened intently; but hearing nothing, closed the door quietly, and somewhat to Poons's alarm turned the key in the lock.

"Now tell me," he demanded, in a voice that was as strange as it was determined; "what do you know? Sit down." This last was a direct command.

Poons felt that nothing was to be gained by silence. He had, so to speak, put his foot in it by allowing himself, through sympathy in his friend's affairs, to betray the fact that he knew what was troubling him. He felt, therefore, that by making a clean breast of it, he might not only mitigate Von Barwig's sufferings but enable him to see what the world, or at least the world of Leipsic, had seen for some time.

Poons was not a rapid thinker, but these thoughts flashed through his mind in less time than it took him to obey Von Barwig. He sat down in the chair indicated by his friend and tried to collect his thoughts.

"What do you know?" repeated Von Barwig. Poons moistened his lips with his tongue, as if to enable him to speak; but words would not come. He loved Anton; he knew that what he had to say would make him suffer; and that he could not bear to see. He tried to speak, faltered "I cannot, I cannot!" and burst into tears. Von Barwig walked up to the window and gazed steadily into the street.

"It's more serious than I thought," he said after a few moments' pause, giving Poons time to recover in some slight degree from his emotion. "It is serious, eh?"

"Yes," assented Poons, relieved that Anton's question required only a monosyllable for an answer.

"Very serious, eh?" asked Von Barwig, steeling himself for the answer he expected.

"Yes, I think so," nodded Poons, gulping down a sob.

"The worst, eh?"

"God, you know what scandal-mongers are; what people say--when they do say--how they talk! They have no mercy, no brains, no sense! What is a woman's reputation to them? They repeat, they--they--the wretches--the murderers--" Poons seemed to be trying to shift the blame on a number of people; it was easier for him to generalise at this moment than to answer his questioner straightforwardly.

"Do they say that my wife--that Madam Von Barwig neglects her home?"

"Yes."

"And her child?"

"No, no!" eagerly interrupted Poons, quite joyous at being able to deny something at last.

"Do they say that she--neglects me, that she doesn't care for me, that--" Von Barwig spoke now with an effort; "that she no longer loves me?"

Poons nodded affirmatively. He was summoning up all his courage for the question that he knew was coming; and it came.

"Do they say, do they mention--his name?"

Poons again nodded affirmatively.

"Ahlmann?"

"Yes."

Von Barwig held his breath for a moment; then literally heaved a sigh. What he most feared had indeed come upon him. The world knew; his heart was on his sleeve for daws to peck at.

"How long have you known this?"

Poons hung his head, he could not answer. He was longing to throw his arms around his friend's neck and cry on his shoulder; and he could think of nothing to say but "Poor Anton! Poor Anton!"

"Don't pity me, damn you! don't pity me!" burst out Von Barwig. "And don't sit there bleating like a lost sheep of Israel! I'm not a woman--tears are no panacea for suffering like mine. Put the world back five years, restore for me the past few months; then I could live life over again, then I could see and know and act differently. Don't sit there like a wailing widow, moaning and moping over other people's miseries! That isn't sympathy, that's weakness! If you want to help me, tell me to be a man, to face my troubles like a man; don't cry like a baby!"

"That's right," assented Poons, "go on; it does you good. Give it to me, I deserve it!"

"Poor old Poons, you do your best! Ah, your love does me good, old friend; but there's hell to face! She threatens to leave me, to leave me because I refused to allow him to come here. I've warned him! And if he shows his face in Leipsic again, I'll kill him! Look!" Von Barwig felt in his inner pocket. "Now you can understand why I couldn't hold the men together at rehearsal this morning. My mind was with her, with him. Ha! the mother of my little girl, my little Helene! That's the pity of it, Poons, that's the pity of it!" and now it was Von Barwig's turn to show weakness. "That's what I can't understand. A woman's love for a man, yes, it can go here, there, anywhere; but the mother instinct, how can that change?"

"Doesn't she love her little girl any more?" asked Poons in simple astonishment.

"She loves *him*," said Anton. "Can there be room for the mother love with such love as he inspires?"

He looked at the letter in his hand and passed it to Poons. "This morning, just as I was leaving for rehearsal, the servant handed me this. My little girl is all I have left now." His voice choked with emotion as he turned once more toward the window.

At the sight of his friend's suffering Poons could no longer contain himself, and he fairly blubbered as he read the following:

"DEAR ANTON: Henry Ahlmann is in Leipsic and I have seen him. I cannot live a lie, so I am going away with him. Believe me, it is better so; I feel that you can never forgive me and that we can never again be happy together. Kiss my darling Helene for me, and oh, Anton, don't tell the little one her unhappy mother's miserable history until she is old enough to understand!

"ELENE VON BARWIG."

"Well, that's conclusive, isn't it?" asked Von Barwig grimly as soon as Poons finished reading.

Poons's voice failed him. Hot, scalding tears were fairly raining down his cheeks as the letter fell out of his trembling hands and fluttered to the floor.

"Well, what's to be done; what's to be done?"

"Then she has gone?"

Von Barwig nodded. "I suppose so! I don't know, I can't tell," he said helplessly. "I didn't try to stop her," he went on after a pause. "What's the use, to what end? Oh, I don't want the entire blame to rest on her shoulders! A beautiful woman, twenty-five years of age, a pampered, petted, spoiled child, craving constant excitement; and he, a handsome, young American, rich and romantic. I, as you know, am a mature man of forty, devoted to an art in which she takes little interest. I introduced them. Ha! that's the irony of it! I brought them together, I left them together, I--it's my fault, Poons--my fault! I neglected her for my work. With me, all was music: the compositions, the rehearsal, the concert, the pupil, the conservatory, the opera, the singer, the player. He used to take her to my concerts; and I,--fool, fool--encouraged him, for it gave me more time to devote to my art. An artist is a selfish dog! He must be, or there is no art. What could I expect? I am fifteen years older than she; ugly----"

"No, no!" blurted out Poons.

"Misshapen, undersized----"

"No, no!"

"My friend can lie, but my looking-glass doesn't. I know, I know! God, how will it all end? How will it all end?"

At this point the door shook a little as though some one were trying to get in.

"She's come back!" almost gasped Anton, and walking firmly to the door, he unlocked and opened it. As he did so, a little fairy creature between three and four years of age, with golden, flaxen curls and blue eyes, bounded into the room, calling out, "Papa! Papa! Where is oo? Where is oo?"

Von Barwig was on his knees in a moment, and the child threw her left arm around his neck and hugged him so tightly that the little doll she held in her right hand was almost crushed between them.

"Helene, Helene! my poor, motherless little baby!" And then for the first time

Von Barwig gave way to tears.

"We are alone, alone, alone! Oh, God! Oh, God!" he sobbed as he rocked from side to side in his agony. Poons crept softly out of the room and closed the door gently after him.

Chapter Two

It was past seven o'clock that evening when Poons returned to Von Barwig's apartment on his way to the Gewandhaus concert. His old overcoat buttoned tightly over his well-worn dress suit covered a palpitating heart; for Poons was afraid. A few minutes before, when he had kissed his motherly wife good-bye and told her to take good, extra good care of their little son August, she had noticed that his hand was trembling. And when he tried to account for his nervous condition by reminding her that Anton Von Barwig's new symphony was to be played that night and that a member of the Royal family was to be present on the occasion, she had shaken her head gravely, accusing him of being a foolish, timid old boy. It needed all the courage he could muster up to enable him to ring the door-bell of Von Barwig's dwelling. There was such a death-like stillness that Poons thought for a moment no one was there; he dreaded he knew not what. As he stood listening to the silence, he thought he heard a child's laughter, and he sighed in relief. The servant came to the door, a sleepy-eyed German **maedchen** as strong as an ox and nearly as stupid. "Oh, it's Herr Poons," she said. "Come in. I tell Herr Von Barwig----"

"Is he--is he? *How* is he?" faltered Poons, much relieved that the girl showed no evidence of acquaintance with the real condition of her master's mind.

"I tell him," repeated the girl stolidly, without answering his question.

Closing the hall door, she ushered him into the studio and left him standing there. Poons looked at his watch; it was a quarter past seven. He still had fifteen minutes to spare before the concert engagement, which began at eight o'clock, called him to the Gewandhaus.

While he was wondering what he could say to his friend, the servant opened the door leading to the living apartments of the family and intimated that he should come in. Poons passed through a magnificently furnished drawing-room and library, and thence into the dining-room.

"This way," said the girl, opening the dining-room door, beyond which was a passage leading to the kitchen and bedrooms. Poons looked surprised, and the girl hastened to say:

"Herr Von Barwig is in the nursery."

"Ah, of course," nodded Poons, as he followed her.

Not very observant usually, Poons noticed that the dinner table was set for two persons. Both places were undisturbed and the food was untouched.

"He has not eaten," thought Poons. "Of course she is not here! Oh, God! that is the tragedy of it! The empty chair, always the empty chair--it is like death!"

As the nursery door opened Poons heard the sound of voices and laughter and, to his utter astonishment, saw his friend Von Barwig on the floor playing with little Helene's dolls' house. Helene was shrieking with childish laughter because Von Barwig pretended to be angry with one of her dolls which would not eat the cake he tried to make it swallow.

As Von Barwig saw his friend, a look of intense pain crossed his face, but he forced himself to smile and say:

"Come in, Herr Doctor Poons, and mend this little girl's eye. See, I've given her cake to eat, but it won't do her eye any good!"

Helene laughed gleefully at the idea of cake being good for a broken eye.

"Good gracious, how did the eye fall out?" said Dr. Poons, shaking his head gravely.

"She fell down and I kicked it," lisped the little one. "I kicked it," she laughed, unconscious that she had committed an unprovoked assault on her plaything. "Mend it; oh, please mend it!"

Poons shook his head gravely. The child mistook this for a confession of his inability to do what she wished.

"Mamma 'll fix it when she comes home. She won't be long, will she?" said the child, somewhat tearfully. She had asked the question many times, and her father seemed unable to answer her.

"I am trying to make her forget," said Anton savagely to Poons, in answer to his look of painful inquiry. "She must forget soon; I've been with her ever since you left me this morning." His arm stole around the child's neck, and drawing her to him gently, he kissed her again and again with such sad, lingering tenderness that the ever-ready tears welled up into Poons's eyes, and he turned his head to conceal them. The child struggled to free herself.

"Papa so rough, eh? Well, he won't be, or Herr Poons will beat him, eh?"

"Surely," assented Poons.

"Papa will be so gentle and so kind," went on Von Barwig tenderly. "He'll love his little girl as no little girl in this wide, wide world was ever loved before, eh?"

Little Helene did not understand, and as she had nothing at this precise moment to occupy her attention, she answered him by asking the one question that absorbed her mind, "Where's mamma?"

Von Barwig and Poons looked at each other helplessly. Apart from the tragedy of two men trying to comfort a little child that had lost its parent, there remained in Von Barwig's mind a sense of the utter inability of the masculine individuality to fill the place of mother in the child's heart. In after years, Von Barwig always remembered the sinking sensation he felt when this fact came home to him in full force.

"Well, one thing," said Anton, as he swallowed something that came in his throat and threatened to choke him, "one thing, she was kind to the little one; the was a kind mother, eh?"

"Kind? kind?" began Poons fiercely. "Is it kind to----"

Von Barwig silenced him with a look.

"Yes, she was a good mother," he admitted conciliatingly. "But, by God, if we don't go we shall be late! Phew!" he whistled as he looked at his watch, "half past seven." Von Barwig sat still for a moment.

"Half past seven? Yes." Then, as if it were slowly dawning upon him that he had duties, he arose, dusting his knees mechanically.

"Half past seven, yes. It begins at eight, eh? and I must dress. Yes, I suppose I must dress!"

The little girl was now putting her dolls back into the dolls' house; the doorway was blocked up and she was pushing one through a broken window in the little house as Von Barwig caught her in his arms and caressed her.

"How can I leave her? Good God, how can I leave her?" he groaned. He stroked her face, her hair, and kissed her again and again.

"She's all I have, all; she's all I want. I won't go to-night, I won't leave her, do you hear? Let Ruhlmeyer conduct to-night. I can't go, I can't leave her alone! Suppose something were to happen to her?"

"But you must go!" said Poons firmly; desperation had given him courage. "You must go!"

Von Barwig looked at him in surprise; Poons's tone sobered him a little.

"For her sake you must work," went on Poons, gaining courage as he saw that his words had an effect on his friend.

"Yes, I must work," assented Von Barwig, feeling the force of Poons's words. "Shall I go, little Helene, my little darling? Shall I go?"

"Yes, go and tell mamma to come," was the little one's reply.

"Come, hurry, Anton! You must dress, you have barely five minutes: five to dress, ten to get to the Gewandhaus."

"Ha! they can wait!" said Von Barwig grimly. "Prince Mecklenburg Strelitz, the Kaiser, all Germany can wait, while I mend the strings of my heart!"

The nurse-maid came in and suggested that it was time to put little *Fraeulein* to bed. Poons looked at her closely; her eyelids were red, for she had been crying.

"Take good care of the little *Fraeulein*," said Von Barwig as he handed her over to the maid. It was long past her bedtime, and the little child had almost fallen asleep in her father's arms.

"Let me kiss her just once more; I won't wake her up!"

The girl burst into tears as Von Barwig bent over the child, kissing her tenderly; then she hurried into the next room with her precious charge.

"She knows?" inquired Poons.

"Yes," nodded Von Barwig; and then, with a sigh, "She knows."

Five minutes later, Von Barwig, accompanied by Poons, left the house and hurriedly took a cab to the concert hall.

Chapter Three

It was noticed by more than one member of the Leipsic Philharmonic Orchestra that Herr Director Von Barwig was in unusually high spirits that evening. Many attributed it to the fact that he was nervous because of the first production of his new symphony. Karlschmidt hinted to his deskmate that Von Barwig was nervous and was trying to conceal it by pretending to be delighted with everything and everybody. This was probably true in a measure; at all events, when he came into the artists' room at the Gewandhaus at about five minutes to eight, he shook hands with everybody, joked with his men, and talked almost incessantly, as if he wanted to keep at high pressure. Poons watched him closely. Von Barwig was unusually pale, and as he slapped his concert meister on the back Poons noticed that, though his face wore a smile, his lips quivered.

"For heaven's sake," he heard him say to the leader of the second violins, "don't play the *pizzicato* in the third movement as if you were picking up eggs!" Poons rejoiced that his friend could forget so easily.

It was, however, when Von Barwig walked out on the platform to the dais, bowed to the immense audience, and turned to his men, that the deadly pallor of his face was most apparent. Some of the audience noticed it as he acknowledged the applause he received. There was not a tremor of hand or muscle, not an undecided movement; merely a deadly pallor of countenance as if he no longer had blood in his veins, but ice. The men felt the absence of the compelling force that always emanated from him, that seemed to ooze from his baton; that psychic something that compelled the player to feel as his director felt--the force we call magnetism. The firmness of mouth showed that the determination to dominate was still there, but the absence of that mental power left only the automatic rhythm and swing, sans heart, sans soul, sans feeling. The beat was the beat of the finely trained academic conductor, but the genius of it was gone. The ghost of a departed Von Barwig was beating time for the Von Barwig that had lived and died that night.

Perhaps the audience did not feel this as much as the men did, for they applauded heartily at the end of the opening number. They did notice that Von Barwig did not acknowledge their applause and seemed to be oblivious of their presence. The fact that an ultra-fashionable audience was present, including a prince and princess of the Royal Family, and the *elite* of Leipsic, to say nothing of the American Ambassador, Mr. Cruger, apparently did not affect Von Barwig in the least. This appealed very much to the democratic instinct of Mr. Cruger, and at the end of the first part he asked his friend, Prince Holberg-Meckstein, to present him to the conductor.

"I will present him to *you*," said his highness, carefully readjusting the pronouns; and he sent for Von Barwig.

"A curious personality!" remarked Mr. Cruger to the prince as Von Barwig bowed himself out of the box a few minutes later.

"Yes, and a fine musician," said the prince. "But he's not at his best to-night."

As Von Barwig passed through the artists' room, Poons approached him. Anton motioned him away as if to say, "Don't speak to me," and Poons walked sadly away.

The second part of the programme was to begin with Von Barwig's latest work.

"Quick, put the score of the symphony on my desk," he said to the librarian, who happened to be passing at the moment. "I intended to conduct it from memory; but I have forgotten."

As the librarian placed the score on the conductor's desk, he thought it strange that a man who had been rehearsing from memory for weeks should so suddenly forget.

Von Barwig opened the score a few moments later, raised his baton, and the wood wind began the new work. He conducted as mechanically as before, for his dead heart could pump no enthusiasm into his work, and the audience suddenly felt a sense of disappointment. But after the first few passages had been played the leader lost his self-consciousness and forgot his surroundings. He began to feel the music, to compose it again, and the mechanism of the conductor was lost in the inspiration of the composer. It was a beautiful movement marked *andante sostenuto*--pathos itself, and Von Barwig drew from his men their very souls, forcing them in turn to draw out of their strings all the suffering he had been going through for the past few days. Then a curious psychic phenomenon took place. Von Barwig completely forgot himself, his audience, his orchestra; he was living in his music, and the music took him back to the precise moment of inspiration. Once more he was in his studio, seated at his work table, looking up from his score into the face of his beloved Elene. She was smiling at him, encouraging him to go on with his work, the work that she had prophesied would make him famous and her the happiest of women. This dream had almost the appearance of reality to Von Barwig. Indeed it was real, as real as reality itself, until the wild applause of an enthusiastic audience awoke him alike to the consciousness of the success of his work and the hopeless misery of his present position; his success in his music only accentuating the failure his life had become.

The playing of this movement made such an impression that Von Barwig was compelled again and again to acknowledge the plaudits of the audience. Indeed, they wanted him to repeat it, but this he steadfastly refused to do. There was a slight intermission between the playing of the first and the second parts of the symphony, and during this pause the librarian handed a note to Von Barwig, whispering to him, "You must read it. The woman is outside in hysterics."

"What woman?" demanded Von Barwig, his thoughts reverting to his wife.

Trembling and fearful of he knew not what the leader read the following hastily scrawled note:

"Come at once. The *Fraeulein* is gone. She has been stolen away. Please come. GRETCHEN."

Von Barwig crushed the note in his hand and looked about helplessly, almost lurching forward in his bewilderment.

"Helene stolen? What did it mean?" He could not understand.

He knew instinctively it was time to go on with the next movement, and that he must make an effort for the sake of others. Already there were signs of impatience in the great audience. Slowly he stepped upon the dais, steadying himself by means of the music-stand. He raised his baton, his men played the opening bars, and as they did so the full meaning of the awful news he had just read flashed upon him. He realised suddenly that his men were no longer with him; the first violin looked up at him panic stricken. He sawed the air wildly as he felt the great audience surging around him and his orchestra swaying to and fro. Then he reeled, stumbled, clutching at the music-stand for support; and fell face forward upon the floor.

*   *   *   *   *

Some six weeks later loving friends had gently nursed him back to life and reason. It was slow work, but Von Barwig weathered the point of death and sailed slowly into the harbour of life. As he grew stronger, he realised by degrees all that had happened. One day he called for his beloved Poons, but they did not dare to tell him that his faithful friend was dead; the shock of that night had brought on a stroke from which Poons never recovered. When they did tell him long afterward, he only smiled, shook his head sadly, and said, "Why not? All is gone! Why should my old friend remain to me?"

When Von Barwig was strong enough he took the train to Berlin and consulted with the police authorities in reference to the whereabouts of his lost wife and child; but they had left no trace behind them except an indication that they had passed through Paris on their way to some unknown destination. He called on Mr. Cruger, the American Ambassador, who could throw no light on the subject. A search of the steamship lists failed to reveal their whereabouts; and at last, though Anton Von Barwig felt that they were hopelessly lost to him, he returned to Leipsic, more than ever determined to find them. It was the only idea he had: to find them--to find them--to find them. His other thoughts were without stimulating power--irresolute, vague, uncertain. This one idea grew and grew until it became an obsession. He could no longer bear the sound of music; so it was no sacrifice to him to give up his profession. He hated the very streets he walked in, for had Elene not walked in them? He must find her; he must find his child. He could hear the little girl calling for him, he kept telling himself. It was his only duty, his only object and mission in life; so it became an ideal, a religion. But where to go, where to go? Finally, he made up his mind to leave Leipsic for Paris and start from there. One day, after living in Paris for some months, the idea occurred to him to go to America, the place of the man's birth. A week later he packed up all his effects and took passage on a steamer sailing for the port of New York.

Chapter Four

It was a hot August afternoon in New York, especially hot in the downtown districts, where it was damp and muggy, for it had been drizzling all the morning. The sun blazing behind the thin vapour-like clouds had converted the rain into steam, and the almost complete absence of a breeze had added to the personal discomfort of those who were compelled to be out of doors. Altogether it was a most uncomfortable afternoon; and the task of running up and down stairs and answering the front door-bell increased the misery of the maid of all work in Miss Husted's furnished-room establishment on Houston Street, near Second Avenue.

"Phew, ain't it a scorcher?" muttered the young woman as she mounted the kitchen stairs in answer to some visitor's second tug at the bell. She walked across the hall that led to the front door.

"Don't the dratted bell keep goin'," she went on as she tugged open the door, which the damp weather had caused to swell and stick to the door-jamb.

"Forgot your key?" she said as she recognised Signor Tagliafico, better known as Fico, the third-floor, hall-bedroom "guest," as Miss Husted insisted on calling her lodgers.

"Forgot your key?" repeated the girl, as the gentleman from Italy shrugged his shoulders and otherwise disported himself in an endeavour to convey to her the news that he had lost his key and felt extremely sorry to trouble her.

"Keys is made to open doors, not to forget," continued the girl, banging the door shut.

The noise brought Miss Husted out into the hall in less time than it takes to state the fact.

"What is it, Thurza?" she asked, showing evidence of being startled out of a doze by the noise.

"Third floor front forgot his key, Miss Houston," said the girl sulkily, as Fico trudged upstairs to his room.

"I wouldn't mind if he wasn't behind three weeks," said Miss Husted, who usually answered to the name of Miss Houston, chiefly because she lived in Houston Street.

"Well, *I* mind it," muttered the girl to herself, "whether he's behind or whether he isn't. It makes work for me, and there ain't enough time for regular, let alone extras," she went on, as she turned to go down stairs to the kitchen.

"Quite right," said Miss Husted, as she closed the door and returned to her room. Experience had taught her that it was useless to argue with Thurza. The girl was open to impression, but not to explanation; once an idea found lodgment in her brain it stayed there, despite all argument to the contrary. It was most mortifying to Miss Husted that Thurza had such deep-rooted prejudices against every guest that found his way into her establishment. Lodgers made work; the more lodgers the more work; ergo, lodgers were enemies, is the way Thurza reasoned it out; and she resumed her occupation of cleaning silver (save the mark) almost as cheerfully as she had left it to answer the door-bell.

"Dear me," sighed Miss Husted, "how hard it is to get help and how much harder it is to keep them! Back again already? Why, Jenny, you must have flown!" this last to a rather pretty little girl who had just entered the door.

"Yes, aunt," replied the girl, "I knew Thurza must be busy--so--I--I hurried."

"I can see that," her aunt said reprovingly, "you are dripping wet; you shouldn't walk so fast in this hot weather."

Jenny was a thoughtful child. She had lived rather an unhappy existence with her parents, for her father had deserted her mother when she was three years old and after her mother's death she had come to her aunt "for a few days" until a home could be found for her. The few days were over some years before, for Miss Husted loved the child far too well to let her go, and gladly made a home for her. Jenny loved her aunt and stayed on. Curiously enough, not a word had ever been spoken between them on the subject, and the little girl just fitted in, adapting herself to Aunt Sarah's ways. Now this process of adjustment was by no means an easy accomplishment, for Aunt Sarah had no sense of time. She thought and felt herself to be just as young as she was years and years ago.

Her looking-glass must have given her several hard jolts, but she either believed a looking-glass to be an illusion or ignored its evidence altogether; for though it showed her the face of a woman near the danger line of fifty, she insisted on considering herself as in the neighbourhood of thirty. She carried herself with the dignity of a duchess; that is, a conventional duchess, and talked habitually with the hauteur and elegance of a stage queen. Her kingdom was the Houston Street establishment, her guests were her subjects, her aristocracy were the foreign gentlemen who occupied rooms in the various parts of her house, mostly hall bedrooms. She doted on fashion, refinement, pungent perfumery and expensive flowers; anything that to her mind suggested social grandeur appealed intensely to her. Even the old house, now situated in an exceedingly unfashionable quarter, held a place in her affections because years before it had been a part of fashionable New York, and she felt quite proud because she was known as Miss Houston of Houston Street. The name suggested a title, and a title of all things was dear to her heart. Perhaps her love for Jenny was stronger because her father was supposed--by his unfortunate wife at least--to have been the scion of a proud and aristocratic family, who had not been too proud, however, to leave her to starve. Altogether, Miss Husted was an exceedingly romantic, high-strung, middle-aged spinster, miles and miles above her station in life, whose heart and purse were open to any foreigner who had discernment enough to see her weakness and tact enough to pander to it by hinting at his noble lineage. This love of things and beings aristocratic was more than a weakness. It was a disease, for it kept poor a good soul, who otherwise might have been, if not well-to-do, at least fairly prosperous.

Jenny, young as she was, knew all this. She knew that Fico, or Signor Tagliafico, was a struggling musician and not an artist in any sense of the word. She knew he was an ordinary Italian fiddler who preferred to fiddle for food rather than to work manually for it. And yet her aunt had confided to her that she was sure he was a count, because one day Miss Husted had asked him the question, and the man, not quite understanding, had smiled and shrugged his shoulders. Still, he had not denied it, so thenceforth was known as Count Fico.

And Pinac, the gentleman who occupied the other back room next to that of Fico? Miss Husted was sure that he was a descendant of the noble refugees from

France, who emigrated during the Reign of Terror in the French Revolution. The romance of this appealed highly to her. Monsieur Pinac was always silent when questioned on this point, but Miss Husted was much interested. His silence surely meant something, and besides, he looked every inch a nobleman with his fashionably cut Van Dyck beard. There was a picture of the Duc de Guise in one of the bedrooms--Heavens only knows where Miss Husted got it, but there it was--and pointing to it with great pride, she defied Monsieur Pinac to deny his relationship to the defunct duke. Pinac did not take the trouble to deny it! As a matter of fact, he was simply an ordinary musician who continued to follow his profession because it paid him better than any other business he could embark in. Music is often the line of easiest resistance, and many there be that slide down its graceful curves. In more senses than one, it is easier to play than to work. But when Miss Husted conferred a patent of nobility on a foreign gentleman, were he an Italian organ-grinder or a French waiter, that title stood, his own protest to the contrary notwithstanding. In this particular view-point Miss Husted was completely opposite to her maid of all work.

Thurza's mental attitude was the socialistic slant that made for the destruction of aristocracy; Miss Husted's system created one of her own. To Thurza foreigners were either "dagoes" or "Dutch"; to Miss Husted they were either "gentlemen" or "noblemen" or both. In this way, perhaps, the balance of harmony was restored in Houston Mansion, as Miss Husted dearly loved to call her home. There was some foundation for believing that the name Houston Mansion was painted on the glass over the front door, but it was so worn that no one could decipher it.

A violent ring at the door-bell interrupted the conversation between Miss Husted and her niece.

"They'll break the bell if they're not careful," remarked the elder lady, arranging her ringlets in the event that it might be some one to see her.

"It's a lady," whispered Jenny to her aunt a few moments later. "She wants a room."

Miss Husted sniffed. "I don't like ladies; they're twice the trouble that gentlemen are, and--I don't know--I don't like 'em. Ladies looking for furnished rooms always have a history--and a past; I don't like 'em."

Jenny nodded without in the least understanding her aunt. She had heard this before, but she knew it was a peculiarity of Miss Husted always to say the same thing under the same circumstances, whether the occasion called for it or not.

"Shall I ask her in, or will you come out into the hall?" went on the child.

"Ask her kindly to step into the reception-room," said her aunt, kicking a feather duster under the sofa and generally tidying up a bit.

A large, stout person of uncertain age stood in the doorway.

"Is this the reception-room?" asked the lady, fixing her glasses and looking about her as if quite prepared to disbelieve any statement Miss Husted was about to make. That lady, much offended, drew herself up stiffly.

"Yes, this is the reception-room," she said, in a tone intended to be frigidly polite. "May I inquire to what am I indebted for the honour of this visit?"

The fat lady sniffed contemptuously and sat down.

"I think it's the sign 'Furnished Rooms' that can claim the honour," she said simply.

"Sit down, Jenny, and stop fidgeting," Miss Husted snapped out, ignoring the fat lady's attempt at smartness.

"I want a room if you have one vacant. My name is Mangenborn."

"Top floor?" inquired Miss Husted.

"I suppose you think a lady of my avoirdupois ought to live on the top floor so as to have plenty of exercise, eh?" inquired Mrs. Mangenborn with an attempt at humour. Then, without waiting for a reply, she went on:

"Well, you've just guessed right! What kind of people do you have in this house?"

"My guests are artists and gentlemen."

"Which?" inquired the stout lady, and laughed; she saw the joke if Miss Husted didn't and was good natured enough to laugh even if it were her own. "Well, I'm an artist," she said after a pause.

"Indeed?" said Miss Husted, and there was a slight inflection of sarcasm in that lady's voice.

Mrs. Mangenborn was either deaf or did not notice it, for she went on unconsciously:

"Yes, I am an artist--a second-sight artist."

"Second-sight?"

"Yes; I tell fortunes, read the future----"

"Oh?" said Miss Husted, and that one word was enough to have driven an ordinary person out of the front door, convinced of being insulted, but Mrs. Mangenborn was not sensitive.

"I should like a cup of tea," she said simply. "It's a very hot day."

The magnificent coolness of this request fairly caught Miss Husted. This woman spoke like one accustomed to command; and much to Jenny's astonishment (she had been listening attentively) her aunt sent her to order tea for two.

Given a person who can tell fortunes, and another person on the lookout for one, a person who has infinite hope in the future, whose whole life indeed is in the future, and it doesn't take long to establish an *entente cordiale*. When Jenny came back a few minutes later, to her utter astonishment she saw the mysterious fat lady dealing cards to her aunt and talking of events past, present, and future; and her aunt chatting as pleasantly as if she had known the woman all her life.

"However can you tell that?" asked Miss Husted as she sipped her tea and cut the cards for the ninetieth time.

"Don't you see the king? That means a visitor!"

"Yes; but how did you know that my best first-floor rooms were to let?"

Mrs. Mangenborn shrugged her shoulders and smiled.

"*That* I cannot tell you; I can't even tell myself; it just comes to me."

She did not remind Miss Husted that the best rooms in most boarding establishments in that locality were usually to let, because the people who could afford to pay the price seldom wanted to live in that neighbourhood; but she did tell her several things that must have pleased her immensely, for in a short while, after Mrs. Mangenborn had disposed of a second cup of tea, that lady was fairly ensconced in a seven-dollar front room on the first floor for a price that did not exceed three dollars. However, if half her predictions came true, it would have been a fine bargain for Miss Husted or any other landlady to have her as a guest.

As Jenny confided to Thurza in the kitchen a few hours later:

"You'll see. If the ground-floor parlor and bedroom aren't let next week, the new lady in the first floor front will get notice to leave because she's told a fortune that won't come true, and aunt will be angry. She keeps her word and she always expects people to keep theirs."

"My fortune never came true," grunted Thurza as she lifted a tub of washing off the table.

"Jenny, Mrs. Mangenborn wants you to go on an errand for her," called her aunt downstairs.

"Thought she wasn't never goin' to take females in her home again," said Thurza, as Jenny went upstairs to obey her aunt's order.

As Jenny closed the front door gently on her way to the stores, she mused sadly on the fact that her aunt, and not Mrs. Mangenborn, had given her the money with which to make the purchases. She hoped with childish optimism that the second-sight lady would pay her back; the other guests never did. Jenny sighed as she thought how much easier it would be on rent-days if auntie didn't advance money.

The front-door bell rang so often that day that Thurza declared it rang when it didn't ring, and was equally positive that the dratted bell didn't ring when it did ring. At all events, when the bell had been nearly jerked out of its socket for the third time, Miss Husted poked her head out of Mrs. Mangenborn's room and shouted for Thurza to hurry up and answer it. As she received no answer, she went down a flight to the head of the kitchen stairs, and gave vent to a most unusual display of temper. This was brought on by the fact that Mrs. Mangenborn had just declared that never in all her born days (to say nothing of her unborn moments) had she seen such a wonderful display of good fortune as that which lay in the cards spread on the table before them; there was a marriage just as sure as death. Mrs. Mangenborn was proceeding to describe the masculine element in the marriage proposition, and Miss Husted was trying to think who it could be, when the bell rang for the third time just as Thurza's head made its appearance above the kitchen stairs. Miss Husted decided to forget her dignity and go to the door herself.

Outside stood a hack piled up with baggage, and on the doorstep, waiting patiently, stood a gentleman who bowed when the door was opened and asked gently with a foreign accent, if Miss Husted had a room for a studio and a bedroom. There was much bustle and excitement, a great deal of noise, and a still greater deal of confusion, but when it had subsided and the hackman had been paid three times as much as he was legally entitled to, the baggage was carried, or rather tumbled, into the rooms engaged by the gentleman with the foreign accent. Miss Husted rushed into Mrs. Mangenborn's room and breathlessly gasped that her fortune had come true, for the front parlor and bedroom were let at their full prices.

"Just think of it, Mrs. Mangborn," as Miss Husted insisted on calling her "guest," "just think of it, full price in summer!"

Mrs. Mangenborn rose to the occasion.

"Why not?" demanded she, as if offended by Miss Husted's enthusiasm, "why not? The cards never lie! How much do you say he is to pay?" she went on, as if Miss Husted had told her and she had forgotten the precise amount.

"Fourteen," replied Miss Husted, "and it's a good price."

"Not bad! But wait, you'll see that's only the beginning," and Mrs. Mangenborn mixed up the cards lying on the table oblivious of the fact that she had just shuffled Miss Husted's marital prospects out of existence.

"Oh, that's nothing," she hastened to say as she saw the expression of alarm on Miss Husted's face. "It'll come out again. It's in the cards and it must come out." Then she asked, "Who is he? What is he?"

"He's an artist of some sort, a fine, noble-looking old gentleman. German! oh such fine, elegant manners; to the manner born I am sure! A musician, I think; he had a violin with him."

Mrs. Mangenborn's nose elevated itself a little.

"No money in music! What's his name?" she asked.

"I don't know," said Miss Husted. "He gave me his card, but I was so flustered I didn't look at it."

She opened the reticule she always carried at her side, containing keys, recipes, receipts, almost everything that could be crowded into it, and after quite a little sifting and sorting she took out a card on which was inscribed:

"Herr Anton Von Barwig."

Chapter Five

There was a decided air of mystery about the new occupant of the parlor-floor suite, or at least so it appeared to Miss Husted of Houston Street. As a matter of fact, Herr Von Barwig minded his own business and evidently expected every one else to do likewise, for he kept his door and his ears closed to all polite advances during the first few days after his arrival at Houston Mansion. Despite Miss Husted's oft-repeated inquiries after the professor's health (the title had been conferred on him by virtue of his possessing a violin and on the arrival of a piano for his room), despite her endeavours to direct conversation into a channel which might lead to a discussion of his personal affairs, Herr Von Barwig remained tacit; hence a mystery attached itself to the personality of the professor. It is a curious fact that the one gentleman of genuine title that found his way into the Houston Street establishment was ruthlessly shorn of his right to distinction and dubbed professor, which sobriquet clung to him for many, many years. However, this did not annoy Herr Von Barwig, for he had not yet realised that in America every concertina and rag-time piano-player, as well as barber, corn-doctor, and teacher of the manly art of boxing, is entitled to the distinction of being called professor.

"The professor has beautiful manners--oh, such beautiful manners," confided Miss Husted to her new friend, Mrs. Mangenborn, about two weeks after his arrival. "Every time I speak he bows, and there's oh, such dignity, such grace in the bending of his head. How polite he is, too; he always says, 'No, madam, thank you;' or 'yes, if madam will be so kind,' and then he bows again and waits for me to go."

"Is that all he says?" inquired Mrs. Mangenborn. "I guess he knows how to keep his mouth shut, then! If you want a man to talk never ask him questions; men are a suspicious lot."

"Ah, but *he* is different," said Miss Husted. "He has such a sad, far-away, wistful look in his noble, dark eyes."

"That may be, but far-away looks don't pay any rent for you! You can't attach any importance to things like that. My first husband had a far-away look, and I haven't seen him for ten years. That Steinway grand the professor's got, did he hire it or buy it? A man's got to have money to support one of those instruments," went on Mrs. Mangenborn.

"I don't know," replied Miss Husted, who could not help thinking that her friend had a somewhat mercenary mind. "No one's been to see him, so he hasn't got it for his friends; his violin has a beautiful sound. Mr. Pinac tells me that it must be a rare old instrument."

The door-bell was heard ringing, but no one seemed to pay any attention to it until they heard the whistle that followed; then everybody bustled about. The postman always created a little excitement in Houston Street, and his arrival was the one occasion on which even Thurza hurried to the door. It was also the one occasion on which she need not have done so, for she invariably found Miss Rusted or one of the guests ahead of her.

"Registered letter for Herr Von Barwig."

"I'll take it to him," said Miss Husted sweetly.

"He's got to come and sign it himself," said the letter-carrier, shaking his head.

"Where's it from?" asked Mrs. Mangenborn, her head appearing over the bannisters.

Miss Husted looked at the letter-carrier inquiringly, but that official appeared not to have heard the question. At all events, he made no reply, and Miss Husted knocked on the professor's door.

"Come in."

Miss Husted opened the door.

"Ah, madam, what can I do for you?" said Von Barwig, rising from the table at which he was writing.

Miss Husted smiled sweetly. She noticed that he was writing music, so he must be a composer as well as a professor.

"Will you please come and sign for a registered letter?" she said.

"Ah, yes! I come at once."

He arose, held the door open for Miss Husted to pass out, bowing to her as she did so, and then coming into the hallway, fulfilled the postal requirements, totally unconscious that several pairs of eyes were watching the operation. The letter-carrier handed him two letters; one bearing the postmark Leipsic, the other that of New York.

Von Barwig returned to his room and read the following from a firm of stock brokers:

"*Herr Anton Von Barwig*.

"DEAR SIR: Pursuant to your instructions, we have sold the balance of the securities you left with us, but they have so depreciated in value during your seven years' absence from Leipsic, that we hesitated to sell them at their present market price. However, your instructions in regard to these securities were definite and we have obeyed them. Hoping this will meet with your satisfaction, we remain,

"Yours obediently,

"BERNSTEIN & DEUTSCH."

A draft on Drexel, Morgan's bank, for $1,000 dropped from Von Barwig's hand; he picked it up mechanically and looked at it.

"The last, the very last, barely one-tenth the price I paid for them," he thought; and sighing, put the draft into a pocketbook and deposited it in an inner pocket.

The other letter was from a detective agency in Eighth Street, and read as follows:

"DEAR SIR: Call on us at your earliest convenience. We have news.

"HATCH & BUCKLEY."

That was all, but it was enough to cause Von Barwig to change hastily from his slippers and dressing-gown to his shoes and hat; and to be out in the street in less than one minute after reading the letter.

"News, news, news! Good God, is it possible? No, no! I mustn't believe it; I dare not. Helene, Helene, my little girl! No, no, I won't; I won't!" and he read the letter again. "After all," he mused, "it may be news of a thousand little girls and yet not of mine. I beg your pardon, madam!" In turning from Houston Street into the Bowery, still reading the letter, he had bumped suddenly into a middle-aged lady, who retaliated by deliberately pushing him back, at the same time asking him a somewhat unnecessary question as to where he was going. Then she had gone on her way without waiting to hear his apology.

Hatch & Buckley's private detective agency, situated just off Broadway and Eighth Street, had a large office divided into several small offices. For some occult reason only one person could get in or out at a time, and this made confidential conversation a necessity rather than a matter of choice. The senior member of the firm was in when Von Barwig called. Be it understood at the beginning that this large, stout personage, who invariably spoke in a whisper, and referred so often to his partner, had no partner but a number of detectives on his staff, to whom he was wont to speak or whisper of as partner when discussing what they had ferreted out or left undiscovered. This man, fat, florid, and fifty, had been a central office detective for many years. After a time, being exceedingly useful in a political sense, he had been admitted to the inner circle at Tammany Hall and was at present one of the leading geniuses in that hallowed body of faithful public servitors.

"Come in, come in," said this gentleman urbanely as Von Barwig stood waiting as patiently as he could for the news he was so anxious to hear.

"Well, I think we've got something," he added.

Von Barwig said nothing; he waited to hear more.

"First of all, business before pleasure," said Mr. Hatch, and suited the action to the word by handing Von Barwig a bill for $556.84, for "services rendered."

"Yes, yes; but tell me the news!" faltered Von Barwig, without looking at the bill. "Have you found her? Tell me!" The pleading look in Von Barwig's face would have melted the heart of any ordinary scoundrel; but Mr. Hatch was no ordinary scoundrel.

"It's customary, Mr. Barwig," he said drily, "to settle one account before opening another."

Von Barwig looked at the bill that had been handed to him, saw the amount, shook his head pathetically, and smiled. "There must be some mistake," he said.

"My partner went to California on this clue and followed it clean to British Columbia; railroad fares alone amount to two fifty; there's hotel bills, carfare; there's salaries, office expenses, stamps; and then--there's me." If Mr. Hatch had put himself first there would have been little need to refer to the other items.

"There's the vouchers," he went on, pushing a lot of papers toward Von Barwig. "Everything O.K.'d; everything on the level, open and above board." He leaned back in his chair as if determined not to say another word until the matter was settled.

"Then you refuse to tell me any more until this is paid?"

"Not at all, not at all! I'd just as leave tell you right now; but it wouldn't be business, it wouldn't be business." He repeated this as if to impress his listener with the importance of the business aspect of the situation being well preserved.

"You are right; it is not business! It is life and death; it's my heart, my soul, my very existence! My little girl, my little Helene is not business."

"I suppose not," assented the fat man, "not to you; but our end of it rests on a commercial basis. We've laid out the money and we're entitled to be paid for it."

"But I have paid you already so much! I cannot afford more. For years I have hunted high and low for my wife and child through city after city for thousands upon thousands of miles. At last I came to you, and there have been months and months of weary waiting, hunting false clues; disappointments upon disappointments."

"I know, I know," nodded the senior partner. "That's part of the game."

"I have spent with you nearly all the money I have, and nothing has come of it. Every now and then you raise my hopes by saying you have found her. Then, when the news comes, you ask for more money and when I have given it, it is again a false clue."

"That ain't our fault!" observed the stout gentleman. "My partner follows a clue, and you can't blame him if it don't turn out exactly the right one. This fellow Ahlmann is an eel; that's what he is, an eel! But I think we've got him now, I'm almost sure!"

"You think?" eagerly inquired Von Barwig.

"Well, of course there's nothing absolutely sure, but this is the last report he's sent in. Seems to me to pretty well cover the case, but it's been a hard job. This fellow Ahlmann has completely covered his tracks."

"The child? She--she lives?"

"Oh, yes; yes!"

"And the mother?"

"I think he's located them all. I can't tell you for sure till I read the report again."

Von Barwig, his hands trembling with excitement, wrote a cheque for the amount required, and with breathless impatience awaited the information as to the whereabouts of his lost wife and child.

"They're in Chicago," said Hatch, taking up the cheque and scanning it.

"Both of them?" asked Von Barwig in a hoarse whisper.

"Both of them," repeated Hatch, conveniently remembering the detail without reading the report. "George, bring me Mr. Bailey's telegram in the Barwig case," and when George, a smart young office boy, brought the required documents, he was quietly instructed by his employer to cash Von Barwig's cheque immediately.

"When will you go?" asked Mr. Hatch.

"As soon as possible."

"To-night?"

"Yes."

"Here's the address," and Mr. Hatch handed him a card. "You'll meet my partner there, 1120 State Avenue; he'll take you to the parties. Shall I get your railroad tickets?"

"No. I--I get them."

"It's twenty-six hours to Chicago; you'll need a Pullman ticket."

"Thank you; I get them."

"Well, just as you say. Good luck to you, Mr. Barwig."

"Thank you," said Von Barwig simply. He did not tell Mr. Hatch that he had nearly come to the end of his resources and that he would ride in the day car. Not that he felt ashamed of not being able to afford luxuries, but he instinctively resented making a confidant of a man like the senior partner of the firm of Hatch & Buckley.

As he walked rapidly toward Houston Street he found himself thinking for the first time since his arrival in America of the question of his future, but this question did not occupy his mind long. Like all his ideas on any subject other than that of his lost wife and child, it was forced into the background. As he neared his rooms in Houston Street his hopes began to rise; and the prospect of going to Chicago, the possibility of seeing his wife and child, began to work in his mind. His heart began to beat tumultuously. This time his dream would come true, and in his mind's eye he clasped his little girl tightly to himself and rained kisses on her little upturned face. He even found it in his heart to forgive the mother; after all, she was the mother of his little one, that he could never forget.

As for Ahlmann, he could not picture him; his mind refused to conjure up a thought of the man. It seemed as if he were dead, and that Von Barwig was on his way to rescue the wife and child from some danger that threatened them. This work of rescue was the fulfilment of an ideal. Nothing should be allowed to stand in the way of it! The senior partner of Hatch & Buckley had been quick to note this condition of mind and to reap the profits that came therefrom. Monomania means money, was a business axiom in that gentleman's office, but he had pumped the stream dry and Von Barwig was now at the end of his resources. By some strange process of thought, Von Barwig recognised this fact, but it seemed to him to mean that because his money had come to an end his search had also come to an end. The result of his trip to Chicago could not but be favourable, because he dared not think of its failure. So great is the influence of hope upon imagination that by the time Von Barwig reached his rooms he was already contemplating the possibility of keeping his wife and child there, at least until he could obtain better quarters for them. So, when he opened the door of his room, and found Jenny there polishing the brass andirons, he took more notice than usual of the little girl, and to her intense joy promised to bring her a box of candy from out West, where he told her he was going as he busied himself packing his handbag.

In a few hours Anton Von Barwig, his heart beating high in expectation, was seated in one of the day coaches of a fast Pennsylvania Railroad train on his way to Chicago.

Chapter Six

Von Barwig had left New York with a light heart. Hope had ripened into expectation, and for the first time since his arrival in America, seven years since, he had felt something like a positive assurance that this time his mission was going to result favourably. Hatch had assured him that his partner had positively found the missing wife and child; and Von Barwig had gradually allowed himself to think it possible, then probable, and finally he became almost certain of the successful result of his journey to Chicago.

As Jenny watched him pack his valise on the afternoon he left for Chicago, she had noticed that now and then his face beamed with happiness, the happiness of expected joy. And when he jokingly asked her how she would like to be his little girl, it made her, so happy that she wanted to throw her arms around his neck and cry on his shoulder. She felt that he was just the kind of father she would like to have, but the conversation didn't get very far, for Von Barwig had a train to catch and was too busy to hear the little girl's response to his question.

Jenny thought he was not quite in earnest, certainly not so deeply in earnest as she was. Her aunt did not quite understand her, and she needed some one to whom she could open her heart. She felt that Mr. Von Barwig would listen to her little confidences and sympathise with her; perhaps even tell her his troubles. Young as the girl was, she felt that the man had suffered. She couldn't tell why, but her little heart had gone out to him in sympathy almost from the moment she saw him. How it was she could not have explained, but she loved him. Jenny thought these things over long after Mr. Von Barwig had departed on his journey. It made her glad to think how happy he was when he left the house with his valise and umbrella, hurrying to catch the little bobtail car that wended its way across town to the Pennsylvania ferry.

So it came about that when Jenny, looking out of the window some few days later, saw him coming up the street slowly, disconsolately, almost dragging himself along, the little girl experienced a great shock. The man seemed to have changed altogether. It was the same dear Mr. Von Barwig, yes, but the eyes of love cannot be deceived; he looked older, and oh, so careworn and tired! She rushed to the door at once, to save him the trouble of finding his night key, and greeted him with affectionate inquiry. To her intense disappointment, he nodded absentmindedly to signify his appreciation of her act. The faint, ghost of a smile came over his face, but he did not look at her. Silently he opened the door to his room and passed into it without speaking, closing the door firmly behind him. Jenny's heart sank; she felt rather than knew that her friend was in trouble, for he did not pat her on the head or pinch her cheek as he had always done before when she opened the door for him.

Her inability to be of any service to him only added to the child's sorrow; tears came into her eyes as she stood looking at the closed door, for she felt completely shut out of his life. At supper that night, when her aunt asked her "what ailed her," and invited Mrs. Mangenborn to look at "Jenny's long face," the child tried to laugh, failed completely, and burst into a flood of tears. Jenny could not have explained to herself the whys and wherefores of her tearful outburst, but the child could not forget poor Von Barwig's drawn, haggard face and its weary, hopeless expression.

"She's a queer child," commented Mrs. Mangenborn, when Jenny had gone to bed that night.

"Her father had blue blood," replied Miss Husted impressively, "and you always find hysterical natures in high-born families."

"I shouldn't wonder," agreed her friend; "something is wrong with the child, that's plain."

"What do you suppose it is," said Miss Husted, rather anxiously. "Perhaps she's working up for an illness! Oh, dear," she went on, almost in tears, for shallow as she was herself, she loved the child deeply, "shall I send for a doctor? I think I'd better; I always feel safer with a doctor in the house."

"Wait till the morning," suggested Mrs. Mangenborn; "if anything's going to develop, you'll know what it is by then."

"Do you think anything will develop?" inquired Miss Husted, clutching Mrs. Mangenborn by the arm.

"I don't know for certain," replied her friend, "but it can't be much anyway, or I'd have seen it there," pointing to a pack of cards on the mantelpiece. "Wait a moment," she said suddenly, and then she knit her brows as if thinking very hard; "didn't the six of spades come out true? Yes, it did!" and she shook her head thoughtfully.

"I shan't feel comfortable till I go and see her," said Miss Husted, now thoroughly alarmed; and taking a lamp from a side table, the good lady went upstairs to look at her niece.

"That six of spades surely came out for something," muttered Mrs. Mangenborn to herself. "Six is tragedy! Well, we must take what comes," she continued philosophically as she helped herself liberally to some chocolate caramels that Miss Husted had thoughtfully, or thoughtlessly, left on the table.

In the meantime, another tragedy of a very different sort was being enacted in the room on the parlor floor--the tragedy of the death of hope. For when Anton Von Barwig closed the door of his room on the evening of his return from Chicago, he closed it finally and forever upon hope, and gave himself up completely to dull, grim, sodden despair. Not only this, but he cursed himself for ever having hoped. He never suspected for a moment that the eminent firm of Hatch & Buckley had wilfully deceived him, for Mr. Hatch's partner almost cried with vexation and disappointment when he found that the woman and child he pointed out were not the "parties" they were looking for. Indeed, Mr. Buckley's grief was so poignant that Von Barwig almost felt sorry for the man, who declared that his professional honour as a detective was ruined from that moment. It was, in this case, for Von Barwig made up his mind at once never to employ him again.

The summer twilight was fast deepening into night as Von Barwig sat staring out of his window, looking at the passers-by and seeing them not. He rebelled against fate, conditions, life; and for the first time in his career he railed at his Creator. He had asked for light, and no light came in answer to his prayer; only more darkness, more disappointment, more loneliness. He sat with bowed head, wondering what was the meaning of it all. Who could solve the problem; who could straighten out his tangled life; who could explain it? Was the devil really and truly greater than God--the God who is Love?

Von Barwig had read Nietzsche, Schopenhauer, Haeckel, all the school of pessimistic philosophers that exercised such a tremendous influence upon the thought of his day; but he had always instinctively rebelled against the nihilism of their creed, the creed of materialism. Yet, at this moment he was perilously near to believing that the force for evil was greater than the force for good. There was no love in his life; and for him love was life itself. As he sat there with eyes fixed and staring, seeing nothing, hearing nothing, he thought over the events that had come to him since his sojourn in America. For the past seven years he had devoted every thought, every energy, and nearly every penny he had to the search for his loved ones. And he had failed, failed, failed.

When the first shock of his loss came upon him in Leipsic he had asked himself the meaning of it, and the answer had come to him that Art had been his mistress, and that she had stepped in between him and the ones he loved. He had been self-ish, he had loved his Art as much, more perhaps, than his own flesh and blood--and this was his punishment. Yet he had given up his mistress, Art; he no longer lived for her; he would live for his wife and child, if he could only find them, if, if, if! He felt that there was indeed nothing to live for! Then why live, he asked himself? Better be dead; far better be dead! Who would care if he were no more? At this moment Von Barwig caught himself up, and realising his own danger refused to allow himself to drift along that line of thought. Life meant nothing to him now, but live he must, live he would; that he was determined on. Complex as the problem was, he would go on with it. He was not a coward, and for this he thanked his Creator.

In thanking Him he gained a little courage, and he asked for a sign, something to indicate that he was not the sport of fate, the creature of circumstance; something, anything, to indicate that God had not completely forgotten him. With bowed head Von Barwig prayed that he might be saved from himself; that thoughts of self-destruction might never again come into his mind; for he felt that he might not always have the power to reject them. He asked that the desire to live might again come upon him; for it dawned upon him that perhaps his duty lay in the direction of serving others. Desire is prayer, and Von Barwig's prayer was answered, for when he looked into the street he saw life once more. Opening his window he heard the voices of the children at play. He saw their joy, and rejoicing with them, he thanked God that he could rejoice. As he arose from his chair he sighed, a deep, deep sigh, and the darkest moment in his life had passed.

"Was that a knock?" Anton asked himself as he turned toward his door. "Surely not a visitor?"

Lighting his lamp, he looked at the cuckoo clock upon the wall. It said a quarter past nine o'clock; he had not heard the cuckoo strike seven, eight, or nine!

"Phew!" he whistled, "I had no idea it was so late." Again the timid little knock.

"Surely I can't be mistaken again," thought Von Barwig, and walking to the door he threw it wide open.

To his utter astonishment, a little girl in a white night-gown stood there, silently sobbing as if her heart would break.

"Why, Jenny, Jenny!" and Von Barwig, taking the trembling child in his arms, placed her gently in his armchair. "Jenny, my dear child."

"I--I--couldn't go to sleep until I'd said good-night; I tried to but I couldn't," sobbed Jenny as soon as she could speak coherently.

"Why, what has happened?" asked Von Barwig, as he covered her with a travelling rug.

"You asked me to be your little girl, and then, when I said 'Yes,' you didn't answer; and I--thought--you--were--angry--with--me--because--because! When--you--came--in, I felt so sorry for you, and you looked so unhappy that I had to come down and ask you to forgive me. I--I just couldn't help--it. You're not angry, are you?"

"My dear, dear little girl. I, angry?" Von Barwig shook his head. "How could I be angry with you? Why should I? Why, it's--it's impossible!" and Von Barwig laughed at the very idea. Jenny sighed deeply and remained silent; she seemed contented simply to be with him.

After a few moments' silence Von Barwig looked at her.

"Is this my answer; is this--my--answer?" he thought, and then he said slowly, "I am glad, more glad than I can ever tell you, that you have come to me at this moment."

He looked at the girl thoughtfully; she was not his little Helene, but he would try to love her as if she were. Von Barwig took her hand in his and tenderly stroked her cheek.

"You shall be my little girl, my little one, eh, eh? You shall!"

"Yes," nodded Jenny, smiling happily, "I'll be your little girl, if you'll have me."

And from that moment Von Barwig never again felt quite alone in the world.

At this instant a loud scream was heard, followed by another, and still another. Von Barwig rushed into the hallway, followed by Jenny.

"She's gone, gone! jumped out of the window!" screamed Miss Husted, from the top floor. "Look! the window's open, and she's gone; jumped out--gone."

"Who, who?" shouted Thurza, rushing upstairs.

"Jenny, Jenny!" wailed Miss Husted--so excited that she was almost beside herself.

Jenny and Von Barwig looked at one another in astonishment and the little girl hurried after Thurza, arriving upstairs just in time to prevent her aunt from going into hysterics.

"Here I am, auntie," she said, and Miss Husted was so delighted to see her niece again, that she forgot to scold her. As she came downstairs after satisfying herself that Jenny was not only safe and sound, but in her usual health--she found Herr Von Barwig at the foot of the stairs waiting for her.

"She is all right, eh, madam?"

"Oh, yes," responded that lady, pleased that Herr Von Barwig should be interested in the welfare of any member of her family.

"She is a good child; I like her very much, very much."

"Yes, Jenny is a very good girl; her father was a member of one of the oldest New York families, quite the aristocrat let me tell you!"

"Ah, yes. Her father is dead?" repeated Von Barwig, "and her mother also?" he asked.

"I am her only living relative," sighed Miss Husted.

"Ah, I am glad of that," said Von Barwig simply, "Yes--I--Jenny and I have come to an understanding. I am her--what you call--not father-in-law--her--her----"

Von Barwig fumbled a little with the English language until he made Miss Husted understand that he had taken her niece under his wing, so to speak; and hoped that she would have no objection. On the contrary, Miss Husted was highly pleased, for one of her lodgers had told her that Von Barwig had been a great man in Germany.

"I shall go out to dinner. Is there a restaurant near here that you can recommend?" asked Von Barwig. "Dinner? Why it's nearly ten o'clock!" replied Miss

Hasted, "let me get you a cup of tea."

"No, thank you, madam. I must go into the street, into the *cafe*, where there is life, and people; I must get away from myself. Here I think too much my own thoughts. Where did you say?"

"Galazatti's across the street is a nice little *cafe*," she replied, "and he serves a nice *table d'hote*."

"Ah, I shall go there, then. Thank you, madame. Good-night!" and Von Barwig bowing to Miss Husted, closed the front door quietly and went into the street.

Chapter Seven

When Anton arose the next morning after a refreshing night's rest, he became conscious that he was looking at the world through different coloured spectacles; and that there was no longer a dull feeling of despair gnawing at his heart. For the first time in many years his plans for the day did not include a search in this or that direction for his lost ones. It was not that he had forgotten, but he thought of them now as dead and gone; and this certainty, this lack of suspense, lightened his heart to such an extent that his manner was almost buoyant. Realising the fact that he had spent nearly all of the large sum of money he brought with him from Germany, he thought of his future, his welfare. To do for others, he must first do for himself; he must think of his music again; in short, he must earn a living. So, after a light breakfast at Galazatti's, he took an inventory of his available assets. They included some old music; some compositions which he would now try to sell; a genuine Amati violin worth at least three thousand dollars; a grand piano; one or two paintings; some silverware, presents, and jewelry; and about eight hundred dollars in cash.

Von Barwig was completely bewildered; he had purposely avoided meeting musicians in New York and scarcely any one knew him; those who had known him by reputation had now completely forgotten his existence. He had not felt sufficient interest in affairs going on around him to realise the state of musical art in America, so he scarcely knew how to begin. It seemed like the commencement of a new life. The period was that between Jenny Lind and Adelina Patti, and he soon realised that musical art was at its lowest ebb. There were one or two ambitious orchestra conductors in America; one in Chicago trying to introduce the Wagnerian polyphonic school, and perhaps one or two in New York; but the public clamoured after divas, prima donnas and tenors with temperaments and vocal pyrotechnic skill. For orchestral music there was little demand. Wagner was as yet unknown to the public--certainly he was unheard except on the rarest occasions and the majority of musicians did not like him because he was difficult to play.

So it happened that Von Barwig's compositions, which were of the modern German school and rather heavy, did not find a ready market, in fact they did not find a market at all. Day after day he would visit the music stores with his music roll tucked under his arm. After a few months the music publishers used to smile when they saw him coming into their places of business, and shake their heads before he had a chance even to show them his manuscripts. As time went on he came to be a byword among them.

"Here comes poor old Von Barwig," they would say, and then they would smile at his earnest face with its sad, longing expression and sympathise with him for his beautiful smile of resignation as he folded up his package of compositions and went sadly away. They admired his technical skill, but thought him very foolish to waste his time on such "stuff" as they called it. They advised him to write for the hour, and not for posterity.

"You must give the public what they want," said Schumein.

"How can you tell what they want if you don't try?" pleaded Von Barwig. "If you give them only what you acknowledge is bad, how will they ever know what is better?"

"It's no use," was Schumein's reply, "music like yours has no market value. We're not in business for our health; once strike a popular tune and you'll be famous!"

Von Barwig had never mentioned his Leipsic reputation, and if he had, in all probability, it would have been useless. Seven years is a long time for even a genius to remain in obscurity.

"Bring in a good waltz," said one.

"What we want is a catchy melody; something that everybody whistles," said another.

Finally they were too busy to see Von Barwig at all; and after waiting hours and hours in vain efforts to obtain an interview, he would walk home slowly, thinking over the events of the day, or trying to create a tune that might make an appeal to the music-loving, or rather music-buying public.

"Alas!" he would say to himself, after giving up the effort. "I do not understand these people. The American people do not like my work." It did not occur to him that the Americans were not a music-loving nation, at least not at that period. And so Anton Von Barwig gradually came out of the world of dreams into the world of life. He had been reborn, of necessity, for he was nearly down to his last penny. He used to talk over the condition of the music market with Tagliafico, our old friend, Fico, of the hall bedroom on the top floor of Miss Husted's establishment, and Pinac, Fico's friend, who occupied the room adjoining. The meeting of these three men, which subsequently resulted in a friendship lasting many years, came about as follows:

While eating dinner at Galazatti's one night, Von Barwig found himself at the same table as Fico. Fico bowed to him and he graciously acknowledged his salute, not knowing who the man was, but vaguely remembering his features. Fico then introduced Pinac, his fellow-lodger. Fico had recognised Von Barwig as the occupant of the first floor and took this opportunity of making the acquaintance of the musician whose music he had so often heard on the piano--for Von Barwig frequently played his own compositions and the strains were wafted through the open window. Pinac was most enthusiastic, for he knew Von Barwig slightly by reputation. He had been in Dresden and he had heard of Anton Von Barwig, the musical conductor. It seemed scarcely possible that the gentleman before him was that great man.

Von Barwig was silent, smiling a little at Pinac's enthusiasm, but as he did not deny his identity Pinac felt sure that he was right. The three men soon became quite friendly and often met in the little *cafe* to talk things over. Galazatti's was frequented chiefly by foreigners and the din of loud voices added to the rattle and clatter of knives and forks made conversation difficult. But its patrons soon became used to this and the *table d'hote* was cheap and good at the price, twenty-five cents. It was a combination of East Side Tivoli and French Brasserie and Hungarian Goulash Rendezvous--a tiny cosmopolis in itself--and it did a rushing business.

So the months dragged along in unending monotony. Poor Von Barwig tried hard to do work that would please the gentlemen who controlled the music trades, but failed. One day, while looking over his manuscripts to discover if possible the cause of his failure, he was struck by the similarity of one of his compositions to another. They all seemed to contain the same melody, in one form or another, and he saw plainly at last that he was subconsciously haunted by the leading motif of the first movement of his last symphony, the symphony that was played on that dreadful night for the first and last time. The inference was plain enough. This melody haunted him, he could not forget it; it showed itself in all his work and he realised that his career as a composer had come to an end.

After that Von Barwig tore up all his compositions and turned his attention to teaching, an occupation he had always hated ever since he had given up the professorship of counterpoint and harmony in the Leipsic Conservatory. Teaching--the very thought had made him shudder. He looked about him and found that New York was fast moving uptown, and that Houston Street was not a good locality for a musical conservatory. People who could afford to study music did not live in that neighbourhood; but he could not summon up sufficient energy or courage to leave the place. He had come to like the old house; it had become a home to him now. He liked Miss Husted, too, though she made him the repository for all her troubles, and then there were Fico, and Pinac and Jenny--he really loved Jenny. His little world was all in Houston Street and he made up his mind not to leave it, even if the location made the getting of pupils harder. Besides he felt that he was not a fashionable teacher; he could teach only those who learned music because they loved it and not because they wanted to be accomplished.

Von Barwig did not speak to his friends of all this; his pride would not allow him to discuss his personal affairs with them. Besides neither Pinac nor Fico could throw much light on the pupil question, for though they were musicians, yes, for they played, they did not teach. Pinac did not even know until Von Barwig showed him how to hold his violin properly he used to grab it with his whole hand instead of by his finger and thumb; and as for Fico, he could not read music until Von Barwig taught him, but played the mandolin, guitar and piano by ear. These men were not only grateful to Von Barwig for his kindness, but they loved him, and recognising in him the real artist had unbounded respect for him. As for Von Barwig, he found them simple fellows, sentimental, unpretentious and good-hearted, and he liked them and felt at ease with them because they did not seek to probe into that part of his life which he preferred should remain unknown to them. They merely accepted him as they found him and for this Von Barwig was grateful. As time went on, Von Barwig found himself badly in need of ready money. One day when Miss Husted came for her rent, he hesitated before he paid her; he had forgotten it was rent day and was unprepared. The poor lady was kindness itself, but her kindness embarrassed Von Barwig extremely, for he had never been in a position in his life where he actually needed cash for his daily wants.

"Leave it a week, a month, a year, my dear professor!" said Miss Husted, and she implored him not to pay her if it afforded him the slightest inconvenience.

"I go to the bank--if you come in an hour I will have it for you," said poor Von Barwig, quite overcome. He did not know what it was to be "behind," and the experience was painful to him.

This was the beginning of the end, and the valuable Amati violin soon went for eight hundred dollars, one-fourth its value, to a scoundrelly violin maker and dealer who told Von Barwig he had tried everywhere but could get no more for it, since there was a doubt as to its genuineness.

Von Barwig took the money, which was further decreased by a twenty per cent. commission. The man told him he was very lucky to get it; and perhaps he was.

This amount tided Von Barwig over for several months, during which time he secured several pupils and seemed for a time to be in a fair way to make a living. Be it understood that he was no longer the Anton Von Barwig who lived in Leipsic ten years before. Gone was the fire of his genius; dead was his ambition. His soul was not in his work--the man was alive, but the artist was dead.

Chapter Eight

And so the years passed away; one, two, three, Von Barwig did not keep count now. One year was just like another, equally profitless, equally monotonous; the struggle for existence just as keen, the interest in this or that pupil just as superficial, the interest in obtaining pupils perhaps the greatest of all. But the drudgery of teaching the young mind to distinguish between crotchet and quaver, and mark time, mark time, wore Von Barwig out.

"Good God," he would think, "will it ever come that time shall cease to be, and I shall cease to mark it?" The old man often smiled as he contrasted the Leipsic days with the present. Then he had but to raise his arm and from a hundred instruments and five hundred voices would vibrate sounds of beauty, of colour, of joy, in harmony and rhythm. Now when he beat time some dirty-fingered little pupil would tinkle out sounds that nearly drove him mad with their monotony. Von Barwig had been compelled to sell his good piano and rent one on the installment plan; a cheap tin-pan affair, with a sounding board that sent forth the most metallic sort of music. This went on until Von Barwig hated the very sound of a musical instrument. He must have suffered terribly, but he made no mention of it. At the close of his day's work he would shut his piano wearily, put away his violin and go to Galazatti's, where he would meet his friends, Fico and Pinac. He did not complain, but they did. Fico was playing the mandolin on a Coney Island boat; Pinac was doing nothing, but sat in Galazatti's all day. When they complained to Von Barwig of their ill luck, their inability to obtain good engagements because they could not get into the Musical Union, Von Barwig did not spare them. He told them plainly that they had talent but that they were lazy; they would neither study nor practise, and yet they expected to enjoy the fruits of labour without its drudgery. Both Fico and Pinac felt that he was right, and from that day forward they did practise and study, with the result that a year or so later they were admitted into the Union; but times were hard and good regular engagements were rare.

One day while Von Barwig was labouring hard to beat time and other musical values into the head of a square-browed, freckle-faced youth of nineteen, whom nature had ordained for the carpenter's bench and not for the piano, a knock came at the door, and on invitation to enter, in came a little fellow not more than nine years of age, black-haired, dark-eyed, of olive complexion, his features plainly bearing the stamp of his Hebraic origin. As he stood at the door trying to speak, Von Barwig could not help commenting on his finely chiselled features and the intelligence and fire in his eyes.

"What can I do for you, little man?" inquired Von Barwig. His soft voice and kindly look of interest gave the boy courage; for he was obviously afraid to speak.

"Come to me," said Von Barwig tenderly, and after he had closed the door, he placed his arm around the boy's neck. The old man's trained eye discerned in a moment the sensitive play of the lad's mouth, the quivering of the nostril that denotes what we call temperament.

"I want to study--I want to learn--and they won't let me," blurted out the boy, bursting into tears.

"Who won't let you?" gently inquired Von Barwig.

"My people," sobbed the child.

"Hully Gee, you're in luck!" interrupted the shock-headed youth. "I wish my people wouldn't let me."

"You go home, Underman! You have no soul; this child has."

"You bet I will!" and with a dart at his hat, the big boy seized it and ran out of the door in a moment.

"So you want to study music and they won't let you?"

"Yes, sir. I--they'll let me play at night, but in the daytime, I--I must work."

In a short half hour Von Barwig made the discovery that the child was a musical genius. He had taken no lessons and yet his manipulation of the keys was marvellous, but all by ear. Chords, arpeggios, diminished sevenths, modulation, expression, all were mixed up in formless melody. The boy knew nothing, but felt everything. In Von Barwig's experience it had generally been the other way.

"Who sent you to me?" asked Von Barwig after he had heard the child play.

"The sign says that you teach music, and I--I--then I saw your name outside." The little fellow seemed to think that he had committed some crime in coming in unasked. Von Barwig put him at his ease, then called in Pinac and Fico, and they listened to the child's playing in open-mouthed astonishment. Bit by bit Von Barwig elicited his history from him. His name, it appeared, was Josef Branski, and he was the oldest of seven children. His father and mother had come from Warsaw, in Poland, and worked in a sweat shop below Grand Street near the river. Josef himself worked there, too, and helped to support his family, who all lived in three small rooms. His parents would miss him and be angry, he said, and this partly accounted for the little fellow's anxiety. Von Barwig shook his head; he already had many pupils who couldn't pay, as well as several who didn't pay, but here was one who had to steal the time in which to learn his beloved art. It would be a crime not to teach the boy, he thought, so he determined to take him as his pupil.

Some six months later an excited Pole bounded into Von Barwig's room and in a mixture of Polish, German and Hebrew threatened Von Barwig with the law if he continued to take his son away from him. He was, as nearly as Von Barwig could make out, little Josef Branski's father. Von Barwig vainly endeavoured to explain to the man that the boy could make his parents rich if they allowed him to study and develop himself as an artist, but they must give him time to practise, instead of compelling him to sew at a machine twelve or fourteen hours a day. The older Branski either could not or would not understand. He declared that he did not want his son to be a worthless musician (for he evidently associated Von Barwig with the gipsy, an inferior type of musician) and could not be made to understand that the boy had talent, even genius. He needed the boy's help and wanted no further interference from Von Barwig. Von Barwig saw that it was useless and gave up trying to dissuade him from his purpose in condemning the boy to the merciless grind of a sweat shop machine. So it was that little Josef came at night only for his lessons. This went on for some time, but Von Barwig shook his head sadly as he saw that the boy was tired out with his day's work and could not take in the instruction. Finally he told Josef that he had better not come again, as the strain of night study following the grind of machine work during the day was plainly telling on his health. But the boy pleaded hard:

"Take away my music and you take away my life," he said. "Some day father and mother will see and then they'll let me study with you."

Von Barwig looked at the boy sadly.

"They love me and they want to see me famous, but they don't understand. They work so hard, they have so little to eat, and there are so many of them. Mother can't work, you know, she has to nurse the baby. I must do all I can; I'm the eldest, it's my duty!"

The boy's eyes filled with tears as he thought of the hardships his parents went through. "Father worked till twelve o'clock last night; he's working now," and the little chap looked at the cuckoo clock, which was just striking ten.

"How long will it be before I can play to the gentlemen you're going to take me to?" he asked wistfully.

"I think you'd better have a little rest before you play to them, Josef. You've been working very hard; up at five, to bed at midnight!" Von Barwig noticed that Josef's face was peaked and white, but his great black eyes looked appealingly at his master.

"But I must play to them; they'll give me money and I can give the money to father. Then he'll believe me, and he'll believe you," said the boy in a tearful voice. His urgent, appealing manner had its effect on Von Barwig.

"I'll take you to-morrow morning," he said. "Will your father let you go?"

"I'll beg him, I'll beg him, oh, so hard, on my bended knees. He won't refuse, he can't refuse! If he does, I--I'll just make an excuse and leave the machine as if I were going for oil, or cotton or something. I'll come! Don't disappoint me, will you?"

And so it was arranged that the boy should call for Von Barwig on the morrow and that they should go to Steinway Hall, where Josef should play before some musical gentlemen that Von Barwig had come to know.

The morning arrived, but little Josef did not appear. After waiting three hours, Von Barwig made up his mind that the father would not let the boy go, so he sadly gave up the idea for that day, and waited till evening for Josef to come as usual for his lesson. When the child did not come, Von Barwig experienced again that sensation of fear, for the first time in several years; and with it came the train of sickening thought, the old dread of impending evil. Von Barwig soon threw this off, and waited for events with as much calmness and patience as he could muster up.

A week passed, and Miss Husted could not understand why Von Barwig spoke in such a low tone when he replied to her cheery good-evening. Mrs. Mangenborn put it down to hard times. Jenny knew something was wrong, for he said very little to her as she swept out his room. She knew something had happened, but experience had taught her that sympathy doesn't ask questions. As for Pinac and Fico, they were too full of their own affairs to notice anything unless it was brought directly to their attention, and as Von Barwig made it a rule never to burden other people with his troubles they were in blissful ignorance of his mental perturbation. So it went on till the tenth day, when Von Barwig made up his mind to go and call on his little pupil and find out what was the matter.

After much hunting and questioning, Von Barwig found the family he was looking for on the fourth floor of a crowded tenement house in Rivington Street. He heard the whirr of sewing machines and as he opened the door he saw the father of his pupil, and several others, all sewing rapidly as if for dear life. The six machines made such a noise he could barely hear the sound of his own voice. As soon as Branski saw Von Barwig, he jumped up from his machine and railed at him in terms of bitter reproach. It was well perhaps that Von Barwig could not understand and that the noise of the machines and the crying of babies prevented his hearing what was said. The father pointed into the next room and motioned him to go in there. Pushing aside a little chintz curtain, for there was no door, Von Barwig saw the object of his search lying on a cot in the corner of a small inner room with no window, only an air shaft for light and air, moaning in the grasp of mortal illness.

The mother sat by the bedside of the sick boy rocking herself slowly, and at the same time holding a babe to her heart. The little one was trying in vain to get sustenance enough to satisfy its pangs of hunger and crying because it couldn't. Another child of two years of age was playing on the floor, banging two pieces of wood together and shouting gleefully when it succeeded in making a noise. The woman looked at her sick son helplessly and then at Von Barwig.

"Doctor?" she asked feebly.

Von Barwig shook his head slowly. He saw that his little pupil was too weak to recognise him and gazed at him too moved to speak. His lips quivered, and kneeling down by the lad's bedside he wept scalding hot tears of agony, for he felt rather than knew that the boy was dying. It appeared from the mother's story that when

Josef had reached home that night he had been in too excited a state to sleep. All night he moaned and tossed--the next morning he was delirious. The prospect of deliverance from his life of drudgery had been too much for him and had resulted in brain fever. The doctor said he had a bad cold, then finally announced that tubercular complications had set in, and as nearly as Von Barwig could find out the boy was now rapidly wasting away with the dreaded white disease. Von Barwig looked around him helplessly; the light was bad, the air rank poison and the noise and commotion distracting.

"What hope could there be for his recovery?" thought Von Barwig, and he then and there resolved on a plan of action. Before he left the house he had given the father all the money he had and secured a room with plenty of light and air and a nurse for the boy. His efforts were crowned with success. In a few weeks little Josef was gently nursed back to life, and at the first signs of returning health Von Barwig saw to it that he was sent South. "His only chance," the doctor had said. It was Von Barwig who gave him that chance, but in order to do so he parted with his last remaining bit of valuable jewelry.

*   *   *   *   *

It was some time before Von Barwig recovered from the effects of witnessing the sufferings of his pupil. When Jenny asked him about Josef Branski he smiled sadly and shook his head.

"The doctor says it may be years before he can touch an instrument again. Poor Josef--his little frame completely went to pieces under the burning fire of his genius; if any one was ever born out of harmony with his surroundings, he was. He might have become a great artist," added Von Barwig thoughtfully and then he sighed. It was a great struggle for him to send the money to keep the little chap alive down South, but he made the sacrifice without a murmur. If only the boy recovered, it would be sufficient reward for all his work. But it was not to be, for a few weeks later they brought him the news that his little pupil had died peacefully, without pain. Von Barwig said nothing--his mouth tightened a little and he smiled, a sad, far-away smile. Miss Husted tried to cheer him up. She had learned from Jenny the details of the affair and her heart went out to the old man in womanly sympathy. She had liked the boy, too, and when he came for his lesson had given him many a slice of cake, for she thought he always looked pinched and hungry, underfed, as she called it.

"Do come and have a bit of dinner with us, professor," she said. With her dinner was a universal panacea, but Von Barwig declined with many thanks. He had grown to like Miss Husted and realised that she was far, far above the average woman of her class. Moreover, he felt that she liked him, and sympathy begets sympathy.

"Professor, you are always doing things for folks, but you never allow folks to do anything for you," said Miss Husted, slightly piqued by his refusal of her invitation.

"Ah, then I accept!" said Von Barwig, seeing that she was hurt, "just to show you that you are more powerful than my own resolutions. But I warn you I shall be sad company; I don't feel quite myself tonight. It is better, far better, that little Josef should have--left us, for I do not think he would have ever been strong enough to play again, but--" and Von Barwig sighed, "it is sad enough. A little light prematurely snuffed out is always sad. Ah, well! I won't make you miserable. Life is full of sorrow for us all; don't let me selfishly add to yours."

At dinner he was the life of the party. He pinched Jenny's cheek; he joked with Miss Husted; he smiled at Thurza, and he even ventured a few remarks to Mrs. Mangenborn, whom he cordially disliked. Every one present thought that Von Barwig was as happy as could be.

That night, after he had closed the door of his room he sighed deeply and looked out of his window into the street at the blinking lamplights. Once more that mournful far-away expression came into his face and he asked himself: "Why? Why is it my fate to lose everything I love? Have I not yet drunk the dregs of my cup of sorrow?"

*   *   *   *   *

"Good-night, professor," came Miss Husted's cheery voice from the hallway, interrupting his reverie.

"Good-night, Mr. Von Barwig," said Jenny, as she passed his room on her way to bed. He opened the door and kissed her tenderly.

"Good-night, good-night, my friends," said Von Barwig. The sound of their voices comforted him not a little and then he thought, "I mustn't be ungrateful; there are many, many kind hearts in this world." And he slept peacefully all that night.

Chapter Nine

The next morning, while Von Barwig was waiting for a pupil--he had very few in these days--Jenny came into his room with a letter, at the sight of which his heart beat rapidly, for it was post-marked Germany. The handwriting was in a boyish scrawl he did not recognise.

"Not many pupils to-day?" ventured Jenny.

"No, they don't come; I'm afraid this is not just exactly the neighbourhood. New York is going uptown. I gave only fifteen lessons last week."

"That's not bad, is it?" asked Jenny.

"Not so bad when they pay, but they don't," laughed Von Barwig, and seeing that his visitor was in no hurry to leave him, Von Barwig ventured to open his letter and read it. He read it again and then looked at Jenny with such a perplexed expression on his face that she was forced to laugh in spite of herself.

"Young Poons is coming," he said finally.

"Is he?" replied Jenny doubtfully.

"Yes, he is coming. He is the son of an old friend; a very dear old friend. His name is August and he wants me to--to give him a start in life. He is a 'cello player. You know what is a 'cello? It's a large violin and stands up when you play it, so," and he took his own violin and placing it between his knees showed her how the 'cello was manipulated.

"He sails on the steamship *City of Berlin*. He is coming here to make his fortune," and Von Barwig laughed at the idea of making a fortune at music in America.

"How old is he?" asked Jenny.

"Hum--he must be seventeen by this time!" Jenny became quite interested. "I knew him when he was quite a little chap; his father was a horn player in my orchestra at--at--" Von Barwig hesitated; "in Germany. I must help him. Yes, Jenny,

I must help him. Poor old August, I must be a father to his son! He was a dear little chap," he said reminiscently. "Tell your aunt we shall want one of her bedrooms on the top floor if it is at liberty."

"The one next to Mr. Pinac is empty. Aunt will be so pleased that a friend of yours is going to take it." And Jenny rushed off to acquaint her aunt with the good news.

Von Barwig told the news of the impending arrival of his friend's son to Pinac and Fico, and the three men went down to the docks to meet him. At the docks they learned that he had arrived with eleven hundred other steerage passengers and had landed at Castle Garden, so they went down to the Battery to try and find him. They found him in an inner room off the immigrants' reception hall, sitting on an old trunk, and busily engaged in trying to prevent his 'cello, which was protected only by a green bag, from being smashed by the rushing, gesticulating crowd of baggage men, porters and immigrants. With his round, smiling face and blond hair he was the picture of his father, and Von Barwig, recognising him in a moment, embraced him cordially.

"I am to be sent back," he cried in German.

"Nonsense!" said Von Barwig, placing his arm around the young man affectionately. After Von Barwig had introduced his friend, they noticed his crestfallen manner.

"What's the matter?" asked Pinac, who could not understand German, but who knew something was wrong, and wanted to show Poons that he knew the ropes in the States. Poons poured out a tale of woe which was intended to touch Von Barwig's heart and gain his sympathy, instead of which it made him laugh heartily.

"Some one is investing his money for him and hasn't come back yet," Von Barwig confided to his friends; and they laughed too. Poons could not understand why the men laughed at his troubles. The simple German lad had been swindled out of all his money, two hundred marks, by the simplest and most transparent of the many methods of swindling, the confidence game, and the immigration authorities had refused to allow him to land, as he had no means of subsistence. Von Barwig had very little money with him, so he consulted with his friends. They were playing in a *cafe* at night and had a few dollars in their pockets, which they cheerfully handed to Von Barwig. Between them they managed to find the necessary money and Poons was allowed to land. On the way uptown the boy was profuse in his gratitude for the money that Von Barwig had sent to his mother while she lived. It was she who had given her son Von Barwig's address and begged him to seek him out in America and greet him for her. Poons was greatly astonished at Von Barwig's appearance and condition, for he had always heard of him as one of the great conductors of Germany. He did not understand how Herr Von Barwig could be so poor, but he accepted the facts as they were and ceased to ask himself any further questions.

In due course they arrived at Miss Husted's and young Poons, bag and baggage and 'cello, was shortly afterward ensconced in a hall bedroom on the top floor of that lady's establishment. Von Barwig hurried to his room, locked the door and looked around him. A little later when he let himself quietly into the street, he had under his arm, carefully wrapped up, his cuckoo clock and a couple of pictures. That night at Galazatti's, when he handed to Pinac and Fico the money he had borrowed from them at Castle Garden and paid for the little dinner which he gave them to celebrate the arrival of Poons in America, they did not suspect that he had spent the very last dollar he had in the world.

*   *   *   *   *

Young Poons was not a success at first. He had a good technique and was a well-grounded musician, but he could not get an engagement suited to him, as he was not in the Union, and the foolish boy would not play dance music. He said he couldn't, and unfortunately the responsibility for his financial condition rested on Von Barwig. It was he who was compelled to make arrangements with Miss Husted and it was a hard blow to him to have the additional incumbrance, especially when times were so hard and pupils so scarce. It may be imagined that Miss Husted did not take very kindly to the new arrival, who was unable to pay even his first week's room rent. Of course she sympathised with his misfortune, but thought he should have taken care of his money and not have handed it to the first person who asked for it, so that now he was a pauper. She discussed this delicate point with Mrs. Mangenborn in the strict privacy of her room, but Jenny's ears were very sharp and her sympathy went out to young Poons. "Poor young man," she thought, "what a pity that he had been robbed." That his mother and father were dead added to the romance, and she felt a sort of a fellow-orphan's interest in him. "Poor boy! robbed of his fortune on his arrival in a strange country; penniless and homeless; can't speak a word of English; as helpless as a child." The maternal instinct in the child was aroused, and his large innocent blue eyes and blond hair made a very strong appeal to her. He needed a mother and she determined to be a mother to him. So, many a little delicacy was left surreptitiously in his room; now a box of chocolates, now a slice of cake, or even a few flowers. When young Poons would thank Miss Husted for these attentions in the choicest German that lady would turn on him and tell him to mind his own business, and he would smile and bow deferentially to her, saying, "Ja, Frau Hooston."

As the weeks went on, the struggle for Von Barwig to pay expenses became greater and greater. Poons saw that it was an effort and determined to sink his pride, so he begged Pinac to help him get something for him to do; anything, anywhere. It was a great day for Poons when Fico announced to him that the proprietor of the *cafe* where they played had given them permission to bring him and his 'cello on trial for a week at a salary of six dollars and his supper, at the end of the night concert. Jenny was quite proud. "I told you that Mr. Poons would succeed," she said joyfully to her aunt.

"Wait," replied Miss Husted, "he's not out of the woods yet."

But she was mistaken, for he held on to his engagement and at the end of the week was taken on permanently. This was most fortunate, for by this time Von Barwig had completely denuded his room of all superfluous articles of value; even the fine old prints that had adorned his bedroom went for a mere trifle. A silver baton that had been given him by the director of the Gewandhaus was the last thing to go. It was quite a wrench to part with it, for it was the last link between Von Barwig and his musical past.

In the meantime he had lowered his prices for music lessons in the hopes of increasing the number of his pupils, and at Miss Husted's suggestion even had a new sign made with large letters in gold-leaf. But pupils did not come, and Von Barwig felt that he was indeed doomed to failure. Everything he touched turned to dross; his one pupil of promise had died; there was no future, no outlook, no hope, and yet he did not give up, nor did he speak of his troubles to his friends. How he kept

Miss Husted paid up she never knew, and yet, punctually every week, he handed to her the sum of money due her. When he suggested taking a smaller room upstairs she offered to lower the price of the room he was occupying. This sacrifice the old man would not accept; so he remained where he was, always hoping, hoping, hoping. He did not complain directly to her, but she knew that he was taking in little or no money. She blamed him for not being more exacting with those who were indebted to him, and as a matter of fact had he been able to collect all that was owing to him he would have been in far better circumstances; but no one seemed to think he needed money--he had such a prosperous air.

"What can I do?" said Von Barwig apologetically, when she told him to sue his delinquent pupils. "I tell them their course of lessons is finished and they make no reply, or if they do, it is an excuse or a promise. I cannot go to law with them, and if I could, just think what it would cost for the lawyer! Besides, they are very poor--these neighbours of ours. Music with them is a luxury, not a necessity. Poor souls, it brings a little joy into their lives! They struggle so hard to get higher in the scale of existence; why should I impede their progress by demanding my pound of flesh? No, my dear Miss Husted, they do the best they can; but they are poor."

"And so are you," replied Miss Husted, shaking her curls.

Von Barwig shook his head dubiously. "I'm afraid--I--I don't put my heart into my work." He did not like to tell her he thought the neighborhood he lived in was partly to blame.

"Who could put soul into a thing like that?" and he pointed to a cheap violin he had bought to play to his pupils when he taught them. "Or that?" and he dropped the lid of his piano to show his contempt for the tin pan, called by courtesy a concert grand. Miss Husted looked sad; the ever-present tear was close at hand and Von Barwig saw it coming.

"But, never mind, my dear Miss Husted; all comes right in the end! It's all for some good or other. I can't see it myself, but I know it's all for my good. Come! Cheer up, cheer up!" and he looked at her with such a beatific smile that she thought for the moment that she was very unhappy and that he was trying to help her.

"Very well, I will," she said resignedly, allowing herself to be comforted.

That was one of Von Barwig's individual traits. No one ever thought of cheering him up, for no one knew that he suffered, except perhaps Jenny. She alone saw through his smile, and felt rather than knew that it hid a heart torn with suffering and emotion.

A few days after this Von Barwig read in one of the papers that a man named Van Praag, whom he knew years before in Berlin as a ticket-taker in one of the theatres, was going to give a series of concerts in one of the large concert halls in New York. He mustered up courage to go and see him. Van Praag received him cordially and invited him to dinner that evening at one of the big hotels. Von Barwig put on his old dress suit, and Houston Mansion quickly recognised the fact. Miss Husted especially was most enthusiastic.

"Oh, professor, how well you look!" she cried. "Mrs. Mangenborn, do come and see the professor with his evening clothes on, he looks a perfect picture!"

Von Barwig was compelled to leave an hour before the time appointed for the dinner, in order to escape from the congratulations of his friends. That night, for the first time in his life, he begged for a position. He had failed at composing, at teaching, at playing, but surely he could still conduct an orchestra. The desire for success grew on him again. Van Praag seemed convinced, and at the end of the dinner, after taking his address, he promised Von Barwig he would do what he could; but he must consult the director first, etc., etc.

Von Barwig went home that night almost happy. A pint of champagne at dinner, with a liqueur afterward, had completely aroused his spirit; and for the first time in many years he felt quite jovial. He went to bed but couldn't go to sleep, so he rose and awakened Pinac and Fico out of their slumbers to tell them the good news, adding that he intended to engage them for his orchestra. Poons, hearing the sound of voices in the room next to his, came in, and the men sat talking over their prospects. Their hopes, their ambitions were about to be realised, and they talked and smoked the cigars Von Barwig had brought home with him until sleep was out of the question; they were too excited to go to bed again. Twice did Miss Husted send up to beg them to make less noise, as the second floor front, Mrs. Mangenborn, had complained that her slumbers were being rudely disturbed. So the men dressed themselves and went down into Von Barwig's rooms, where they sat till daylight, talking and smoking; after which they all went out to breakfast at Galazatti's.

As the weeks went by and Von Barwig received no word from Van Praag the certainty of the engagement died out and became merely a hope. Finally Von Barwig came to the conclusion that Van Praag had forgotten, and wrote to him reminding him of his promise. He received no answer to his letter, and even the hope of getting the engagement died out some few months after its birth.

Chapter Ten

The winter had now fairly set in and it was remembered by New Yorkers as the hardest in many years. Miss Husted declared it was the coldest in her experience, for the plumber's presence was constantly required to thaw out the frozen pipes. Certainly Von Barwig remembered it because he had to wrap blankets around him to keep warm while he was copying music at a few cents a page. He had other uses for the money that coal would cost; besides it was very expensive. So he preferred to write in bed rather than spend money for fuel, until one day some sixty odd pages of music were returned to him, because they were so badly written as to be almost illegible. The fact is, the old man's hands trembled so with the cold that he could not hold his pen tightly. After this loss he gave up copying music, and so even this last meagre means of getting money was denied him.

As he walked up and down his room, feeling intuitively that it was breakfast time, he became really angry with himself for his repeated failures. Lately he had been thinking of his wife and child; but fourteen years had somewhat benumbed his memory. When he thought of the happiness of his life with them, it was more as a happy dream that he delighted to ponder over than a tangible something of which he had been robbed. The wound was there but the pain had ceased.

"Are you coming out to breakfast?" said Pinac's voice outside.

"Come on, Anton," shouted Fico, "it's late!"

"I've had my breakfast," said Von Barwig, and he felt that he was lying in a good cause. The men would have torn down the door and carried him over to the restaurant by main force had they guessed the truth. "Thank God it hasn't come to that," he thought.

"He is an early bird," commented Pinac, and he went out humming the latest music-hall ditty which he was playing nightly to the patrons of the *cafe*. Poons went along; he had no more idea of his benefactor's condition than the man in the moon. The three men had not seen much of him lately, for they always left him to himself when he signified by his silence that he wanted to be alone. They respected his dignity, his slightest suggestion was law to them; they loved him, so they left him alone.

"Come on, you wretch," said Von Barwig to his violin, after the men had gone, "you are the last of the Mohicans!" and, polishing it, he put it in its case, having determined to sell it.

"This will be the first meal with which you have provided me," he said, shaking his fist at it, "so at last you are going to accomplish something, you cheap wooden cigar-box of a fiddle! I cannot play you to advantage but I can eat you. That's all you are good for--a few dinners and breakfasts!" He went out into the street with the violin under his cloak, and from Houston Street he turned into the Bowery. There was no elevated road at that time and the thundering, ear-splitting, overhead noises heard nowadays were not yet in existence. Still it was noisy, a perfect bedlam of jabbering foreigners, who crowded this busiest of busy streets as they crowded no other section of this cosmopolitan city. Von Barwig, usually so sensitive to noises, apparently did not notice this babel. Curiously enough his thoughts were miles away from New York, and the idea that he was going to sell his violin to buy a breakfast was not borne in upon him with sufficient force to prevent his thinking of something else. Although it was very cold he did not notice the weather, so he did not walk fast. His progress was a mechanical movement, for in fancy he was in Leipsic again, walking down the August Platz. It was a pleasant day dream, one from which Von Barwig did not like to awaken himself. He pictured to himself the joy, the happiness of his loved ones when they saw him, and thus he felt the reflex of this joy. These mental pictures were almost real to him, and he enjoyed them while they lasted, though he knew that they were not real.

"It is better to dream than to think of the present," he said to himself. "What is there going on about me but misery and starvation and folly? Why should I focus my mind on the evils of existence, analyse them, make them my bosom companions to the exclusion of all joy? No, I will think of those things that make for happiness. Little Helene shall be my companion. These shadows" (and he looked at the people who passed him), "these caricatures of life shall not find a place in my mind. I will shut them out and in that way they shall cease to exist for me; since what we do not know cannot make us suffer."

Von Barwig walked down the crowded thoroughfare, barely conscious that he was dreaming, yet in his dreams finding peace. The old man knew that there was a musical instrument shop somewhere in the neighbourhood, but it is quite possible that he would have passed it by had not the sound of a loud, roaring voice, accompanied by the banging of a big drum, attracted, or rather demanded his attention and aroused him from his day dream.

"Eat 'em alive, eat 'em alive!" bellowed the voice. Bang! bang! went the drum. "Bosco, Bosco, the armless wonder," bang! bang! "bites their heads off and eats their bodies; eats 'em alive, eats 'em alive!" Bang! bang! "Bosco, Bosco!" the drum punctuating each phrase, making a hideous, ear-splitting duet.

"What hellish syncopation!" thought poor Von Barwig mechanically, as he looked at the individual from whom issued the voice that sounded so like the bellowing of a bull.

The owner of this extraordinary vocal organ was a big, fat, florid-faced individual with a dark, bluish-red complexion. He wore a flaring diamond ring around a glaring red necktie; and a loud checked suit that matched his voice perfectly. In fact, his whole make-up harmonised remarkably with the unearthly noise that issued from his throat. He was standing before a flashy-fronted building, on which was painted in large yellow letters, intended to be gold, the legend "Dime Museum." In the front entrance were several cheap wax figures of a theatrical nature, and some still cheaper scenes, showing the figure of a nude savage without arms, biting the head off a huge fish and eating it alive apparently. On the canvas were also painted pictures of a wild man from Borneo, a tattooed man, a skeleton, numerous fat ladies, mermaids, sylphs, and fauns; the whole forming a group of pictures and figures calculated to arrest the attention of the passers-by and attract them into the "theatretorium," as he of the loud voice called it.

It was not the paintings that caught Von Barwig's attention; it was the voice that offended his sensitive ear. He looked at the man in astonishment; never in his life had he heard such an utter lack of music in a human voice, such volume of tone, such a surplusage of quantity and an absence of quality. Barwig was fascinated and wondered how it could be possible. At this moment he caught the man's eye, and then a strange thing happened. The man stopped roaring, and, looking over at Von Barwig, in a more natural tone called out:

"Say, professor, I want to see you."

"Are you speaking to me?" said Von Barwig; his voice faltering.

"Yes," replied the showman, "that's just what I am." Coming over to Von Barwig he took him by the arm and led him almost by force into the entrance of the Museum. "Say, professor," he asked, "how would you like a job?"

"A job?" Von Barwig repeated helplessly, trying to realise the meaning of the man's words.

"A job; yes, to be sure. Can you thump the ivories?"

"Thump the ivories?" Von Barwig looked so mystified that the man volunteered an explanation.

"Play the pianner," and suiting the action to the word he perforated the air with ten large fingers.

"I play--yes. I--I play a little--not well----"

"Well, do you want the job? We've got a day professor, but we need a night professor. Day professor plays from eight till eight; night professor from eight till two or three. Depends on the crowds. Come on, now; I like your looks. Say the word and the job is yours."

It was not pride that made Von Barwig silent when he wanted to speak; he simply did not grasp the man's meaning.

"I see you've got your fiddle there. You can play the incidental music for the dramas with that; and you can play the pianner for the curios and the intermissions. Dollar a night; what do you say?"

"A dollar a night!" Von Barwig at last caught the man's meaning. He wanted him to play for that amount, at night, and it would not interfere with his teaching in the daytime.

"I only play a very little, just enough to show my pupils," he said deprecatingly.

"Oh, you're all right! You can read music, can't you?"

Von Barwig smiled. "Yes," he replied simply.

"Well, you'll get on to it."

But Von Barwig still held back.

"What's the matter, ain't it enough?"

Von Barwig was silent.

"Damn it all," the showman blurted out. "I'll risk it; a dollar and a half a night. Your long hair is worth that; you look the goods. I'll make a special feature of you--a real professor. Come on inside and take a look at the place. A dollar and a half a night, eight till three; is it a bargain?"

Von Barwig paused, then drew a long deep breath and nodded affirmatively.

"You'll be fine--fine," said he of the big voice. "I can see it in your eye; you ain't one of them smart felleys."

He grabbed the hand of his new attraction and shook it heartily. "Say, George," he roared, "come here! This is the new night professor."

George, the young man who was beating the drum, ceased that occupation and came over to the showman and Von Barwig.

"What's your name?" the showman suddenly asked Von Barwig.

"Anton Von Barwig," came the reply in a low tone.

"Well, Anton, my name is Costello, Al Costello." Then with dignity, "Professor Anton, shake hands with George Pike--he's my assistant. This is the new night professor, George."

"Happy to meet you, professor," said that individual, grasping Von Barwig's hand and shaking it effusively. This hand-shaking process seemed a part of the theatrical trade.

"Say, George, take him inside and introduce him to the curios and just tell 'em from me that if they don't treat him better than they did the other night professor, by the eternal jumpin' Jerusalem, I'll fire the whole bunch!" With that Mr. Costello slapped Von Barwig on the back, and resumed his occupation of attracting public attention.

As George and Von Barwig passed the turnstile and went up the passage that led into the main hall, the huge voice outside continued to roar.

"Bosco, Bosco, the armless wonder! Bites their heads off and eats their bodies; eats them alive, eats them alive!" And so Anton Von Barwig became the night professor in a dime museum on the Bowery.

It astonished even Von Barwig himself, when he found how easily he adapted himself to his new position. In a very short time he found his occupation far less irksome and tedious than he had expected. As to the disgrace of appearing nightly in a dime museum, Von Barwig felt it keenly enough, but he preferred to pay his way and suffer himself, rather than to make others suffer through his inability to make sufficient money to meet his expenses. Not a word escaped him as to his new engagement, for he was determined not to parade his shame before his friends' eyes until it became absolutely necessary for them to know.

His duties were simple enough in their way; he extemporised incidental music on the piano or violin while the curios were being exhibited, and during the progress of the little abbreviated dramas that were played by the troupe of actors in the theatre upstairs. It did not add to Von Barwig's happiness that Mr. Costello always insisted upon calling the attention of the audience to the special music as played by "Professor *An-tone* of Germany, Europe," and would point at him and start clapping until the audience gave him the round of applause that he felt the professor was entitled to. To Von Barwig's astonishment and embarrassment, Costello took a violent fancy to him, and would talk to him whenever a chance offered itself.

"Professor," he would say, "you're different from the gang that hangs around here. I like to talk to you; it does me good. You don't never try to give me no songs and dances about how much more you're worth than I'm paying you, and how much more you know than the day professor. You ain't forever talkin' about yourself."

Von Barwig accepted this praise philosophically. He didn't in the least understand it, but he felt that Mr. Costello intended to be complimentary. He was grateful to him, too, for the man had raised his salary to two dollars a night without being asked, and on several occasions had let him go home early. Besides that, he treated Von Barwig with far more consideration and respect than he did any one else, even his own wife. The latter liked the professor and told her husband she was sure he had seen better days.

This deference made things much easier for the night professor, who otherwise would have suffered many an indignity. Indeed the position seemed to call for special insult from any one who chose to bestow it. He heard the day professor roundly abused on several occasions because he did not play to suit the performers. Not only insults, but cushions were flung at him, and Von Barwig determined if ever this happened to him he would leave at once. He was willing to sacrifice his dignity and his pride, but not his self-respect. Thanks to Mr. Costello nothing happened to mar the harmony of his existence there. The curios were very fond of Von Barwig, and he took quite an interest in them. Poor, crippled human beings, the sadness of their existence aroused his sympathy; their very affliction earning a livelihood for them. Was life not a living hell for them?

He found on closer intimacy with them that it was not, for they enjoyed life after their own manner and were capable of real affection. The midgets always shook hands with him every evening when he came to play. They were a loving little pair, brother, and sister, and they grew quite fond of him. Von Barwig, for his part, used to look upon them as children, although they were both well past forty years of age. Once he saluted the "little girl," as he called her, with a kiss, and he was quite astonished when she blushed. Her brother clapped his hands and enjoyed what he called the fun. But it was the untoward affection of the fat lady that nearly brought about a catastrophe, for her constant smile at the professor aroused the jealousy of the living skeleton and brought about an ultimatum from that gentleman in the shape of a challenge to fight a duel to the death. The fat lady was an agreeable individual. She seemed to have one occupation only, that of sitting in a rocking chair and rocking and fanning herself by the hour. The skeleton was quite sure that the professor was trying to win her affections, but as a matter of fact, Von Barwig was so fascinated by her constant rocking and fanning that he simply could not help looking at her, and she evidently could not help smiling. As he explained to the skeleton, her tempo was against the beat, or in other words, the rhythm of her rocking and fanning conflicted with the rhythm of the music he was playing. The skeleton did not altogether understand Von Barwig's explanation, but he accepted it willingly, for it was clear that the professor had withdrawn from the candidacy for the fat lady's affections!

It must by no means be understood, however, that Von Barwig liked his new occupation. On the contrary, it grieved his very soul; but it was far less painful than he had anticipated. Mr. Costello seemed to realise that his night professor was not in his element and he made it as easy for him as possible. The weary months went on, and Von Barwig by teaching during the day and working at night just barely made ends meet.

"I am getting thinner and thinner," thought he as a ring slipped from his finger

and rolled under the old sofa which had been in his room for a long time. In looking for it he came across an old portmanteau which had been slipped under the sofa
and had entirely escaped his memory during his residence in Miss Husted's house.
He opened it and his heart beat rapidly as he saw the case of pistols he had brought
from Leipsic intending to force Ahlmann to fight a duel. He looked at them--there
they lay, old-fashioned, duelling pistols--weapons for the shedding of blood. He
had found no use for them in all these years and now he would not use them if he
could, so he gently laid them down on the piano and looked further into the portmanteau.

Within its depths, among many relics of the past he found one or two of his
compositions, pieces for the piano. He lifted them up and underneath lay the symphony played by his orchestra the night she left him--the symphony that had never
been heard in its entirety. He let the lid of the portmanteau fall. The dust flew up
in his face, but he did not notice it, for memories of that fatal night came thronging
into his brain and he could think of nothing but that never-to-be-forgotten scene.
A great longing to hear that music again came upon him, a longing he could not
resist. It was dusk and the gas lamps were being lit when he sat down at the piano.
How long he played he never knew, for when they found him several hours later,
it was quite dark and the old man was completely unconscious; his head had fallen
on his arm which rested on the keyboard of the piano.

*   *   *   *   *

Mr. Costello was quite disturbed at the absence of "Professor Antone of Germany" that night, and when, the next night, Von Barwig walked into the Museum,
his violin under his arm as usual, he was greeted quite effusively.

"Well, well, well, profess'! So you didn't give us the shake after all! Say, George,
he's come back!" bawled Costello at the top of his voice.

"Yes," said Von Barwig simply, "I've come back."

The midgets laughed, the skeleton scowled, the fat lady smiled; and the old
man took out his violin and prepared to go to work.

Chapter Eleven

Miss Husted was a woman of few ideas, but once an idea obtained lodgment in her brain it was by no means an easy matter for her to rid herself of it. She pondered over it and thought it out until it became too big for one person to hold. Then, under the ban of secrecy, she confided it to another, and another, and another, until it became everybody's secret. She went through this process in regard to her aversion to young Poons, whom she suspected in one way or another of being a burden to "the dear professor." In addition she had a haunting dread that Mr. Poons was in love with her niece. Jenny was now nearly nineteen years of age, and although she looked barely sixteen, she had developed into a remarkably good-looking young woman, a fact which young Poons had evidently noticed.

Miss Husted trembled with dismay when she saw Poons look at Jenny. She was very grateful that he couldn't speak to her in English, and still more grateful that Jenny couldn't understand German. Mrs. Mangenborn, aided and abetted by the cards, had predicted a most advantageous marriage for her niece; indeed the cards had pointed to either a title or a million, or both, and Miss Husted dreaded lest any premature, ill-considered love match should interfere with this happy prediction. She declared vehemently that Jenny was too young "even to look at a man."

Now Jenny had no idea that she liked young Poons. She was interested in him because she was sorry for him, and she was sorry for him because her aunt was always speaking against him. So Miss Husted brought about the very condition she most dreaded, for her niece began to like the young man from the moment her aunt forbade her to speak to him. This secret was originally Miss Husted's, but after she had begged Pinac to tell Poons not to behave like a moon-calf, had asked Fico to prevent the young German from sighing audibly whenever he saw Jenny, and had finally told Von Barwig she wouldn't keep Poons in the house at any price, everybody in the house began to suspect something. This suspicion ripened into certainty, and with the solitary exception of Miss Husted everybody sympathised with the young pair and aided and abetted them in their love-making.

But this was not the only awful secret that was troubling Miss Husted's innermost soul. For some time she had been troubled and depressed, for she had found several pawn tickets in Von Barwig's room. She had also missed several ornaments, pictures and even garments that had formerly been conspicuous possessions. His fur-lined coat was gone; and the cuckoo clock, what had become of it? When she saw the pawn tickets she knew, and the knowledge troubled her, for she realised how very badly the professor must need money to pledge articles of such small value. She pondered over her discovery until it became too big for her to bear alone, so she confided it first to Skippy, the little black and tan terrier that the professor had given her as a Christmas gift, and then not getting much response from that quarter she told her secret to Mrs. Mangenborn. She had suspected all along that poor, dear Professor Barwig was not doing well, but she never dreamed it had come to this. Tears came into the good woman's eyes as she showed Mrs. Mangenborn the pawn tickets and tearfully asked her what she could do. Mrs. Mangenborn, being a practical person, suggested reducing his rent and Miss Husted made up her mind to do this forthwith.

She could hear the strains of music coming from his room, so she picked up the little dog, which was now her constant companion, and knocked at the door. Receiving no reply she opened it and walked in. The three men who were playing stopped; Jenny, who was there also, looked very guilty, and began dusting the furniture. Pinac was playing his violin, Poons the 'cello and Fico was at the piano, with Jenny apparently as the audience.

"Isn't Professor Barwig here?" inquired Miss Husted, surprised at his room being occupied during his absence.

"No, Miss Owstong," said Pinac, always the spokesman of the trio. He spoke English slightly better than Fico, who could barely make himself understood. There was an awkward pause. "He lets us come down here to play. We practise to go into the Union. We use his piano; he is very kind," Pinac explained.

At this point the unfortunate Poons dropped his bow and in picking it up, knocked his music stand over. When Miss Husted glared at him, Poons grinned guiltily, and stole a glance in the direction of Jenny. Miss Husted followed this glance with her eye and rather testily suggested to her niece that the bell was ringing and there was no one to answer it. Jenny, who was glad to get out alive, hurriedly made her escape. Poons, sighing deeply, went into the alcove and looked out of the window. Miss Husted sat down, looked around the room pathetically, then followed Poons's example and sighed.

"Gentlemen," she began; then hesitated. After all it was the professor's secret. Perhaps they knew; if not, 'twas better they should. The men looked at each other inquiringly, and waited for her to speak.

"I'm very glad I've found you together--very glad. Do you notice any change in me?"

Pinac and Fico shook their heads, mainly because they were mystified.

"I haven't been sociable lately; not at all like myself," went on Miss Husted, "I'm so upset."

"That's all right," said Fico, who didn't know what else to say.

"Sure," nodded Pinac, who felt he had to add his share to the conversation; then they picked up their music and started to leave the room, but Miss Husted held up her hand and signified that she wanted them to remain. When they came back to her she looked around the room pathetically once more, and began plaintively:

"I said to myself, 'These foreign gentlemen will miss your cheery word in the hall and on the stairs.'"

The men began to feel very uncomfortable, for they had missed nothing. Pinac thought she referred in some way to Poons, and tried to catch his eye and motion to him to get out of the room, but that lovelorn youth was mooning out of the window, so Pinac nodded sympathetically at Miss Husted and said, "Oui, oui. Yes, oh, yes!"

Fico looked very grave and muttered: "Too bad; too bad!"

Again Miss Husted looked around the room very mysteriously and motioned to the men to come closer. They obeyed, somewhat apprehensively this time.

"What did it all mean?" they thought. "Why this mystery?"

"I've something to tell you in confidence," she said finally. She tried to open her reticule and finding Skippy in the way, she handed the little animal to Fico, saying:

"Will one of you gentlemen please hold Skippy while I find those tickets? He just had a bath and if he rolls over he'll get soiled."

Fico took the dog, which promptly yelped, so he hurriedly handed it to Pinac. Pinac, who was afraid of dogs, transferred the animal to Poons. Poons, anxious to be of some service to Miss Husted, tried to pet the dog, but looking at Miss Husted for approval instead of watching the beast, he held it so awkwardly that its head hung down and its tail stuck up in the air. Miss Husted, in the act of pulling pawn tickets out of her reticule, caught sight of the unfortunate animal suspended in mid air, and jumped up quickly.

"Look at him! Look how the stupid, stupid fellow is holding Skippy! All the blood will rush into his poor little head. The dog, the dog; you foolish fellow; the d-o-g, dog! I can't make him understand. Please tell him, Mr. Pinac."

"Hund--hund!" shouted Fico to Poons.

"Le chien--Le chien! Idiot, stupid!" said Pinac.

Poons was so startled by hearing them all shout at him at once that he dropped the dog into Von Barwig's coal scuttle, whence it finally issued covered with coal dust and ran yelping into Miss Husted's arms. That lady petted the frightened animal while Pinac pushed the unfortunate Poons out of the room.

When Miss Husted had completely recovered herself, she held up the pawn tickets.

"I found them," she said dolefully, "under that pile of music."

"Gritt Scott!" said Pinac. He knew at a glance what they were; experience had taught him.

"Are they of Von Barwig?" he inquired.

Fico took three or four of the tickets. "From Anton; yes," and then he sighed and shook his head.

The men knew Von Barwig was poor, but they had no idea to what extent his poverty had reached.

"His cuckoo clock: nine dollars!" read Fico.

"That was the first thing I missed--that cuckoo, evenings," sighed Miss Husted.

"Mozart, gone!" almost shouted Pinac, pointing to the spot on the wall where that musician's portrait had once reposed. "And Beethoven! And where is Gluck?"

Then looking around: "Nom de Dieu! even his metronome have gone--his metronome! Dieu, Dieu!"

"I should say it was dear, dear!" said Miss Husted, who slightly misunderstood Pinac.

And so the truth dawned upon them. For months, for years he had deceived them with his smile, his optimism, his gay manner and cheery word, and above all by the open-hearted manner in which he gave away to all who came to him.

"All these years has Professor Von Barwig been in my house and he has paid me like a gentleman. He pays me now, how does he do it? Oh, dear!" Miss Husted tried hard not to cry, but the tears would come. The men looked on sadly; they had always accepted his bounty, and now they were reproaching themselves.

Miss Husted's feelings made her reminiscent, and when she was reminiscent she invariably exaggerated--in retrospect she saw everything as she would have liked it to have been. "When he first came here what a man he was! And this, what a neighbourhood then, an elegant residential district. I had a position then, I could recommend him; everybody knew Miss Houston of Houston Street." In spite of her sorrow she felt proud of the past.

The men looked at each other. They had heard this for the past fifteen years. It meant a long session and they wanted to practise their music; so Pinac merely nodded, and Fico shook his head gravely.

"Why, I was pointed out by everybody as Miss Houston of Houston Street. I was a landmark; a sight."

"Yes," said Pinac unconsciously. "You were; and you are still."

Miss Husted looked at him sharply. "Was he venturing to laugh at her?" she thought. But his sad face belied any such intention.

"How things have changed?" went on Miss Husted tremulously. "There's not a child in this neighbourhood that can afford to pay for his lesson! And when they can't afford it, he won't take the money! He gives away the very bread out of his mouth."

Pinac and Fico shifted uncomfortably.

"Everything he had of value has gone long ago. Do you remember that beautiful violin?"

"Ah, yes! his Amati. Yes, yes! He bought instead a cheap one. I wondered why, but did not ask him."

"And still he pays me. Where does he get it?" asked Miss Husted tearfully. "What is he doing out every night, nearly all night?"

The men looked at each other; this was another revelation. They were out at night themselves and so did not know of his absence.

"There's something done up to go to pawn now," said Miss Husted, pointing to a box wrapped up in a paper on the piano. It was Von Barwig's case of pistols. Pinac and Fico looked at each other in astonishment.

"Pistols for duel!" said Pinac at once. He had seen them in the theatre, long, thin, single barrel pistols.

"Sometimes I feel that he came to this country purposely to take vengeance on some one," said Miss Husted mysteriously. The men were much impressed, but neither of them spoke.

"I don't believe the poor man has his meals half the time," went on Miss Husted, somewhat irrelevantly. "I am almost sure he doesn't."

"We ask him to dine the evening," said Fico, with a look of triumph, feeling that he had not only discovered the problem but had also solved it.

"Yes," assented Pinac, "we ask him."

At this moment Poons came back into the room, having forgotten his music.

Miss Husted was so wrapped up in her thoughts that she had no time to frown at him.

A door bang was heard, and her sharp ears detected the sound. "There he is now," she said. "Please don't tell him that I spoke of his affairs. You know how sensitive he is."

A key was heard in the door; Von Barwig evidently thought the room was empty. As he came in, followed by Jenny, the sad expression on his face changed.

"Ah," he said, with a sigh of satisfaction; "when I set foot here, I am among friends. So glad, so glad! Welcome to you all."

Miss Husted, making a few lame excuses, hurried out. She felt that she had been guilty of an indiscretion in betraying the professor's secret to his friends.

Von Barwig greeted his friends warmly.

"Well, how is the little *hausfrau*?" he said as he handed Jenny a flower that he had brought for her. "Beauty is a fairy, eh? Sometimes it hides in a flower, sometimes in a fresh young face," and he pinched her cheek tenderly. "Here blooms a rose; not picked, not picked, August!" Poons smiled and shook his head.

"He doesn't understand me," said Von Barwig. "The son of my old friend has been six months in this country, and not a word of English can he speak."

"Never mind, Jenny! I find you a splendid fellow; one who can speak his own mind in his own language. Not a selfish fellow like these bachelors. Bah! a bachelor is not a citizen of his country; he is not even civilised. He is--a nondescript--a--a----"

The men were looking at him sadly as if trying to read his innermost thoughts. They seemed to have realised for the first time that his gaiety was forced. His spirits this afternoon were unusually high; and it made the reality stand out in greater contrast. Pinac felt that he might resent any reference to his financial condition, so he did not speak of it.

"It is a long time since we have had a nice little dinner together," he said in his Gallic way.

"Yes," assented Von Barwig, "a long time!"

"A dinner during which we can exchange confidences," ventured Fico, interspersing his English with Italian, and a word or two of slang. Pinac gave Fico a look of warning.

"He means a 'art to 'art talk," explained Pinac.

"Excellent, excellent!" said Von Barwig, rubbing his hands, and going over to the window he pulled up the blind.

"He falls into our trap very easily," whispered Pinac to Fico; "but be careful!"

Poons looked on and smiled as usual.

"I should like nothing better," said Von Barwig. "You shall all dine with me," and before his friends could remonstrate he had invited Poons to the banquet.

"But I asked you!" said Pinac.

"He ask you," repeated Fico.

"I ask you; we all ask you," asserted Pinac.

"In my apartment!" demanded Von Barwig, with some slight show of dignity. "Come, come! The matter is settled. It is good to have old friends at the table. We won't go to the restaurant; it's too noisy there; we shall dine here. Galazatti will send over a dinner without extra charge, if we order enough."

"I am not hungry," began Fico, but Von Barwig silenced him with a look.

"Then please find your appetite at once," he said.

They saw it was useless to remonstrate with him and for a moment remained silent, but Pinac determined to make another effort.

"You cannot afford such expense," he began. "It is too much."

"Pardon me," said Von Barwig, with quiet dignity, "I can always afford to invite my friends to dinner. I have had lessons all day, ever since early morning. Please, my dear Pinac, and you, Fico, old friend, do not refer to the financial side of our little festivity. It robs it of the zest of enjoyment, of comradeship. Let us eat and drink and be merry! The question is, what shall we have for dinner, not who shall pay for it?" And then without awaiting a reply, he opened the door and called for Jenny.

Pinac and Fico looked at each other. It was evident to them that Miss Husted had exaggerated Von Barwig's poverty, so their spirits rose at once.

"Jenny! We take dinner here. Get me the *menu*, Poons. Jenny, you will ask your good aunt, Miss Husted, to dine with us *en famille*--one of our old-time dinners. Now, what shall we have?" he said, scanning the well-thumbed *menu* that Poons had handed to him.

"It is an old one," suggested Fico.

"It is always the same. It is only the date they change," said Von Barwig. Pinac looked over his shoulder at the *menu*.

"*Chicken a la Marengo*," said the Frenchman, "with a *soupcon* of garlic."

"No," said Von Barwig decidedly, "Miss Husted doesn't like garlic!"

"*A la Polenta* is better," suggested the Italian.

"*Ein Bischen Limburger*," put in Poons, which was instantly frowned upon by all.

Jenny was asked to take down the order, and the process of selecting the dishes for the dinner was gone through; each ordering according to his own taste. Jenny tried to write down everything they wanted, but gave it up after she had filled three pages of suggestions and scratched them out again. Finally Von Barwig ordered a nice little dinner, including spaghetti and garlic. As Jenny was about to take the order to Galazatti's, Miss Husted made her appearance. Jenny told her that the professor had invited her to dinner, and she realised in a moment what had happened.

It was the old story; the professor was to be the host. She suggested that she herself get up a little dinner for the men, but Von Barwig wouldn't hear of putting her to the trouble and so his ideas were carried out as usual. It was really a most enjoyable dinner! To this day Miss Husted speaks of it as one of those gala Bohemian affairs that must be seen and heard and eaten to be appreciated. As she afterward told her friend, Mrs. Mangenborn, they had a hip, hip hurray of a time. The dear professor was just as jolly as he could be. Even Poons was tolerable, although she would not for worlds sit next to him at the table. It was simply impossible for her to describe the dinner in detail, but how Fico swallowed the spaghetti without losing it down his shirt front was a mystery. How the man got so much on his fork and swallowed it down by the yard nobody knew, it was simply a sublime feat! But the toasts they drank (with the last of the professor's claret), the songs they sang, the art they discussed! Every word was a scream of laughter.

"Just listen to this," said Miss Husted, laughing at the very memory of the joke. "Young Poons asked what was garlic, and the professor said: 'Garlic is a vegetable limburger!' The idea of such a thing!" Even Mrs. Mangenborn consented to smile.

"And when Mr. Fico said, 'Wine is the enemy of mankind,' Mr. Pinac jumped up and said, 'Is it? Then give me my enemy, that I may drink him down.' Oh, it was a most enjoyable affair. I can't tell you all that was said," went on Miss Husted. "But how the wit did flow! Wit and wine; no, wit and water; there wasn't much wine. We didn't in the least mind the noise that the Donizetti family made overhead; though once when the chandelier nearly came down the professor did say they ought to live in the cellar! I think I'll give them notice next week," she added thoughtfully, "though God knows I need the money."

"What about the pawn tickets?" asked Mrs. Mangenborn.

"Not a word was said about them," replied Miss Husted. "I don't know what to think! The professor was just--oh, he was--well, we had a great time. There's something about Bohemia that appeals to my innermost nature. Give me a Bohemian dinner every time!" she said, when she had spoken her final word on the subject.

"He must have money in the bank," commented Mrs. Mangenborn.

Miss Husted shook her head. "I don't think so," she said.

On the same evening the collection agent for the Blickner Piano Company called on Professor Von Barwig, and presented him with a "final notice."

"I intended to pay you to-day," said Von Barwig. "I will pay you next week. Won't you please wait? I have two lessons to-morrow."

"You'll pay, or we'll take the piano away; that's all! You're six weeks behind."

"I had the money and I intended to give it to you to-day," Von Barwig pleaded. "But--some friends came to dinner, and--" He paused, and then smiled as it occurred to him how thoughtless he had been. The collector left the notice in Von Barwig's possession, and walked away without further comment.

Chapter Twelve

Affairs had not been going along very smoothly at the Museum. About this time, there came into existence a new tempo in music that appealed chiefly to people whose musical tastes were not yet developed, or who had no musical taste or ear whatsoever. Now the performers at Costello's Museum, who were called artists on the playbills, insisted that the "Night Profess'" play their accompaniments to their acts in this new style of musical rhythm--ragtime as it was most appropriately called. But Von Barwig, being a musician, whose music lay in his soul and not merely in his feet and fingers, could not do this. He worked hard to get it, but could not, and the artists complained to the manager. As a result Mr. Costello called upon Von Barwig at his lodgings; much to the professor's astonishment and dismay.

"Say, who was that freak that poked her head out or the door as I came in?" said that gentleman, as soon as he had banged the door shut, and seated himself comfortably in Von Barwig's armchair.

"Freak? Freak? we have no freaks here! Oh," and a faint smile stole over Von Barwig's features, which he tried hard to repress. "You mean perhaps Miss Husted?"

"Do I?" inquired Costello, "well, p'raps I do! She's of the vintage of 1776, and looks like a waxwork edition of ----"

"Please, please!" remonstrated Von Barwig. "She is a lady, a most hospitable, kind-hearted lady! You would like her if you knew her, really----"

"Maybe so," said Costello, somewhat dubiously; and then he blurted out: "Well, profess', I've come on a professional visit! I want to put you wise before you turn up to play to-night."

Von Barwig looked pained. Costello was bawling at the top of his voice, and he was afraid that the household would hear.

"Hush, please! You speak so loud. As you know, my visits to the Museum are, in a sense, a secret. I keep my private and my professional life apart, as it were. Forgive me, but please, please, don't speak loudly! I do not wish it known; for they think that I--they do not know that I--have--" Von Barwig was about to say, "fallen so low," but he did not wish to hurt the amiable Costello's feelings; so he paused.

"That's all right, profess'," broke in Costello; "I'm having a little trouble with my main attraction, Bosco, the armless wonder. I wish she was a tongueless wonder! She has no arms, but my God; how she can talk! I left her taking it out of the day professor; she was swearing a blue streak. Ain't it funny how these stars kick?" and Mr. Costello bit the end off a cigar, viciously lit it, and puffed furiously at it till the room was clouded with smoke. Von Barwig was silent. He was waiting for Mr. Costello to tell him the worst, that he could not come again. His heart began to beat; what should he do if he lost his position?

"She says your music is queering her act," said Mr. Costello finally, "she says you don't give it to her thumpin' enough; she wants ragtime or she can't work."

"I will do my best," said the old man simply. "I try hard to please her; indeed I do!"

"I know you do, I know you do, profess'! But, say, you can't do anything with them guys! You know I like you, you've got such damned elegant manners--the gentleman all over. Yes, sir, you're a twenty-two karat gentleman; you're the first professor the freaks darsent josh!"

Von Barwig bowed his head. He was grateful to Costello; the man had made his hideous task almost bearable.

"Now I don't want to lose her and I don't want to lose you," Costello went on, "but things have got to go right, see? They've got to! You're one of them kind that can take a tip. Give her what she wants! What's the difference? You're a gentleman--she's a lady! She doesn't know any better!"

"I am so sorry, so very sorry to trouble--" faltered Von Barwig.

"You're all right, profess'," broke in Costello, "you earn your money if it is small pay; but the job goes against you, now don't it?" His voice was almost soft. "You ain't used to our kind, are you?" The man's brusque kindness touched Von Barwig, and he choked up a little as he spoke:

"Well--I--I--I have had higher thoughts. Here in Houston Street life is strange, and I must take what I find. Times are a little hard, a little hard, and the parents of my pupils are pushed for money. They don't pay, otherwise, perhaps I--" and Von Barwig sighed.

"You ain't suited, that's what's the matter!"

"Oh, yes; oh, yes! I--" broke in Von Barwig, afraid that Costello might dispense with his services altogether. "I acknowledge the curios came a little on my nerves at first. It was all so strange: the people staring, the midgets chattering, the stout lady fanning, fanning, always fanning, the lecturing of the lecturer; and you at the door always calling 'Insides, insides!'"

Costello laughed, "You mean 'Insi-i-ide.'"

"Yes, insides," went on Von Barwig, unconsciously making the same mistake. Then he added, trying to convince himself, "Better times will come soon and then, perhaps, we shall part, but for the present I remain, eh, yes?"

Costello nodded. "As long as you like, profess'; as long as you like!" and he held out his hand for Von Barwig to shake. As Von Barwig did so, he said: "I shall always remember it was your money that helped me to bridge over--my--my difficulties----"

"That's all right, that's all right!" asserted Costello. "You're worth the money or you wouldn't get it. But don't forget, when the lecturer says, 'Bosco, Bosco, the armless wonder!' play up lively, see? and when he says, 'Bites their heads off and eats their bodies; eats 'em alive, eats 'em alive!' give it to her thumpin'!"

Here Von Barwig drew a deep breath. He was tired, tired unto his very soul of the whole business; but he had to go on.

"Yes," he said, with a pathetic smile, "she shall eat 'em alive yet livelier!"

This appeared to satisfy Costello, and shaking hands with Von Barwig once more, he went out and left him standing in the middle of the room. Von Barwig's eye fell on a daguerreotype of Mendelssohn, and it called him back to Leipsic. "Eat 'em alive, eat 'em alive, eat 'em alive!" rang in his ears. "Good God, to what have I fallen, to what have I fallen?" he cried to himself; then he stopped. "I must have more courage. I am a coward, I am always railing at fate! Who can tell what the future shall have in store for me?" Then he thought of the songs he had found in his old trunk with his symphony. He hastily opened the trunk, took them out and hurried uptown for the purpose of selling them, but the symphony he did not take-

-he had not the courage to sell that.

It was some years since Von Barwig had tried to dispose of his compositions and he made the rounds of the various music publishers with as little success as usual. "There is no demand for my music," he thought, and he went into a fashionable music emporium, as a last hope.

The clerks at Schumein's recognised him in a moment; his was a face one could not forget. Mr. Schumein, the head of the firm, could not see him; he was busy.

"I will wait," said Von Barwig, and he sat down.

"I'm afraid he'll be busy all the afternoon," said the clerk apprehensively.

"I can wait all the afternoon, if necessary," said Von Barwig. He was tired and was glad to sit down.

"Suppose you leave your songs here and I'll hand them to our reader," suggested the clerk, after Von Barwig had been waiting over two hours.

"They won't see me," thought Von Barwig, "I can no longer obtain an interview. I am not worth seeing," and he smiled to himself as he thought of the days when people used to wait for hours to see him. "Well," he spoke aloud, "I will leave them; and to-morrow I will call for the answer."

"Better leave it till next week; our reader is very busy," said the clerk, a little impatiently.

"I will call again next week," said Von Barwig patiently.

"What's your address?" asked the clerk.

Von Barwig told him and he wrote it on the back of the manuscript. "All right, I'll attend to it," and the young man threw the songs carelessly into a drawer in his desk. Von Barwig thanked him, bowed politely, and walked slowly out.

"Who is that?" asked a young lady who had just arrived in a fashionable carriage and pair. She had been watching Von Barwig for the past few moments and was struck by the sweet, gentle sadness of his face.

"He's a sort of a composer, miss; that is, he writes songs and things. He's a music master, I fancy, in one of the poorer quarters of the city," said the clerk, taking out the manuscript he had just thrown into a drawer.

"Yes," he added, as she saw the address, "he has a studio at 970 Houston Street. Rather far downtown," he added.

"Nine hundred and seventy Houston Street," repeated the girl; "that must be near our settlement headquarters." She made some purchases, and a few moments later the footman opened the door, and she was whisked rapidly away by a pair of fine blooded horses.

"Who is that?" asked a fellow-clerk.

"Why don't you know?" asked the other with a slight tinge of superiority. "It's Miss Stanton, the heiress."

"Is that so? She's a beauty!"

"Yes," went on his informant, "her father is only worth about twenty-five millions!"

The other clerk whistled.

During Von Barwig's absence from his room that morning, young Poons had taken possession of it for the purpose of practising on his 'cello, but this was not his only reason. Jenny invariably made it a point to straighten out Von Barwig's room at just about the time that Poons happened to arrive. There he could look at her and speak to her in little broken bits of the English language, without fear of being interrupted by Miss Husted. Jenny's knowledge of German was as hopelessly nil as his ideas of English; so they made up their minds to study "each other's language from each other." To help matters along, they bought two English-German "Conversation Made Easy" books, and in the security of Von Barwig's studio they exchanged cut and dried sentences by the page, neither understanding what the other said. On this particular morning young Poons, with the assistance of Fico, had written out an English sentence, which he had recited to himself dozens of times that morning, for he had made up his mind to declare himself.

The opportunity came quickly. Poons had scarcely been practising three minutes before the door opened, and in walked Jenny with Mr. Barwig's table-cloth.

"Ach, Fraeulein Chenny!" said Poons, blushing.

"Mr. Poons," gasped Jenny, in complete astonishment, although she must have heard him playing as she came through the hall.

"Ach, Fraeulein Chenny," he repeated, trying to remember his declaration, but by this time the English sentence he had learned by heart had completely left him.

"I could not speak to you for two days because auntie, that is, Miss Husted, was watching," said Jenny, laying the cloth. Poons nodded and smiled. "She was watching," said Jenny, but he made no sign. "Verstay? Verstay?" she repeated, making her little stock of German go as far as she could.

"Nein! Ich--" said Poons hopelessly. He was hunting for the piece of paper with his declaration of love on it, and was having a great deal of trouble finding it. Where was it? He knew it was in one of his pockets; but which one? He looked very awkward and embarrassed.

"Have you your lessons learned?" asked Jenny, taking out her English-German "Conversation Made Easy" book, and hoping to help him out by starting on a topic.

"Nein," replied Poons, who knew what she meant when he saw the book. Then he added in German that he had been so thoroughly occupied in practising that he had no time, but that he had something of great importance that he wanted to say to her.

Jenny almost shook her head off trying to make it clear that she didn't understand a word he said.

"Fraeulein Chenny," he began again, but gave it up. He opened the lesson book and read in English, with a strong German accent, "Heff you die--hett of--die poy--found?" Then he looked at her ardently, as if he had just uttered the most delicate sentiment. Jenny smiled, and read what she considered to be an appropriate answer.

"Nein, ich hab die slissell meine--Grossmutter----"

She looked at him for approval,

"Schluessel," corrected Poons.

"Slissell," repeated Jenny.

"Schluess----"

"Sliss----"

Poons gave up trying and went back to his book, reading the following with deep-bated breath and loving emphasis.

"Vich---iss--to der hotel--die--vay?"

Jenny's reply came with business-like rapidity.

"Der pantoffle ist in die zimmer----"

"Puntoffel," corrected Poons.

"Pantoffle," responded his pupil.

"Tsimmer," said he.

"Zimmer," repeated she, placing the accent strongly on the "Z"; and so the lesson went on. Suddenly a smile of joy spread itself over Poons's features. In searching for his handkerchief he had fished out a piece of paper from his hip-pocket. Joy! it was the lost declaration of dependence! He opened it, and read her the following with such ardent tenderness and affection, that the girl's heart fairly beat double time.

"Fraeulein Chenny," he began, putting the piece of paper in the book and pretending that it was part of his lesson. "Fraeulein Chenny, I cannot mit you life midout--you liff," and then, feeling that he had somewhat entangled his words, he repeated: "I cannot life midout--you--Chenny--you Chenny midout." Jenny looked at him in perplexity. His manner, the words--all were so strange!

"That isn't in the lesson," she managed to gasp, holding down her head bashfully.

"I cannot life midout you liff! Luff, Chenny, luff!" he added. He meant love, for he knew the meaning of that, and he waited for her answer. Perhaps she did not understand, but if she did, all she seemed able to say was:

"That isn't in my lesson, Mr. Poons; it isn't in my lesson!"

What Poons said in response to Jenny's statement will never be known, for at that precise moment in walked Von Barwig, who had just returned from his weary, useless effort to sell his compositions. His face brightened up as he saw the young lovers, and a beautiful smile chased away the lines of sorrow and suffering. There was no mistaking Poon's attitude. His eyes were full of love, and he held Jenny's hand in his. Although she indignantly snatched it away as soon as the door opened, probably thinking it was her aunt, Von Barwig saw the action, and it brought joy to his poor, bruised old heart.

"Come here, Jenny," he said. She nestled by his side.

"Poons," he said sternly in German, "how long has this been going on?"

"I don't know, Herr Von Barwig," replied Poons, in a low voice.

"Jenny, do you approve of his action?"

"I don't know, professor, I--" Jenny laid her head on his shoulder and Von Barwig knew that she loved the young man.

"Scoundrel!" began Von Barwig, turning to Poons. He tried to be serious, but the expression on Poons's face made him smile in spite of himself. Poons begged him to speak to Jenny for him; he pleaded so hard that Jenny asked Von Barwig if he was talking about her.

"Ask him if he likes me!" said Jenny innocently.

"I will," replied Von Barwig, and he turned to Poons. "Do you love her?" he asked.

Poons's reply was a torrent of burning love, a flood of words that let loose the pent-up emotion of a highly strung musical temperament that for months had longed for utterance. The way he poured out the German language surprised both his hearers; it seemed as if he could not restrain himself. In vain did Von Barwig try to stem the onward rush of the tidal wave of talk, for declaration followed on declaration, until Poons had completely poured out all he had wanted to tell Jenny for months. He only stopped then because he had fairly exhausted the subject.

"What did he say?" asked Jenny anxiously.

"He said, yes," said Von Barwig, with a faint smile.

Jenny looked at him shyly, and held out her hand.

"Go on, love, you loon!" said Von Barwig to Poons in German, "you have caught your fish. Don't dangle it too long on the hook!"

Poons acted on the suggestion, and took Jenny in his arms and kissed her. The old man looked on approvingly; his eyes were moist with tears, but his thoughts were far away from the lovers. He loved them, yes; they were good children, good; dear, children, but his heart yearned for his own flesh and blood. It did not satisfy him that Jenny put her arms around his neck and kissed him gratefully, or that Poons embraced him and cried over him. Their happiness only emphasised his misery. He wanted his own flesh and blood; he wanted his wife and his little Helene.

But, feeling that he was selfish, he kissed them both affectionately, and promised he would speak to Miss Husted for them at the first opportunity. He did not have to wait long, for a few moments later Miss Husted came into the room with a letter for the "professor," and saw enough to convince her that Poons and her niece were more than friends. Poons wanted to pour out his heart to Miss Husted and tell her all, but Von Barwig promptly squelched this impulse, and sent him out of the room. Jenny followed him, and Von Barwig faced Miss Husted alone.

"They are charming young people," began Von Barwig.

"Yes, when they're apart," she replied.

"Now what have you against young Poons?" he asked conciliatingly.

"Nothing," replied Miss Husted, "but I don't like him!"

"Ah, if you knew his father!"

"I don't see how that would make any difference; it's the young man himself I object to! Besides, I have tremendous prospects for Jenny; she is going to marry a rich man, a very rich man."

"This is news," said Von Barwig.

"Yes," replied Miss Husted.

"Who is the gentleman?" asked Von Barwig.

"We don't know him yet; he--" Miss Husted hesitated.

"Ah, I see!" said Von Barwig, a flood of light breaking in on him.

"But I know he will come!"

Von Barwig shook his head. "You have been consulting Mrs. Mangenborn, the lady who promises you a fortune for fifty cents. Ah, my dear Miss Husted, when will you understand life as it is? You take the false for the real and the real for the false!"

"I take Mr. Poons for a fool!" said Miss Husted with some asperity, "and I am not far wrong."

"On the contrary," assented Von Barwig, "to some extent you are right, quite right! But he is young, and he is in love. To you, perhaps; love is foolishness; but love is all there is in life." There was quite a pause. Miss Husted toyed with the letter she had not yet given to the professor.

"You may be right, of course," said Miss Husted after a while. She was more placid now, more like herself. In thought she had gone back many years to a certain episode, the memory of which softened her toward love's young dream, and even toward Poons.

Von Barwig looked at her a moment, then took her hand in his.

"Is it possible, dear lady, that you, in your woman's heart, never wished that you had something to take care of besides Skippy?"

"Yes, but Mr. Poons is not--" began Miss Husted, and then she blurted out "I can't understand him; he can't understand me. I might talk to him for a week and he wouldn't know what I was talking about!"

"Yes, but Jenny understands him. What joy have you in life alone? Think of the joy of seeing a young couple begin life, just like two young birds in a little bird's nest! God put love into their hearts; can you stop them? No, neither you nor I can forbid! As well try to count the sands of the sea, as well try to stop the waves, the tides!"

Miss Husted did not reply for a moment. It was evident that Von Barwig had made some impression on her, but she would not admit it.

"I had built such hopes on Jenny," she said, shaking her head sadly.

"Can you tell how Poons will turn out?" inquired Von Barwig, feeling that he was gaining ground.

Miss Husted elevated her nose slightly, and handed the professor his letter. "He'll turn out of this house if he makes love to my niece!" she said.

"Give the matter a little thought," urged Von Barwig. "They both love you," he added.

Miss Husted sighed deeply as if thoroughly disappointed. Then she began to whimper. She told Von Barwig the story of Jenny's life; which story, with variations, he had heard annually for many years. He listened patiently, and agreed with her. Finally he extracted from her a promise to suspend action in reference to Poons until she had given the matter more thought.

"But in the meantime," insisted Miss Husted, "they must not speak!"

Knowing the extent of their knowledge of each other's language, Von Barwig readily promised on behalf of Poons to obey her injunction to the letter, and she left the room in a state of resignation.

Von Barwig opened his letter, his eyes fairly glittering with excitement as he read the following:

"MY DEAR VON BARWIG: No doubt you thought I had forgotten you, but such is not the case. Your appointment as conductor of the 'Harmony Hall Concerts' has been passed on favourably by the promoters of the venture. None of them knew you or had ever heard of you, but I soon won them over, and I am now empowered to offer you a liberal salary during the engagement. So come up to the hall at your earliest convenience and let us discuss details.

"Yours always faithfully,

"HERMANN VAN PRAAG."

P.S. "We are having some trouble with the Unions, but I do not anticipate any serious impediment to our progress."

Von Barwig's blood ran hot and cold; his heart beat so rapidly he could hear it. He read the letter again and again. His first impulse was to rush out into the hall to tell all his friends; to shout, to dance, to, give way to excitement. This he resisted. Then a great calm came over him; the end of his ill luck had come at last. It was a long lane, but the turning was there and he had reached it. Deep, deep down in his heart the man thanked God for His kindness. And as he read the letter once more, he wept tears of joy, for he felt that his deliverance was at hand. At last, at last, when well on the brink of failure, of despair, perhaps of starvation, this great joy had come to him!

In order to realise it to its fullest possible extent he sat down in his armchair and thought it all out. He could give engagements to Poons, to Fico, to Pinac. Pinac was a fairly good violin player, both he and Fico played well enough to sit at the back desk of the second violins. Poons would, of course, be one of his 'cellists. And he, himself? He need never go to the dreadful Museum again; for this alone he was grateful. Yes, he could share his good fortune with his friends; he could even make it possible for Poons to marry Jenny. These thoughts filled him with such wild excitement that he could restrain himself no longer. He rushed out into the hall, and called up the stairway for his friends. They were in, he knew, for he could hear them practising. As soon as they heard his voice they came trooping down the stairs, making so much noise that Miss Husted rushed out of her room and asked whether the house was on fire.

They all crowded pell-mell into Von Barwig's room. Was this the usually calm, dignified professor? Could it really be Von Barwig who was now almost shouting at the top of his voice, telling them to send in their resignations from the *cafe*, that they need play no more at a wretched twenty-five cent *table d'hote* for their existence. He would provide for them, he would engage them forthwith for his orchestra. By degrees they understood, and when they did understand they made his little outburst of enthusiasm appear almost feeble and weak-kneed compared to the wild, unrestrained, excited, and enthusiastic yells of joy that they let loose. They embraced each other and danced around the room. They hugged Miss Husted. Poons even dared to kiss her, and although she slapped his face, she joined in the Latin-Franco-Teutonic *melee* of joy as though she herself had been one of them. In fact, she was one of them! Even then their happiness did not come to an end, for they ordered a good dinner for themselves at Galazatti's.

"To hell with the *cafe*," said Fico as he wrote to his employer, the proprietor of the restaurant, saying they did not intend to play that night, and could never come again.

"*Table d'hote*, nothing! Not for me, never again," said Pinac as he indited his resignation. "A bas le *cafe*!"

"I don't trouble to write at all," said Poons in German, "I simply don't go."

Presently the dinner came, and what a dinner it was. The (California) wine flowed like water, and this was true literally, for more than once Von Barwig was compelled to put water in the demijohn to make it last out. They all talked at once, and everybody ate, drank and made merry. Miss Husted sang a song!

After the rattle and banging of plates, knives and forks had subsided and the coffee had been brought in, Von Barwig was called upon to make a speech. Somehow or other his mind reverted to the last speech he had made, so many, many years ago, when he had accepted the conductorship of the Leipsic Philharmonic Orchestra. It seemed strange to him now, nearly twenty years later, that he should be called upon to speak on an almost similar occasion. Then, too, there had been a banquet. He made a few remarks appropriate to the occasion and finally drank a toast to the standard of musical purity.

This was Pinac's opportunity. "No, no, Von Barwig!" he said, "we are not fit to drink such a toast! We are in the gutter. It is you, my friend, you alone of all these present, who does not sink himself to play for money at a *cafe* on Liberty Street. To Von Barwig, the artist!"

The rattle of plates, knives and forks attested the popularity of this sentiment; then Fico began:

"It is you only who keeps up the standard." More applause. "You are the standard bearer, the general. You lead; we follow," at which the clapping was vociferous.

Von Barwig felt keenly the falsity of his position at that moment. He thought of the deception, the lie he was practising on them. He had sunk lower than they, far lower, for he was playing in a dime museum. He could not bear their praises; for he knew he did not deserve them. He inwardly determined to tell them the truth, but not at that moment, for he did not want to dampen their spirits. As the cognac and cigars were placed on the table Miss Husted rose grandly, and stated that the ladies would now withdraw; whereupon she and Jenny left the room, proudly curt-seying themselves out. "***La grande dame***!" said Pinac as he bowed low to her. The men then talked over their prospects, their hopes, even getting so far as to discuss the opening programme. An idea occurred to Von Barwig, "Why not open with his symphony?" The men almost cheered at the idea, so he unlocked the little trunk and took it out. There it was, covered with the dust of years and almost coffee-coloured. As he took it out of the trunk, something fell out from between the pages and dropped upon the floor. He picked it up, and his heart stood still for a moment as he glanced at it, for it was a miniature portrait of his wife. He thrust it hastily in his pocket and went on distributing the parts of the symphony.

"You, the first violin, Pinac," and he handed him his part. "For you, Fico, the second violin. Poons, the 'cello, of course," and the men hurried to get their instruments.

Chapter Thirteen

It was late the following morning when Von Barwig returned from his interview with Van Praag. All the details had been settled satisfactorily, and his three friends were to be engaged. Von Barwig had not yet left the Museum; his sense of obligation to Costello was too great to permit him to desert him without notice, so it was understood that he was to leave at the end of the week. How Von Barwig welcomed the thought of that Saturday night, and it was only Wednesday!

When Von Barwig came in, the men were in his room practising their parts of the symphony. His arrival put an end to further work. They wanted to talk about their "grand new engagement," as Pinac called it.

Von Barwig produced some cigars that Van Praag had forced on him, and the men sat talking of their prospects, and smoking until the room looked like an inferno.

While they were debating as to where they should dine that night, there was a knock at the door, and, Von Barwig hastened to open it. A somewhat portly, rather well-dressed, middle-aged individual entered. He was followed by another person, a tall, lantern-jawed man of the artisan type, who looked around defiantly as he came into the room.

"Does Anton Von Barwig live here?" demanded the first comer.

Von Barwig did not know the gentleman who made the inquiry.

"Why, it is Schwarz! how do you do, Mr. Schwarz?" said Pinac, coming forward and shaking hands with him, and he then introduced him to Von Barwig as Mr. Wolf Schwarz, the Secretary of the Amalgamated Musical Association.

Mr. Schwarz then introduced his companion as Mr. Ryan, the representative of the Brickmakers' Union. "Shake hands with Professor Von Barwig, Mr. Ryan," said Schwarz. Mr. Ryan did so with such enthusiasm that Von Barwig was glad to withdraw his hand.

Mr. Schwarz was an Americanised German, far more American than the most dyed-in-the-wool, natural-born citizen of the United States. Had any one called him a German, he would have repudiated the suggestion as an insult. He knew the American Constitution backward, and he determined that others should know it, too. His demand for his rights as an American citizen was the predominating characteristic of his nature, for he was a born demagogue of the most pronounced type. It did not take Mr. Schwarz long to make clear the object of his visit.

"You don't come to our rooms very much, Von Barwig," he said.

Von Barwig pleaded stress of business as an excuse.

"If you had," went on Mr. Schwarz, taking up the thread of his remarks without noticing Von Barwig's apology, "you'd know that Van Praag and those fellows up at Harmony Hall are on the black-list."

"Black-list?" said Von Barwig apprehensively.

"Mr. Ryan here represents a delegation from the Brickmakers' Union," stated Mr. Schwarz, coughing and clearing his throat, thus indicating the importance of the statement that he was about to make.

"Well?" asked Von Barwig, who did not see the value of the information just furnished by Mr. Schwarz.

"Well," repeated Mr. Schwarz, "The Brickmakers' Union has just affiliated with our musical association."

"Music and bricks--affiliated!" The idea rather appealed to Von Barwig's sense of humour and he laughed. "Music and bricks," he repeated, but this attempt at pleasantry did not meet with much response from Mr. Schwarz. That gentleman merely shrugged his shoulders while Mr. Ryan, the brickmakers' delegate, contented himself with squirting some tobacco juice into the adjacent fireplace and tilting his hat, which he had neglected to remove, over one eye, while he surveyed Von Barwig with an unpleasant stare from the other, thus indicating that he wanted no nonsense.

"Music and bricks," repeated Von Barwig, who evidently enjoyed the incongruity of the combination. Then noticing that Ryan was standing he said with a smile, "Brother artist, be seated!" Pinac and Fico roared with laughter. Mr. Ryan sat down, mumbling to himself that that sort of sarcasm didn't go with him; he was a workman, not an artist. Von Barwig apologised and then, looking at Schwarz, waited for him to speak. A very awkward pause ensued.

"You've had an offer from the Harmony Hall Concerts, under the management of Van Praag," stated Schwarz.

"Yes," assented Von Barwig, who began to perceive for the first time that his visitors had come on a matter of more or less serious Import.

"Well," began Schwarz, "you've got to hold off for the present."

"I do not understand," said Von Barwig.

"You've got to throw up the job," broke in Mr. Ryan, emphasising the statement by allowing his walking stick to fall heavily on a pile of music which lay on the piano.

Von Barwig looked at him but did not speak.

"You can't go on," said Schwarz.

"Not while scabs are working there," added Mr. Ryan sententiously.

Von Barwig tried to speak but could not; words would not come. His heart had almost stopped beating. Finally he managed to gasp, "What does it mean; all this?"

"Our association has been notified that Van Praag is having his new music hall built with non-union bricks, and----"

"Scabs," broke in Mr. Ryan, once more banging the inoffensive music with his stick. "Scabs! We called out our men and they put in scab carpenters. The carpenters went out and the plumbers have gone out; they've all gone out, and now it's only fair--that--you should go out. Stick together and we'll win; in other words, 'united we stand, divided we fall.' Am I right, Schwarz?"

Mr. Schwarz did not commit himself as to the merits of the case; he was not there for that purpose. He was there to carry out the wishes of the association, so he merely contented himself with saying that the musicians would undoubtedly have to go out under the term of the affiliation.

"Music and bricks has got to stand by each other," said Mr. Ryan, unconsciously quoting Von Barwig. "They've got to, or there'll be no music; and no bricks."

Music and bricks, then, was no longer a joke. It was a reality, a dreadful impossibility that had become true; and Von Barwig's heart sank as he looked at his friends, and saw by their faces that they, too, realised what it meant. They were in the midst of a sympathetic strike; the question of the right or wrong of it did not appear. It was immaterial; right or wrong, they must go out because others went; those were the orders from headquarters.

"Of course, Von Barwig, you'll stand for whatever the Amalgamated stands for?" said Schwarz.

"You'll resign until the matter is settled, I presume?" queried Mr. Ryan. Von Barwig shook his head. A faint "no" issued from his throat, which had literally dried up from fear; the fear of losing the happiness he had had just now, the fear of going back to that dreaded night-drudgery again. All their hopes were shattered, their anticipations were not to be realised.

"Of course--I--I am of the Union. I stand by the Union--of course. I--but it's--it's hard!" Then with an effort, "It will not last long, eh?"

"No," said Mr. Ryan, "it won't last a month! We'll put them out of business if it does. They'll weaken, Mr. Barwig, you'll see! They'll weaken all right." The ashen appearance of Von Barwig's face, the abject despair he saw depicted there aroused the man's sympathy. "It won't be long, Mr. Barwig," he repeated in a softened voice. "I know it's hard, but what are we to do? If we don't stand together, we'll be swamped."

"That's right," said Schwarz.

"It ain't sympathy; it's self-defence, Barwig," declared Mr. Ryan, uttering what he thought was a great truth.

"Yes, yes," muttered Von Barwig. Hope had gone completely from him now.

"Self-defence," he repeated, and then he laughed bitterly. "The art of music progresses. Wagner should be glad that he is dead."

"Wagner? Who is Wagner?" inquired Mr. Ryan.

"No one, no one!" replied Von Barwig, shaking his head, "he did not belong to the Union----"

"Then he's a scab," remarked Mr. Ryan.

Von Barwig looked at him and burst out laughing, the laughter of despair. Pinac and Fico looked at each other. Von Barwig's laugh grated harshly on their ears; they did not like to see their beloved friend act in that manner. Pinac touched him gently on the arm and looked appealingly at him. Von Barwig nodded, then rising from his chair, with his habitual gentleness, suggested that the interview was at an end. Messrs. Schwarz and Ryan bowed themselves out and the four friends were left there alone with their misery.

Von Barwig turned to his friends. It was for them that his heart bled, for they had resigned their positions at his request. For the first time since their friendship he had been the cause of misfortune coming to them. He felt it more than all the disappointments that he had experienced during his stay in America. "I am accursed," he thought, "doomed always to disappointments, and I am now a curse to others, to those I love." He tried to tell them how grieved he was at their misfortune, but they would not allow him to apologise, so he sat down in his old armchair and tried to smoke, but he could not. His heart was as heavy as lead. They saw this and they felt for him; they felt his sufferings more than they did their own.

"We have resign from the *cafe*, yes, but we are glad, damn glad," said Pinac, lying like a true Gallic gentleman. "Von Barwig, I tell you we are deuced damn glad," he repeated with emphasis.

Von Barwig silently shook his hand and smiled.

"I said to hell with the *cafe*--I say it now!" ejaculated Fico. "The *cafe* to hell, and many of him!"

"My beautiful 'cello is wasted in that food hole," said Poons to Von Barwig in German, then he laughed and told him a funny story that he had read that day in the *Fliegende Blaetter*. He did his best to make the old man laugh with him, but Von Barwig only smiled sadly. He did not speak; his heart was too heavy.

"It won't last long! You see, it won't last long!" said Pinac, again trying to comfort him. "Come, boys, we go upstairs and play. We play for you, Anton, eh?"

Von Barwig made no reply. The men looked at each other significantly and tried to cheer him up by striking up a song and marching around the room; but they saw that the iron had entered deep, deep into his soul, and that he was thoroughly disheartened.

"Come! We go and play; perhaps that will arouse him," whispered Pinac to the others. And they marched out of the room singing the refrain of one of the student glees that Von Barwig had taught them.

Von Barwig sat there quite still for a long time. His thoughts were formless. In a chaotic way he realised that he had played the game of life and had lost; he seemed to feel instinctively that the end had come. He had the Museum to go to, that could supply his daily needs, but he was tired, oh, so tired of the struggle. There was nothing to look forward to--nothing, nothing. He arose with a deep, deep sigh.

"I am tired," he said to himself, "tired out completely. I am like an old broken-down violin that can no longer emit a sound. My heart is gone; there is no sounding post; I am finished. I have been finished a long time, only I did not know it." He arose slowly from his chair and took his pipe off the mantelpiece. As he slowly filled it his eyes lighted on a wooden baton that lay on the mantelpiece. He took it up and looked at it. It was the baton with which he conducted his last symphony. He smiled and shook his head. "I am through; thoroughly and completely through," and he broke the conductor's wand in pieces and threw them into the fire. "That finishes me!" he said. "I am snapped; broken in little bits. I did not ask to live, but now,--now, I ask to die! To die, that is all I ask, to die." He took out the little miniature of his wife and looked at it long and tenderly. "Elene, Elene! My wife, where are you? If you knew what I go through you would come to me! Give me the sign I wait for so long, that I may find you."

He listened, but no answer came; then a new thought came to him.

"I go back home, home; for here I am a stranger; they do not know me. The way is long, so long--" and then he started, for he heard the strains of the second movement of his symphony which was being played in the room above. It brought him back to himself, and he listened--listened as one who hears a voice from the dead. It seemed to him that the requiem of all his hopes was being played. He was still looking at the picture of his wife when Jenny entered. She had come to fetch the lamp, to fill it with oil. The short winter afternoon was drawing to a close and the dusk was deepening into darkness. The red rays of the setting sun came in through the window and as it bathed him in its crimson glow it made a sort of a halo around the old man's head. Jenny gazed at him for a long time and was surprised that he did not speak; but Von Barwig was not conscious of her presence. She looked at him more closely and saw the tears in his eyes; then she came over to him and nestled closely by his side. In a moment her woman's instinct divined his need of sympathy and her heart went out to him.

"Don't look like that," she pleaded, "I can't bear to see it! I've always known that something troubled you, that you've something to bear that you've kept back from us. Tell me, tell me! Don't keep it to yourself, it's eating your heart out. You know I love you; don't--don't keep it back," and she placed her arm around his neck and wept as if her heart would break. Her action brought Von Barwig to himself and he patted her gently on the back. "Why, Jenny, my little Jenny! Yes, I know you love me, and I--I tell you. Yes, Jenny, I tell you----"

Jenny nestled closer to him; it was a sorrowful moment for the old man, and he needed some one to lead him into the light. Slowly, slowly, but surely the young girl led him out of his mental chaos. His heart had been perilously near the breaking point, but he could think more calmly now.

"I--when--I came over to this country I--I looked for some one that I never found. I have--no luck, Jenny, no luck," he said in a broken voice, "and I bring no luck to others." He paused and then went on: "I stay here no longer, Jenny. I go back; it's better! Yes, I go back to my own country."

"Oh, no, don't go back!" pleaded the girl.

"Yes, I go; I must go," the old man said.

She clung tightly to him now, as if she would not let him go. He smiled at her but shook his head. "It is better," he said gravely, "far better. I cannot trust myself here alone; it is too much alone! I love you all, but I am alone. There is an aching void which must be filled. I cannot trust myself alone any longer."

She did not understand him, nor did she inquire of him his meaning. She only clung to him, as if determined not to lose him.

"When you are married, Jenny," he went on, "I shall not be here. But keep well to the house, love your husband, stay at home. Don't search here, there, everywhere for excitement! The real happiness for the mother is always in the home; always, always! One imprudent step and the mother's happiness goes, and the father's, too," he added pathetically.

"Whose picture is that?" asked Jenny, as she caught sight of the miniature in Von Barwig's hand.

"The mother, my wife;" he said in a low, sad voice.

"Ah!" and Jenny looked closely at the picture.

"The mother who loved not the home, and from that's come all the sorrow! She loved not the home." Von Barwig's words came quickly now, and were interspersed with dry, inarticulate sobs. "The mother of my little girl, for whose memory I love you. Ah, keep to the home, Jenny, for God's sake! Always the home!"

Jenny nodded. "Where are they?" she asked, pointing to the portrait.

"Ah, where are they?" he almost sobbed. "For sixteen years I have not seen my own flesh and blood! He, my friend who did this to me, robbed me of them, and took them far, far away from me. I mustn't say more!"

Jenny understood; she no longer looked tenderly at the portrait. She pointed to it almost in horror. "She was not a good woman?"

Von Barwig was shocked. Here was the verdict of the world, through the mouth of a child. He had never thought of his wife as bad.

"She was a good woman; not bad, not bad! No, no, Jenny! I thought of nothing but my art, of music, of fame, fortune. One night, the night of the big concert, when I came home she had gone and she had taken with her my little Helene. It was the night that symphony was played. Listen, you hear, you hear? It's the second movement. It was a wonderful success, but ah, Jenny, that night I won the world's applause, but I lost my own soul!"

The strains of the music came through the open door. Jenny looked at him. He was listening eagerly now. In the red glow of the late afternoon sun his eyes sparkled with unnatural excitement.

"It takes me home," he said, and then he looked at the picture. "Not bad; oh, no, Jenny; she is not bad!"

Jenny shook her head. She hated the woman from that moment.

"She is bad," she thought, "or how could she have done it?" But she did not speak, and the old man went on:

"I am not angry! No, mein Gott, no! I only want my little girl. Anything to have her back, my baby, my little baby girl, gone these sixteen years! My little baby!"

"Yes, but she wouldn't be a baby now," broke in Jenny.

Von Barwig, about to speak, stopped suddenly. "Of course not; I never thought of that!" Then he shook his head violently.

"I cannot think of her as anything but a baby!"

"Yes, but she'd be a grown-up young lady," insisted Jenny.

"How old was she when you--when she--when you left her."

"Three years and two months," said Von Barwig softly.

"Then she'd be nineteen," said Jenny, "just my age; big, grown-up young lady."

"She is my little baby," repeated Von Barwig plaintively. "I can see her now so plainly; always playing with her little doll--the doll with one eye out. That was the doll she loved, Jenny; the doll she had when I last saw her."

The old man was calm now. The idea that the girl was a grown-up young woman, although obvious enough, changed his train of thought. For the moment it took his attention from the immediate cause of his unhappiness, and brought his imagination into play.

"A grown-up young lady!" he mused. "Yes, of course! But I can't see her as grown up; I can't see her, Jenny. I can only remember her as a wee tot walking around with her one-eyed doll; the eye she kicked out! I remember that so well."

In spite of his misery, the old man laughed aloud as he recalled the circumstance that led up to the loss of the eye. The consternation in the face of the child as she handed him the piece of broken eye had made him laugh; and he laughed now hysterically as he recalled the incident. Jenny seeing him laugh, laughed too.

"Thank God he can still laugh," she thought.

"Ah, well!" he went on, drawing a deep breath. "They are gone, and I--look no more. My search is over, Jenny, over and done. But I go back; I see once more my Leipsic. There they know me! Here I am an outcast, a beggar."

Jenny could only shake her head and look at him helplessly. She realised that any effort she might make to influence him to change his plans would be useless; and more and more did she hate the woman who had been the cause of all his misery, the woman whose portrait he looked at so lovingly.

"A beggar," Von Barwig repeated to himself. "Yes, that's it! I can fall no lower, I give up!"

The fortune of the broken-spirited, broken-hearted old man was now at its lowest ebb; and he gave up the fight. There was a long silence. Jenny was thinking hard. What could she say or do; how could she help him?

A knock at the door broke the stillness, which had become almost oppressive.

Chapter Fourteen

C ome in," said Von Barwig wearily. He barely looked at the door as it opened. In the ordinary course of events it was likely to be the laundry boy, or Thurza with coal, or one of the musicians who lived in the house, or perhaps a collector. It might have been almost any one but the liveried footman who now stood at the door, hat in hand, with a look of inquiry upon his face. Von Barwig stared at the man in astonishment. Liveries in Houston Street were most uncommon.

"Excuse me, sir, I am looking for a Mr. Von Barwig," he said. "I was directed to come here. Is this the right place, sir?" The man's manner was polite enough, but there was a decided attitude of superiority in his somewhat supercilious tone. Jenny made her escape hastily.

Von Barwig could not collect his thoughts. He simply looked at the man and made no reply.

"He's a music master in the neighbourhood, I believe, sir," went on the servant. "A music master," he repeated.

"Yes, he was; but he is no more," said Von Barwig, who now realised that the man wanted to find him.

"Dead, sir?"

"No, I am Mr. Von Barwig. I teach, but I give up. You hear? I have finished; I give up, I give up!" he repeated in a voice quivering with emotion as he walked up to the window. There was such utter pathos in the old man's bearing that it caused even the footman to turn and look at the speaker more closely. There was a pause; the servant appeared uncertain what to do.

"Did you find him, Joles?" asked some one coming into the room. The voice was that of a young lady, who was accompanied by a little boy carrying a violin case. At the sound of her voice Von Barwig started as if he had been shot, and with a half articulate cry he turned and gazed in the direction from whence the voice came. He saw in the dim twilight, for the sun had now nearly gone down, the half-blurred vision of a young lady dressed in the height of fashion. Her features he could not distinguish, as her back was to the window, but he could see that she was a handsome young woman of about twenty years of age. As Von Barwig turned toward her she looked at her note-book and asked if he were Herr Von Barwig.

The old man bowed, tried to speak, but could not. His tongue cleaved to the roof of his mouth. He pointed to a chair, and indicated that she should be seated. She noticed his embarrassment and addressed the servant.

"You had better wait for me downstairs, Joles," she said quickly. Then as the man closed the door behind him she turned to Von Barwig, and spoke in a rich, warm, contralto voice that vibrated with youth and health. "You teach music, do you not? At least they said you did!"

Von Barwig swallowed a huge lump in his throat. "I did, but--not now; I have given up." She looked at him but did not seem to understand. "Lieber Gott, Lieber Gott!" broke from him in spite of his efforts to suppress himself. "Elene, Elene!" Then he looked more closely at her and shook his head.

"So you are not teaching any longer? Ah, what a pity!" she said. "They speak so well of you in the neighbourhood. Perhaps I may be able to induce you to change your mind!"

Von Barwig was now slowly gaining mastery over himself.

"Perhaps," he said, with a great effort at self-control.

"You do not know me, Herr Von Barwig?"

The old man's eyes glowed like live coals. "Elene, Elene!" he murmured. "The living image! Lieber Gott, the living image!"

"I am Miss Helene Stanton," she said with unconscious dignity. "You may have heard of me," she added with a smile.

Miss Stanton's name was a household word in New York, especially in that quarter of the city where her large charities had done so much to alleviate the sufferings of the poor. Von Barwig had heard the name many times, but at that moment he did not recognise it, although it was the name of the greatest heiress in New York.

His ear caught the word "Helene" and he could only repeat it over and over again.

"Elene, Elene!"

"Helene," corrected Miss Stanton.

"Ah, in my language it is Elene; yes, Elene!" Then a great hope took possession of him. "Some one has sent you to me?" he asked. "Some one has sent you?"

"Not exactly," she replied, "but you were well recommended." The old man's manner, his emotion, his earnestness, somewhat embarrassed her. "Why does he look at me so earnestly?" she thought. Perhaps it was a mannerism peculiar to a man of his years.

Then she went on: "I am connected with mission work in the neighbourhood here. I go among the poor a great deal--"

"Ah, charity!" he said. "Yes." And then he went up to the window and pulled up the blinds as far as they would go that he might get more of the fast-fading light.

"I saw you a few days ago at Schumein's, the music publishers, and your name was suggested to me by one of the young ladies at the mission as music master."

"Ah, you desire to take lessons?" he asked eagerly.

Miss Stanton smiled. "No, the child. Come here, Danny," and the boy came toward her.

Von Barwig had seen no one but her. The little boy had remained in the corner of the room, where the shadow of evening made it too dark to distinguish the outline of his form.

"Ah, the boy?" he said with a tone or disappointment in his voice. "Not you, the boy? He needs instruction?" Then he looked at her again. It was too dark for him to see the colour of her eyes. He went to the door. "Jenny," he called, only he pronounced it "Chenny"; "a lamp if you please."

"How courteous and dignified his manner is!" thought Miss Stanton, "even in the most commonplace and trivial details of life a man's breeding shows itself."

"We think the boy is a genius," she said aloud, "but his parents are very poor and cannot afford to pay for his tuition."

"It is a poor neighbourhood," said Von Barwig, "but there will be no charge. I will teach him for--for you!" He had already forgotten that he had decided to take no more pupils.

"I have taken charge of his future," said Miss Stanton pointedly; "and of course shall defray all the expense of his tuition myself. I have the consent of his parents----"

Jenny came in with a large lamp and placed it on the piano. Von Barwig could now see his visitor's face, and his heart beat rapidly.

"Tell me," he said, forcing himself to be calm, "your father and mother? Are they----?"

Miss Stanton drew herself up slightly. "I am speaking of his parents," she said.

"Yes, his parents, of course! Yes, but your father--your mother," he asked insistently. "Is she--is she--living?"

The deep earnestness and anxiety with which Von Barwig put this question made it clear to Miss Stanton that it was not merely idle curiosity that prompted him to ask, so stifling her first impulse to ignore the question altogether she replied rather abruptly:

"No, she is not living." Then she added formally, "but that is quite apart from the subject we are discussing."

Von Barwig did not hear the latter part of her answer. His eyes were riveted on her. He could only repeat, "Dead--dead." Then he looked at her and slowly shook his head in mournful tenderness, repeating the words, "Dead--dead."

To her own surprise Miss Stanton did not resent this sympathy.

"I take an especial interest in this boy because his sister is one of the maids in my father's home," she began.

Von Barwig's face fell. "Ah," he said, "you have a father. Fool that I am," he went on. "Yes, of course; you have a father, and it is not----"

At this point Miss Stanton made up her mind that Herr Von Barwig did not understand English quite as well as he spoke it, for she repeated rather sharply this time that she was discussing the boy's musical education, not her own. Then she added that there remained only the question of terms to discuss and she would detain him no longer.

Von Barwig did not hear her. He could only mutter to himself in German, "A father, she has a father!" Then he told the boy to call the next afternoon and he would hear him play. The lad thanked him and went home to his parents.

After the boy's departure, Miss Stanton repeated her request to be allowed to discuss the terms for the boy's tuition; and when the music master made no response she said: "Very well; whatever your charges are I will pay them."

"There will be none," said Von Barwig decidedly.

"But I wish to defray the entire expense," said Miss Stanton, greatly mystified at Von Barwig's refusal to receive payment for his work.

"I cannot take money from you," he said.

"Cannot take money from me? I do not understand you!" and Miss Stanton arose. "Please explain." There was an awkward pause.

Von Barwig saw that he had made a mistake. "I like to help all children," he said somewhat lamely. "You are engaged in work of charity; I do my share," he added.

The explanation only partially satisfied her, and she regarded him doubtfully.

Von Barwig realised now that he had shown himself over-anxious. "I do something for him, I shall take an interest in him," he said, "because you brought him here."

"What a strange man!" she thought as she looked at him in surprise. "A poor, struggling musician with the air and grace of a nobleman conferring a favour on a lady of his own class!" Then she looked around the studio with its old-fashioned piano and the stacks of old music lying about here and there; a violin with one or two bows and resin boxes in the corner, some music stands, Poons's 'cello case, a broken metronome; and on the walls some cheap pictures of the old musicians. In a fit of generosity, Miss Husted had bought them and put them on the walls. Von Barwig had not the heart to remove them, although cheap art did not appeal to him.

Miss Stanton looked at them now, and then at him, and a deep feeling of pity came into her heart. "He has so little," she thought, "yet he is willing to give; and he gives with the air of a prince!"

"I cannot allow you to--to--" she began. "You are not rich, and yet you wish to teach for nothing. Surely your time is--is valuable----"

"I have more than I need," he replied with quiet dignity.

The heiress to twenty-five millions felt the rebuff and she liked him all the more for it, but she would not accept his offer without an effort to prevent the sacrifice.

"Why should you sacrifice yourself?" she asked.

"It is no sacrifice to--ah--please, please! Put it down to the whim of an old man--what you will; but don't deny me this pleasure! Don't, please!"

His pleading look disarmed her and she gave up trying to dissuade him.

"Very well," she said. "It shall be as you wish."

She could not help liking him, she said to herself. His manner, at first a little embarrassing, now interested her strangely. He reminded her of a German nobleman she had met in Washington at the German Embassy. His grace, his bearing, his whole demeanour was noble and dignified in the extreme. Under ordinary circumstances, she would have regarded his offer to teach her little charge for nothing as a gross breach of politeness, but with him she did not feel angry in the least.

"It's curious," she said, "I came here with a good object in view; and you calmly appropriate my good intentions and make them your own, and what is still more strange I allow you to do so."

"Ah, don't say that!" still the tearful, pleading voice that moved her so.

"Yes, I allow you to do so," she persisted, and then she added, "Do you know, Herr Barwig, I like you, in spite of a strong temptation to be very angry with you?"

She had now moved around to the piano.

"You know," she said enthusiastically, "I love music and musical people. Some of the very greatest artists come to my father's musicales."

"My father," the words made Von Barwig's heart sink. "My father!"

She sat down at the piano; he raised the lamp and looked into her eyes, and as he stood there with the lamp uplifted she looked into his face.

"Of whom do you remind me?" she said quickly. "Don't move----"

There was a deep silence. The old man could hear his heart beat.

"Of whom, of whom?" he gasped. "Go on; tell me! Try to remember! For God's sake try to remember!"

"There, now, it's gone!" she said. "I can't think," she added after a pause, greatly surprised at his look. "You know somehow or other I always feel at home with musicians. What a busy little studio this is," she went on, looking around. "You're quite successful, aren't you?"

Von Barwig nodded.

"It must be very gratifying to earn a lot of money through your own efforts; not for the mere money, but for the success. I'm glad you're successful!" she said with such feeling that it surprised even herself.

"Why?" asked Von Barwig. "Why are you glad?"

"I don't know. I suppose--" she paused. She did not like to say it was because she had thought he was very poor and was delighted to find that he was not; so she said it was because of his kindness to the boy, "and because I--I love music," she added.

"You play?" he inquired.

"A little."

"Play for me." The words came almost unbidden. It was an impulse to which he responded because he could not help it. "Play for me," he pleaded.

She ran her hands idly over the keys. "I ought to be angry," she thought, "he, a mere music master, to ask me to play for him as if he were an equal."

But the gentle expression on the old man's face as he regarded her with a tender smile was so full of hallowed affection and respect that she could not utter the words which came to her lips. She merely looked at him and returned his smile with one of her own and Heaven opened for the old man. She began to play.

"You know I play very little," she said.

"I love to hear music from your fingers," was all he could say.

Miss Stanton listened a moment.

"What music is that?" She heard the men upstairs playing. "It's very pretty," she added. They both listened for a few moments. "It's really beautiful! Can I get it? I'd like to know that melody."

"I make for you a piano score. It's the music they played the night that she, that she--" his breath came quickly. "Lieber Gott! Elene; so like Elene, so like!" he said, as he gazed at her.

Miss Stanton took off her gloves and began to play. She had hardly struck the opening chords of a simple pianoforte piece when there came a knock at the door. Before Von Barwig could speak a man entered. She stopped playing and Von Barwig's heart sank as he recognised the collector for the pianoforte house.

"I am engaged, sir. If you please, another time!"

"I've called for the piano," said the man, taking some papers out of his pocket.

"Another time, for God's sake!" pleaded Von Barwig. "Please go on, Miss Stanton."

"I want the piano or the money," said the man automatically.

"I have not--now. To-morrow I will call."

"The money or the piano is my instructions," said the collector. Von Barwig stood as if stricken dumb. The shame, the degradation were too great. He appealed to the man with outstretched hands. Tears were in his eyes, but the man did not look at him; he went into the hall, opened the front door, and yelled out, "Come on, Bill----"

Miss Stanton arose from the piano and walked over to the window. "It is a very busy view from here, isn't it?" she said; "gracious, how crowded the streets are!"

Poor Von Barwig's cup of misery was now full. She had been a witness of his poverty. His lies about his success and his pupils were all laid bare to her; he was disgraced forever in her eyes. He had lied to her, and she had found him out.

The collector came back with the men and the process of moving the piano began. Von Barwig's sense of humour came to his rescue.

"Thank heaven they are taking that box of discords away at last! What a piano! Did you notice it, Miss Stanton?"

Miss Stanton had noticed it, and nodded, "I did indeed," she said.

"Not one note in harmonious relationship with another," went on Von Barwig, trying to smile as they upset his music on the floor. "Not a sharp or a flat that is on good terms with his neighbour."

The only reply the piano mover made was to drop one of the piano legs heavily on the floor, making the dust fly.

"The black and white keys forever at war with each other," said Von Barwig, forcing a laugh, in which his visitor joined. Seeing her merriment, Von Barwig began to recover his spirits. "The next time you call, Miss Stanton," he said, "I will have here an instrument that shall contain at least a faint suggestion of music. In the meantime I am most thankful that I have no longer to listen to a piano that sounds like a banjo."

The whole situation appealed forcefully to Miss Stanton's sense of humour, and she thoroughly enjoyed the old man's jesting. "If he can rise above a condition like that," she thought, "he must be a splendid man." She longed to comfort, to help him; but how?

As the men finally took out the piano, Von Barwig pretended to breathe a sigh of relief.

"I'm glad it's gone," he said, "you can't tell what a relief!" He laughed, but his laugh did not deceive her; her musical ear recognised its artificiality in a moment. She could feel rather than see he was suffering, and she felt for him.

They were left standing alone together. The room looked quite empty without the piano; it was like the breaking up of a home. Neither of them spoke for a moment, and Von Barwig could see that she had found him out again.

"What an awful liar she must think I am," thought he.

"Poor, dear old man trying to conceal his poverty," thought she. Then an idea came to her.

"I want you to come and see me, Herr Von Barwig," she said. "I am going to take up piano study again, and I want you to help me. I shall be at home to-morrow afternoon at three. Of course you must be very busy, but if you have no other engagement will you call?"

"I will call, madam. I--I am--not engaged at that hour," said Von Barwig gratefully, as he bowed to her. Miss Stanton acknowledged the bow.

"You won't find me a very apt pupil, but you'll take me, won't you? Do, please take me!"

The old man could not speak; too many conflicting thoughts were working in his mind. "Take her! Good God--" The very idea overwhelmed him.

"You will take me, won't you?" she urged gently.

He took the card, and nodded. He dared not trust himself to speak; he would have broken down and he knew it.

"Good-bye!" she said. "Good-bye; it's getting so late, I must go!" She held out her hand. He took it and kissed it reverently, bowing his head as if she were a queen.

"Good-bye," she said again at the hall door. "Don't forget!" she added, as she waved her hand from the carriage window. Joles slammed the door shut and got on the box, and she was driven away.

The old man watched the carriage until it was out of sight, returning to his room in a dream. He could not realise or explain his feelings. He had been happy, perfectly happy; that was all he knew. He had been at rest, contented, satisfied for a few brief moments, and that glimpse of heaven had put new, strange thoughts into his life--thoughts that made his blood pulsate. He recognised that life had taken on a new aspect; how or why he knew not. A strange young lady had called upon him, and had left a card; he was to see her again, and his whole life was changed. This was the only point that was clear to him, that his life had changed. How long he sat there, trying to think it out and understand, he knew not.

The old crack-faced clock, with one hand, that Miss Husted had put on the mantelpiece, struck the hour with its old cracked bell, and it startled him. He had heard it hundreds of times, but now its weird, metallic tone jarred on the harmony of his feelings. He counted the strokes; five, six, seven, eight. Eight o'clock! He started up, for his dream had come to an end, and he came back to earth again, back into the world of Houston Street, back to the Bowery, to Costello, to the Museum, to his nightly labour for his daily bread. Mechanically he changed his velvet jacket for his street dress, and hastily put on his cape coat and hat. "No, it's not a dream!" he told himself, as he read the card she had given him. "Miss Helene Stanton, Fifth Avenue and Fifty-seventh Street." He put the card carefully in his pocket-book and placing his violin case under his arm started to go out. Then remembering that the lamp was still burning, he went back and carefully turned it out.

"Fifth Avenue, and Fifty-seventh Street," he said to himself; "to-morrow at three, to-morrow at three."

He went into the street and the noise and bustle of the Bowery jarred upon his sensitive ear. "To-morrow at three," he joyfully sang to himself. "To-morrow at three!" But high above the din and rattle of traffic and street noises, high above Von Barwig's song, rang out Costello's voice as if to drown his happiness.

"Eat 'em alive," it said. "Eat 'em alive; eat 'em alive!" Von Barwig heard it; shuddered, and sang no more. "Eat 'em alive," he muttered mournfully to himself. "Eat 'em alive--eat 'em alive."

Chapter Fifteen

Von Barwig arose at daybreak, for a great hope had come to him. At last life held out a promise; of what he knew not. He only knew that he experienced a sensation of joy, and his great, loving heart throbbed in response. His cheerfulness communicated itself to his friends upstairs, for they came into his room and insisted on his accompanying them to breakfast at Galazatti's. They were all in high spirits. Pinac and Fico were determined to let him see that the loss of their positions had not caused them any uneasiness.

"Bah! we get the engagement back again," laughed Fico.

Pinac snapped his fingers. "The *cafe*! Pouf, pouf, pouf!"

Poons grinned amiably. He had been warned by the others, notably by Pinac in very bad German, not to let Von Barwig see that they felt down in the mouth. He kept a smile on his face when he thought of it, and was exceedingly sorrowful when he didn't; so the expression on his face altered from time to time, much to Von Barwig's astonishment. Once, during breakfast, Pinac heard Poons sigh and kicked him under the table, whereupon he immediately grinned. Von Barwig saw this lightning change and wondered what was the matter.

"Are you in pain?" he asked.

"No," replied Poons, trying to smile, but only succeeding in grinning. Then he laughed with real tears in his eyes.

"Are you laughing or crying?" asked Von Barwig. "If you are laughing, please cry; and if you are crying, for heaven's sake laugh."

Poons nodded. "I am very happy," he said tearfully, "so happy."

"Then you don't know how to show it," commented Von Barwig; whereupon they all laughed at him until he laughed too, in spite of himself. They joked all through the breakfast. So noisy were they that they attracted the attention of Galazatti, the proprietor or the *cafe*, who came over to the four friends and shook hands with them. He had served them for many years, and he was glad to see them enjoy themselves.

"How is the good lady of your house?" he asked.

"Miss Husted is at the top of the notch," replied Pinac, who generally constituted himself spokesman for the party. "We are all top of the notch," he added, "eh, Poonsie?" slapping the young man on the back.

"What a strange thing is this human existence!" thought Von Barwig, as he left his friends and walked back to his studio alone. "Here I am in the middle of Houston Street, giving music instructions for fifty cents per lesson, playing out nights in a dime museum, and yet my heart, my mind is with this daughter of a great millionaire. To-day at three I shall be with her, and I can think of nothing else. What is she to me that I should care so much? A chance likeness, perhaps no likeness at all except that which exists in my brain! Am I mad? Is this world of shadows real? What does it all mean? Who will tear the veil from this mystery, and tell me why one human being is so much more to us than another, why one human being so resembles another, and yet is not that one?"

From time to time he looked at the clock wishing the time would pass more quickly. He brushed his clothes very carefully that morning. The frock coat he had worn for a dozen years now proved its claim to being made of the finest texture, for it responded splendidly to the brush, and gave up most of its spots; but it still retained its shine. When he had put on a clean collar and cuffs and his best white dress shirt, Von Barwig looked at himself in the glass.

"If only this shine on my coat were transferred to my boots, what a happy transformation!" thought Von Barwig. "Still, if that button on my sleeve is transferred to my coat, it will restore the balance of harmony," so Jenny's services were called into requisition.

"Where are you going this morning?" she asked as she stitched on the button.

"To a new pupil," replied Von Barwig as carelessly as he could, though his heart fairly bumped as he spoke. He did not like to speak of his visitor of yesterday afternoon to others. It was too sacred a subject to be mentioned in Houston Street.

"The young lady that came yesterday?" inquired Jenny, but Von Barwig made no reply. Jenny looked at him closely; his silence chilled her. There was an imperceptible change in him, she thought. She could not say exactly what it was, but it seemed to her that when his eyes rested on her it was no longer with the same glance of lingering affection that he had always bestowed on her. Now he barely glanced at her, and his eyes did not rest on her for a moment. The girl's sensitive nature made her conscious that he did not think of her when he spoke to her.

"What's her name?" asked Jenny, after a long pause, during which Von Barwig put on his cape coat. Once more he did not appear to hear her, and Jenny repeated the question. "What's her name, Herr Von Barwig?" This time she spoke with directness.

"I beg your pardon," said Von Barwig, with unconscious dignity. It was the old Leipsic conductor that spoke, and there was such unbending sternness and severity in the tone of his voice, such coldness in his eye, that Jenny shrank back and looked at him as if he had struck her.

"Oh, Herr Von Barwig," she gasped, and burst into tears.

"Jenny, Jenny, my little Jenny! What is it, what did I say?" he asked in genuine distress. His thoughts had been miles away.

"I didn't mean to--to--be--rude," she sobbed. "I--I only--you looked so--so happy! I--wanted to know."

"Come, come!" he said, taking her in his arms, and patting her affectionately on the cheek. "Don't cry! I meant nothing, my child; only I did not want to speak of matters that--that you could not understand. Come, it is two o'clock, and I must go," and he kissed her tenderly on the forehead. "You are all right now, eh?" he said, as she smiled.

"Forgive me, won't you?" asked Jenny, who was now comforted. He still loved her; that was all she asked.

As he walked up Third Avenue and turned into Union Square, he went into a florist's.

"A bunch of violets, please," he said, and the young man tied up a very small quantity of violets with a very large silk tassel and a lot of green leaves, tin foil, oil paper and wire; putting the whole into a box, which he carefully tied up with more ribbon.

"What a ceremony over a few violets!" thought Von Barwig, as he laid a twenty-five cent piece on the counter.

"One dollar, please," said the young man, surveying the quarter with a somewhat pitying smile.

Von Barwig's heart sank. He had forgotten that it was winter, that flowers were expensive, that coloured cardboard and tin foil and ribbon cost money, too. He searched his pockets and found the necessary dollar, but it was within a few cents of all he had. "They are not too good for her," thought Von Barwig as he carried the box away. He walked up Broadway into Fifth Avenue, and stopped at the corner of Fifty-seventh Street. The number he sought was inscribed on the door of a large brownstone mansion with a most imposing entrance, one of those palatial residences that cover the space of four ordinary houses and stamp its owner as a multi-millionaire. As he nervously pulled the bell, he upbraided himself for having dared to think that she was like his child. It was a trick of the fading light, an optical illusion. His reflection was cut short, for the door was opened by a man-servant.

"Have you a card?" inquired the footman, as Von Barwig asked for Miss Stanton.

The old man shook his head.

"Herr Von Barwig is the name; I have an appointment."

"You can wait in there; I'll see if Miss Stanton is in," said the flunky, as he turned on his heel. Such nondescript visitors were most unusual.

"An old person without a card, Mr. Joles," he confided to that individual below stairs; "name Barkwick or something, says he has an appointment. Quite genteel, but--" and he shrugged his shoulders significantly.

Joles made no reply, but went up to interview Mr. "Barkwick." The Stantons had so many applications from persons who needed charity for themselves or others that the standing order had gone forth to admit no stranger, under any pretext, unless of course he had complete credentials.

Herr Von Barwig was standing in the reception-room, hat in hand, when Joles entered.

"No card, eh? Ah--um--dear me," and Mr. Joles rubbed his chin in a perplexed way. He looked around, none of the pictures were missing, nor had the statuary been removed. But Denning shouldn't have asked the stranger into the reception-room.

Von Barwig ventured to say that he had an appointment. Mr. Joles nodded.

"Oh, you have an appointment! Written?"

"No," replied Von Barwig.

"Oh, verbal? At what hour?" questioned Mr. Joles.

"Three," answered Von Barwig.

"Are you quite sure?" inquired Mr. Joles doubtfully. "I have received no orders."

Von Barwig remained silent. What could he say? The man evidently doubted his word.

"If you will please tell her," he said gently.

"I am not at all sure that Miss Stanton is in," said Mr. Joles, and he stood there as if in doubt as to how to proceed. But any further question as to Miss Stanton's being in or out was settled by the young lady herself, who dashed into the room in evident haste.

"I beg your pardon, Herr Von Barwig; I forgot to leave word that you were coming! Forgive me, won't you?" and she held out her hand to him in such a friendly manner that it drew from the servant a faint apology.

"I beg your pardon, sir," he began.

"It's all right, Joles," said Miss Stanton, cutting him rather short. She evidently did not value that gentleman's explanations very highly, and took it for granted that Herr Von Barwig didn't care to hear them. Joles bowed and left the room.

"Well! I'm right glad to see you. It's a long way up town, isn't it?"

Von Barwig nodded. He could not speak; he could only look at her.

"For me?" she asked as he held out the box of violets. "Oh, how kind, how thoughtful!" she murmured, as he bowed in response to her question. She opened the box. "Violets in winter are a luxury, you know!"

Von Barwig smiled with pleasure; he was almost too happy.

"I congratulate myself on having pleased you," he managed to say.

"Now do sit down and talk to me!" she said, placing a chair for him and almost pushing him into it. He looked rather perplexed.

"I thought," he began.

"You surely didn't expect me to take a lesson to-day, did you?" she said, and then she went on: "Oh dear me, no; not to-day! To-morrow. Besides, my music room is upstairs; this is not my part of the house at all. How about the little boy?

When does he begin? Do you think he has talent?"

Von Barwig looked bewildered. He had not only forgotten the appointment he had made with the boy to hear him play, but he had forgotten his very existence.

"I--it is not settled," he faltered. "To-morrow perhaps. Yes, to-morrow, he will call and then I will let you know."

"Oh, I thought you were to hear him to-day! I was rather anxious to know what you thought."

Von Barwig felt quite guilty.

"Do you know I've been thinking of you quite a great deal," she said.

"You are too kind," he replied in a low voice.

Miss Stanton was evidently in a very communicative frame of mind, for from that moment she talked rapidly on current musical topics. She knew the latest operas, and loved the spirit of unrest, the unsettled minor chords of the new school of music; preferred the *leit motif* to the *aria*, music drama to opera, and was altogether exceedingly modern in her tastes. She did not like recitative in music, and preferred Wagner and Tschaikowsky to Bach and Verdi. She loved to be stirred up, she said. She liked Beethoven, yes, but he was too mathematical. As for Handel, he was uninteresting in the extreme; and so she went on and on.

The old man could only gaze at her in silence. There she sat, the living image of his dead wife, talking musical matters in a foreign tongue; an absolute stranger to him, and yet he felt drawn toward her in a strange and unusual way. Who was she? What was she? Had the dead come to life? What had happened? He could only look at her, and feel so very, very happy. What did it all mean?

"How is your father?" he asked when there was a lull in the conversation, brought about by Miss Stanton's pausing to breathe.

Her face fell. "He is in Europe," she said, and did not continue the subject.

Von Barwig noticed that her face saddened when she spoke of her father's absence.

"She must love him very much," he thought, and the thought brought him to his senses.

"Don't be a fool, Barwig," he said to himself. "Her father is a multi-millionaire, one of the great men of the country. Her mother is dead, and you must content yourself with having dreamed that she was yours. You must not look at her, you understand? Don't look at her, or she will suspect what you think and you will be turned away. You have had your dream. Now wake up, wake up!"

It was time for him to awaken, for she was asking him if he thought that musical genius was allied to madness.

"I--I don't know," he replied. "I am not a genius!"

"Will you play for me?" he said, to hide his confusion.

"Not now," she replied. "I have an engagement. Come to-morrow at this hour. I'll leave word this time," she added with a smile. "Mr. Stanton is so particular about callers that no one can get near me without being personally guaranteed by Joles or Mr. Ditson."

"You haven't seen Mr. Ditson, have you? He is father's secretary. I don't like him, and I'm so sorry. I can't bear not to like any one," and she sighed.

Von Barwig was looking at her again; in spite of himself he could not keep his eyes from her.

"Of what were you thinking when you looked at me in that way?" she asked, with a curious smile.

"I--I--don't know," said Von Barwig, rather startled, and this was literally true.

"You're thinking that I am a great rattle-box, aren't you? Now, confess! I am talking a great deal, am I not? But I can't seem to help it! I'm not always like this; indeed I'm not," she said earnestly. "It's a positive luxury to utter the first thought that comes into one's mind--a luxury I seldom get, I can tell you! Somehow or other you drew me out, and I allowed myself to ramble on and on without in the least knowing why. Can you explain it?" she asked laughingly.

He shook his head. "Perhaps you feel that I am interested in you, if you will pardon the liberty I take in saying so."

"Very likely," she said thoughtfully. There was a long pause, for they were so occupied with their own thoughts that neither spoke. The reaction had set in, and she was now strangely quiet; indeed she hardly spoke again that afternoon. After a while Von Barwig rose to take his leave.

"Have I offended her?" he asked himself, as he left the house. "How dare I tell her that I am interested in her! What impertinence, what a liberty! Who am I that I should dare to say such a thing! You old fool!" he now addressed himself directly. "You have happiness well within your grasp, and instead of gently taking it to yourself you grab it with both hands and pluck it up by the roots. You have offended her and she won't see you again. You'll see, you won't be admitted to the house!" The old man almost cried as he thought of his temerity, his folly, his stupidity. He walked faster and faster in his excitement. "I must curb my unfortunate tongue; I must, I will, if I ever get another chance!" He sighed deeply. "And yet--why should she press my hand and ask me to come to-morrow and be sure not to forget the hour? She has forgiven me, yes, yes, she likes me; I know she does, but I must be careful!" And so he walked rapidly home to his lodgings, alternately in a heaven of joy or in a hell of despair.

Chapter Sixteen

"What a strange old man," mused Helene, as she sat in a box that night at the Academy of Music and listened to an aria from "William Tell." "Why do I think of him so constantly?"

"My dear Helene, you are not a very attentive hostess," said Charlotte Wendall, a tall brunette. It was after the curtain had fallen on the act, and the box was filled up with visitors. There was always a crowd in the Stanton box on the grand tier when Helene Stanton was present.

"My cousin Beverly has spoken to you twice, and you have not even intimated that you are aware of his presence."

Charlotte Wendall, as a classmate of Helene's at Vassar, took a school friend's privilege of saying just what she thought. Besides, Helene was fond of her, and permitted her to say what she pleased.

"Won't you speak to me?" pleaded Beverly. "I do so want to be noticed! I'll be satisfied with a glance in my direction."

Beverly Cruger had recently finished a post-graduate course at Harvard and was just budding into the diplomatic service. He was a fine manly looking chap of twenty-seven, and as he looked down into Helene Stanton's face, his pleading eyes attested to the fact that he was more than merely interested in her.

"I beg your pardon," said Helene, shaking hands with him warmly.

"Helene is very pensive to-night. I can't make her out," interposed Octavie, a pretty little blonde sprite, and a perfect antithesis to her sister Charlotte. "She is thinking of some one who is not here."

"Quite true," nodded Helene, smiling.

"Happy fellow," murmured Beverly.

"On the contrary," said Helene, who had sharp ears. "The fellow I am thinking about is very unhappy."

"Ah, one of those sad affairs, with languishing eyes, who simpers and sighs!" said Charlotte laughingly, bursting into what she called poetry.

Helene smiled a little. "You'd never guess," she said thoughtfully. Then, after a pause, "I am thinking of a musician, a music master who lives downtown in one of the little side streets of our crowded city. He is an artist and a gentleman, who has in all probability devoted the best years of his life to his music; and he has made a failure of it."

"Did he tell you his story?" asked Beverly, slightly interested.

Helene shook her head. "He told me he was a great success, a flourishing artist, a rich man (in her enthusiasm Helene exaggerated slightly), and not three minutes afterward the very piano on which he made his living was taken away from him because he had not sufficient money to pay for its hire. It was the most pitiful thing I ever saw; I simply can't forget it!"

"Poor chap! Can't we do anything for him?" asked Beverly, now thoroughly interested.

"He is very proud. I took one of our mission boys there, a lad who has great talent for music, and this strange individual refused to take any compensation for teaching him. He insisted on taking him for nothing, and said he loved children."

"I should say he was a strange individual," commented Beverly. "He ought to feel highly flattered at the interest you are taking in him."

"You want to look out for these *distingue* foreigners, Helene! You're an heiress, you know," said Octavie, who was an omnivorous newspaper reader.

"Yes," said Helene, and then she was silent. Beverly Cruger looked at her. Her face, usually happy and smiling, was sad and thoughtful.

"This stranger has made quite an impression on her," he thought. "What is his name?" he asked, a strange sense of annoyance creeping over him in spite of himself.

"Herr Von Barwig," replied Helene.

"Oh, a nobleman," broke in the irrepressible Octavie, who read novels as well as the newspapers; "a German nobleman! It is a romance, isn't it? Is he a count, or a baron; or a--prince, perhaps?"

"He didn't tell me," replied Helene, who could not help smiling at the curiosity she had aroused. They were all looking at her very anxiously now, even Mrs. Van

Arsdale, the girls' chaperone, was interested.

"He didn't tell me," repeated Helene; "really he didn't."

"Oh, well, he will!" said Beverly, forcing a smile. He did not like to admit to himself that he was not exactly enjoying Helene's romance.

"I am going to see him to-morrow, and I'll make it a point to ask him," said Helene, with a mischievous twinkle in her eye. She rather enjoyed Beverly's obvious consternation.

"To-morrow? You see him to-morrow?" asked Beverly, and his heart sank. The lights were lowered and the next act had begun before she could make any reply, and then it was too late. He had known her only a few months, but in that brief time he had seen a great deal of her. He loved her; of that he was quite sure. It was her immense wealth that prevented him from asking her to be his wife. But for that he would have spoken a score of times.

"Where were you?" asked his mother as he returned to his seat beside her in the stall.

"In box 39," he replied.

"Mr. Stanton's box?" she asked.

"Yes," said Beverly. "I wanted to see Charlotte and Octavie."

"And Miss Stanton?" added his mother. Beverly made no reply.

"You were at her house yesterday," said Mrs. Cruger.

"Yes."

"Beverly, you must be careful! Your father objects to Miss Stanton."

"Objects to her friendship for my cousins?"

"No, to your friendship for her," replied his mother. "You have already shown her marked attention. She is a very beautiful girl, and he is afraid that the intimacy may ripen into something more than mere friendship."

Beverly was unusually silent during the progress of the opera, and when they arrived home he went straight to his father's study.

Andrew Cruger occupied a position of leadership in New York society that practically made his position unassailable. He was not a rich man, but he was the most highly respected diplomat in America; a scholarly gentleman, the friend of kings and presidents. He had been of the greatest possible assistance to the secretaries of state of both parties in solving international problems. The respect of the entire world was his and he was far more solicitous about his good name than about his financial [Transcriber's note: A line of the book appears to be missing here, but the sentence probably ends with "affairs", "business", or something similar.]

"What is your objection to Miss Stanton, father?" demanded Beverly in a somewhat excited manner.

"I have no objection to her, my boy," replied his father. Then, seeing that his son was terribly in earnest, he said in a more serious tone, "There is some question as to her father's social integrity."

"What has that to do with Miss Stanton?" asked Beverly.

"Nothing, my boy. And may I ask, what has the entire question to do with us?"

"I love her, father. I want to make her my wife."

Andrew Cruger put down the pen with which he was writing and looked at his son.

"That's very serious," he said, and walking over to the fireplace he leaned against the mantelpiece. "You are slated by the incoming administration for one of the under secretaryships of the German Legation. You are on the threshold of a great career. A marriage with Henry Stanton's daughter would not affect you at this stage, but when you rise to the dignity of ambassadorial honour, as in the course of events you logically will, your wife, my lad, must be beyond the breath of calumny. No scandal, no mystery must attach itself to her name."

"What's there against Miss Stanton, father? Won't you tell me?" asked Beverly.

"Nothing against *her*! Henry Stanton's early life is shrouded in mystery. He inherited his immense fortune from his uncle. Who her mother was, no one seems to know, and there lies the mystery. Mr. Stanton's immense works of charity have succeeded to some extent in getting him a foothold in New York, but the foundation of his social position is very insecure. I need scarcely tell you, Beverly, that although money is a lever that can do much to help a man along in society, it is almost utterly valueless in the diplomatic world. In that smallest of small worlds one's name, one's record, one's wife, one's family must be almost immaculate, subject to the most minute scrutiny. You are in the diplomatic world; your name will pass muster. But what of the woman you propose to make your wife?"

Beverly was silent. He had hitherto heard nothing against Henry Stanton, much less against his daughter.

"It will make no difference to me," he said firmly. "I love her, and, father, in saying this I mean no disrespect to your authority, but, if she will accept me, I intend to marry her."

Andrew Cruger made no answer. He merely lowered his head and looked at his son.

"When?" he asked briefly.

"I have not spoken to her yet," said Beverly.

Old Cruger looked at him quizzically.

"Perhaps I've been a little premature," suggested Beverly. The elder Cruger shrugged his shoulders. "That is the chief characteristic of American youth," he said, with a slight smile.

"I should never think of settling the question of dates, or of doing anything final until I had consulted you and my mother. Nor would I speak to her without first asking your consent," he added, to please his father.

Andrew Cruger smiled once more. "Suppose I refuse my consent?" he asked.

"Well," Beverly hesitated.

"You'll marry her without it? Of course you will! That's if she'll have you, my boy. The authority of parents is only nominal; therefore I content myself with warning you that you may ruin your career by such a marriage."

"I'll risk it," said Beverly.

"In other words you will give up your career?"

"Yes," replied Beverly.

"Quite so," agreed old Cruger. "But if you are too willing to take the risk, too indifferent as to your future, the world, our world, which after all is the only world, may say that your wife's fortune made it unnecessary for you to bother about a career or even about having to earn your own living."

Beverly looked indignant.

"You know the world, particularly our section of it, has rather an unpleasant way of putting things. I should not like to have a son of mine accused of such motives even though I knew it to be untrue."

Beverly was silent. He dimly saw that his father was right.

"Think it over," suggested old Cruger.

"Have I your consent?" asked Beverly.

"Don't put me in the position of being compelled to say, 'Bless you, my child,' after I have damned you for disobedience," said the elder Cruger laughingly. "Be quite sure, my boy, that I shall adapt myself to conditions. If I say 'yes,' it is because I know you will do as you please in any event, and I don't want to cloud your happiness by interposing useless objections. I merely warn you! Good-night, Beverly."

"Good-night, father." Beverly left the room and the elder Cruger returned to his work.

It was about five minutes before three the next afternoon when Anton Von Barwig's card was brought up to Helene's room by Joles. Herr Von Barwig had evidently taken the precaution to have his name printed on a piece of pasteboard, so as not to offend Joles's delicate sense of propriety.

"Will you see him, miss?" asked the man-servant; glancing at the cardboard somewhat suspiciously.

"Ask him up at once, please," said Miss Stanton, in such a decided tone that Joles hastened to obey her orders.

Helene was perplexed; she had been thinking all the morning of the false position she found herself in. She had told the old music master that she could not play at all, or could only play a little, and that she wanted to take piano lessons. At the very outset he would discover that she was quite a good amateur pianoforte player, with a fine musical ear, and then he would see through her ruse and refuse to teach her. She felt that he would see her pretences were only for the purpose of getting him to give her lessons and she was afraid that he would be very much offended.

"After all, what does it matter?" she asked herself; and the answer came quickly, "It does matter." The more she thought of this the more perplexed she became. Why should she care one way or the other? Who was this man that she should consider his feelings toward her? The whole thing was ridiculous! Yet Von Barwig made an irresistible appeal to her, and she felt that she must rest contented with the fact as it was, without seeking to know how or why. One point, however, stood out very clearly: Beverly Cruger had been obviously jealous last night at the opera. Octavie's silly prattle about a young and handsome foreign nobleman had had a marked effect upon him, and Helene's heart beat slightly faster as she pondered over this phase of the matter.

"He's actually jealous," she thought, and she enjoyed the idea. Beverly's earnest manliness made her admire him greatly. It almost reconciled her to Octavie's silliness! He was so different from the swarm of social bees who sipped only the sweets of pleasure. He was a worker, a sincere worker, and his promised appointment to the diplomatic service, notwithstanding his youth, attested the fact that he was unusual. "He takes an interest in his country's welfare," thought Helene, "and does not ignore it as does the world in which he lives and moves. He is a patriot; he loves his country. He is unselfish, too. A good-looking society man who is unselfish, what an anomaly!" Helene felt rather grateful to the innocent cause of Beverly Cruger's jealousy, and when he entered the room she greeted him with a beaming smile.

"I am so pleased to see you," she said unaffectedly.

Von Barwig had a little paper parcel in his hand. He carefully removed the paper, putting it in his pocket, and then held out a very tiny bunch of violets.

"You are spoiling me," declared Helene, as she took them from him. She had a large bouquet of orchids in her corsage, which she quickly removed, and placed the violets there instead.

"I think violets are far prettier than orchids," she said.

Von Barwig looked rather dubious. He was pleased, but he doubted.

"Do sit down!" she said, and he went toward the piano. "Not at the piano; here," said Helene, seating him beside her. "Now, listen to me, sir! You must not bring me expensive flowers every time you call."

"They are not expensive," said Von Barwig with a smile. "It is the box and the ribbon that costs. You may have observed that I avoided them on this occasion."

"Well, what shall we talk about?" asked Helene, after a pause.

"Talk about?" repeated Von Barwig, slightly perplexed. "Our music lesson!"

"Oh, I don't feel like taking a lesson to-day," said Helene. "I want to talk."

"Yes, but I--it is I who must talk, if I am to teach," faltered Von Barwig in a low voice. He didn't want to go too far, for he had heard that American heiresses were capricious and whimsical and that they took likes and dislikes very suddenly. He did not want her to dislike him, so he would humour her; but he also wanted to teach her.

"You know," she said confidentially, "I think I have a rather discontented nature. Certain people have a horrible effect on me. I want to run about, play, sing, read, quarrel, do anything rather than talk to them. But you, how I like to talk to you! You have a sort of a--what shall I call it--an all-pervading calmness, that communicates itself to me, and soothes my ruffled feelings. I don't seem to feel in a hurry when you're here. And when you smile, as you're smiling now, I don't know why, but I feel just happy, and contented with myself. Do you understand what I mean?" The girl had a far-away expression in her eyes, as if she were day-dreaming. The old man regarded her with a smile.

"You are trying to put me at my ease," he said finally, "and you have succeeded, but we make no progress at our music."

"What music have you brought?" she asked.

"I cannot tell what books you will need until I hear you," he replied.

"You'd better get me Bach's studies," she said carelessly.

"Won't you play?" he asked, "and then I can judge."

"Not now," replied Helene, and then she went on again, telling him of herself, her life, her aims and ambitions, her predilections and prejudices. She seldom referred to her father, and mentioned her mother only occasionally. "How I do ramble on, don't I? I seem to have known you for years."

"You are very happy, are you not?" he asked.

"Oh, yes, I suppose so!" she replied. There seemed to be a tinge of sadness in her manner, a sort of mental reservation as to her happiness that she did not like to confess even to herself. "Yes, I *think* I am," she said finally.

"Why not?" he answered. "Here all is peaceful, beautiful and harmonious. What surroundings you have!" and he looked around, "beautiful art objects to look at, the beautiful park at your very window. Here all is beauty, joy, peace, without and within. Your architect was a fine artist, or is it your own taste--all this?"

Helene nodded. "I designed this part of the house myself," she replied. "The tapestry and pictures and statuary of course add greatly to its general appearance, but you are quite right--the architect was an artist."

"He must have been," commented Von Barwig, looking about approvingly.

"Are you looking at that cabinet, the one with the dolls in it? That's a sixteenth century piece; it belonged to Maria Theresa. Father brought it from Paris himself. It's beautiful, isn't it? I keep all my dolls in it, and some day I'll show them to you. I have a great collection; but I don't suppose you take much interest in dolls," said

Helene.

"Your father--he must be a fine man," said Von Barwig with a sigh. "I have heard so much of his goodness to the poor, his charity, his interest in church matters----"

"Yes, he is very good," said Helene, without any enthusiasm in her voice. "There is not a hospital or a church or an asylum that doesn't number him among its patrons. Yes, he is really a very good man I suppose," repeated Helene as if she were trying to assure herself of his goodness. "He lays more corner stones and endows more orphanages than any man in America. He makes beautiful speeches; no public dinner seems to be complete without him. He knows just what to say and how to say it, and what is better than all, he knows when not to say anything!"

Von Barwig nodded. "It's a great gift, that of speech," he said. "I despair of ever being able to speak this language with fluency."

"But you speak English splendidly," said Helene.

"My accent is terrible," said Von Barwig. "Can you not hear it?"

"Your accent is beautiful to me, a rich German aristocratic roundness of expression, with nothing in the least harsh or grating to the ear. I just love to hear you talk!" declared Helene.

"Really?" asked Von Barwig in surprise.

"Really!" responded Helene with positive emphasis.

"Ah, you spoil me, young lady; you spoil me! But come, just a few bars on the piano, that I may see where my young pupil stands."

Helene looked at him and laughed mischievously.

"Very well," she said, rising with evident reluctance. "I will play you 'The Maiden's Prayer'----"

"Hum," said Von Barwig dubiously. "She has prayed so many times this poor maiden; it is time she should be answered. However, it is for you to decide!"

Helene seated herself at the piano and played that well-known and sorely tried air through as badly as she possibly could. When she had finished she placed her elbows on the keyboard and said: "How do you like this maiden's prayer?"

Von Barwig looked at her critically. "You can do better than that," he said.

"How do you know?" she asked quickly.

"Because, at some points you added notes of your own. You increased the bass, greatly improving the original harmony of the composition," replied Von Barwig. "You have talent," he added. "Badly as you play, badly as you execute, your talent stands out. No one can add to the composer's work without having musical ideas of his own."

"He has found me out already," thought Helene. Then she mechanically picked a tune on the piano with one finger.

Von Barwig's trained musical ear caught the melody in a moment.

"Where did you hear that?" he asked quickly.

"At your house," she answered, "the night I brought Danny to you. I have a very keen ear for music," she added.

"You gave me quite a start," he said. "It is my symphony, my dead and buried work. To hear that music from you was startling." There was a pause. "Do you know the bass part?" he asked.

She closed the piano quickly with a bang. "What do you think of Danny?" she asked, ignoring his question.

"What a curious girl!" thought Von Barwig, and then he said aloud, "The boy has possibilities, and so have you," he added.

Helene laughed. "It's a shame to deceive him," she thought.

"Herr Von Barwig," she began, "I want to be serious a moment. I'm afraid I've been guilty of a little--what shall I call it? Indiscretion? No, deception; that's better. I have deceived you--" She paused; the look of deep consternation on Von Barwig's face arrested her. "What's the matter?" she asked.

The old man gazed at her. "I don't know," he said, swallowing a lump in his throat "The fear that something had happened to prevent the--continuation--of--I am so happy here--I--" He apparently was unable to explain his meaning, for he stopped short.

"Go on," she said.

Von Barwig shook his head. "You look so serious," he said after a pause. "I thought perhaps something had happened to prevent my coming here, and the thought made me very unhappy. I am a foolish old man, eh? But, I am so happy here, so happy! I try to explain," he said. "Everything I have had in this world, everything I love I have lost! I am afraid to love anything for fear that I shall lose it. That's superstition, is it not? You tell me you have deceived me, and immediately

I think she is going to tell me that she will no longer deceive me, that she does not like me for a music master! I know," he added plaintively, "that I am foolish. But my life here since I have been in this country has made of me a coward. Forgive me; please forgive me!"

The girl's eyes filled with tears. "No, no!" she said gently. "You need not fear. I shall never want any other music master but you, never!"

Chapter Seventeen

Pinac and Fico noticed it and so did Miss Husted. Poons probably would have noticed it, too, if he had not been in love. But Jenny was the only one who really felt the change in Professor Von Barwig. Try as he would, the old man could not conceal from them the fact that "something had happened." Not that he was not just as affable to Miss Husted as ever, not that he was any less warm in his manner toward his friends, but there was something missing and Jenny was the only one who came anywhere near guessing the truth. "He has found some one whom he loves more than us," thought she, and she felt glad at heart for his sake; though she did not understand.

"He feels so bad with himself that we have lost our engagement through him that he cannot come over it," said Fico in answer to Pinac's query as to what was the matter with Von Barwig. They knew there was no chance now of their getting the symphony engagement, for Van Praag, hampered by creditors, unable to carry out his contracts owing to the strike, had gone into bankruptcy and retired from the venture with the loss of all his money. He wrote a letter to Von Barwig saying he was going back to Germany, where musical art was one thing and bricks another. Von Barwig sadly showed them the letter, but his mind was so taken up with his new pupil that he did not feel the loss of the engagement as they did.

And yet his financial position was daily growing worse and worse, for he had practically no pupils at all--that is, no paying pupils. Besides this, the weather was so cold and business had dropped off to such an extent at the Museum that Costello had been compelled to reduce Von Barwig's salary fifty per cent. "A half a loaf is better than none," he had told the night professor as he handed him his envelope with half salary in it; so Von Barwig had been compelled to take what he could get. He now seriously considered moving upstairs.

"We haven't a room vacant," said Miss Husted in a decided tone; "and if we had," tenderly, "no, professor, no top floor for you! I couldn't bear the idea of it; I couldn't really! Pay me when you get it," she said when the old man pleaded that he must live within his means.

"But I may never get it," expostulated the professor.

"Oh, yes, you will," confidently replied Miss Husted. "Mrs. Mangenborn says it is in the cards that great fortune is coming to you."

"In the next world, perhaps," said Von Barwig, laughing in spite of himself.

"Besides," went on Miss Husted, "it doesn't matter one way or the other. I could never bear the idea. Stay here for my sake," she pleaded when she saw that the professor was obstinate; and so he remained in his old rooms, though he squeezed every penny in order to pay her.

On the afternoon following his interview with his father, Beverly Cruger made up his mind to speak to Helene, to ask her to be his wife. He called at her home, and was informed by Joles that she was engaged; that a German gentleman was giving her music instruction, and that her orders were that she was not to be disturbed. Beverly left his card, intending to call the next day, but the fates were against him, and he was sent for by the State Department in regard to his diplomatic position and had to go to Washington. On his return to New York a week later, he again called on Miss Stanton. To his astonishment and, it must be confessed, to his extreme annoyance, he found Miss Stanton again "engaged." Herr Von Barwig, her music master, was there. "Please take up my card, Joles, and tell Miss Stanton that I wish to see her on a matter of the utmost importance--the utmost importance," repeated Beverly.

"Yes, sir," replied Joles.

"Herr Von Barwig appears to be **persona gratissima**," thought Beverly, and then it occurred to him that it was very strange that an accomplished musician like Helene Stanton should take music lessons. "He must be a very superior sort of a musical personage, very superior indeed." Beverly would not acknowledge even to himself that he resented Herr Von Barwig's presence at the Stantons'. "How can our American women be so deceived by the artificial deference, the insincere, highly polished politeness of these foreigners!" he mused. "Von Barwig is probably an offshoot of some noble German house, but she's not apt to be attracted by an empty title!" He had loved her for months, he told himself, and each time he had made up his mind to speak this foreigner had been the means of preventing him.

"Send him up please, Joles. I want you to meet Mr. Cruger, Herr Von Barwig," said Helene as she glanced at the card Joles handed her, and rose from the piano where she was taking a lesson. "I haven't seen him for days and days; I wondered what had become of him."

Von Barwig noticed the heightened colour in Miss Stanton's cheeks and he made a mental note that he must like Mr. Beverly Cruger, too, yet, if the truth must be known, he felt a pang of regret. "She loves him," he said to himself, "she will forget me."

"Shall we not continue the lesson?" he said aloud.

Helene shook her head. "No more to-day," she said.

"Then Miss Stanton will perhaps pardon my leaving," said Von Barwig.

"On the contrary, Herr Professor, Miss Stanton insists on your remaining," said Helene, motioning him to a seat. Von Barwig bowed deferentially.

"You have disappointed me to-day," he said. "Ach, your tempos change--like the winds! At one moment it is 6-8, the next 2-4, and almost in the same measure, you play 4-4. At one moment you play with your thumbs, like a little girl; at another, you play like a professional, an artist. I cannot understand it. Technically I don't know where you are. I am puzzled! I admit it; I am puzzled," and he looked at her in perplexed uncertainty.

Helene's only answer was a ripple of laughter. She was beginning to enjoy her own cleverness in deceiving him, and his confusion endeared him to her more than ever. The greater his perplexity the more she sympathised with him.

"Poor old gentleman," she thought, "It is downright wicked of me to deceive him. But what can I do? If I let him know I don't need his services he will not come."

"I have made up my mind to bring you some simple exercises for our next lesson, Miss Stanton. No more Bach and unevenly played Beethoven!" said Von Barwig. "It is necessary that we begin at the beginning and work up. That's it! We begin all over again, at the very beginning, and work up to the top. Then you will have some style, some form, some technique that you can call your own."

"Oh, dear, you're not going to make me play exercises, are you? Oh, Herr Von

Barwig, dear Herr Von Barwig, please don't!" said Helene, with such a pleading accent that Von Barwig was compelled to smile.

"It just serves me right," she thought. "I shall literally have to face the music," she said to herself with a laugh.

Beverly Cruger heard that laugh as he came into the room, and he made up his mind that Herr Von Barwig was one of those highly entertaining foreigners who appeal to the feminine mind with their superficial brilliancy and capture all before them.

"Herr Von Barwig, this is Mr. Beverly Cruger," broke in Helene, and Mr. Cruger was formally introduced to his rival.

Beverly could hardly repress a smile as his eyes fell on the slim figure of the poor, grey-headed, homely old artist. Was this the noble young foreigner, the handsome German music master he had pictured to himself? Was this Helene's romance?

"Gott in Himmel, what a squeeze he gives the hand!" thought Von Barwig, as he tried to release his injured digits from the vice that held them.

"I am so glad to see you, Herr Von Barwig," said Beverly; and he meant it.

"Yes, and I, too," groaned Von Barwig as he rubbed his fingers. "A fine fellow," he thought. "Such a welcome as that must come from the heart. But ach Gott, what a muscle! It's like iron!"

Helene was surprised. Beverly Cruger was far and away the most undemonstrative man of her acquaintance, and his cordial greeting of her old music master went straight to her heart. "He likes him because--perhaps, because I do," she thought.

"Do you know you remind me very much of a splendid bust of Beethoven I saw in the British Museum? Upon my word you do!"

Von Barwig bowed.

"Oh, I think Mozart rather than Beethoven," suggested Helene. "He's not stern enough for Beethoven."

Again Von Barwig bowed.

Beverly Cruger shook his head. "Beethoven," he said, looking at Von Barwig critically. "Still--well--I'm not sure, perhaps----"

"Mozart," insisted Helene.

"Are you sure you don't mean Liszt? We really do look alike!" Von Barwig said, with a twinkle in his eye. Then he added, "Ah, you are very kind to me, very kind! Dear me, I am afraid you spoil me. Those are the giants, the leaders of a great art. I am the most humble of all its followers. Even to resemble them is in itself a great honour."

Helene could never quite clearly remember how or when Von Barwig took his leave that memorable afternoon, but when he came on the following day to give his lesson she held both his hands in hers.

"You shall be the first one to hear the news," she said almost in a whisper. "I'm so happy, so very, very happy!" He looked at her, and understood.

"Herr Cruger?" he asked. She nodded affirmatively.

"How did you know?"

"Ah! He is an excellent young man; I approve very highly of him." Then he was afraid of his own temerity. "What right had he to approve? He must curb his tongue," he thought. "I beg your pardon! I mean he is a most excellent gentleman."

Helene hardly heard him, for her thoughts were far away at that moment. "I wonder what father will say?" she said.

Von Barwig started. The word father sounded strange, as if a discord had been struck in the midst of a beautiful harmony. "Why should I feel like that?" he asked himself. "Barwig, you are a fool, a madman! Mr. Stanton is her father; I must love him, too. My heart must not beat every time I hear his name. Come! Let us go to work; our studies--" he said aloud, tapping the book. "We must go to work. I have brought with me the book of exercises."

"No! no study to-day. But please don't go--just yet," she added as Von Barwig prepared to take his departure. "Sit down! I am going to be very angry with you."

"Angry with me?" the old man smiled. He knew it was only the girl's way of finding some little trivial fault with him. "Angry with me," he repeated. "And you said you were so very, very happy."

"Yes, I forgot when you came in that I ought to be very angry with you."

"Ah, you ought to be, but you are not! No, surely not," said Von Barwig gently.

"Why did you send me back my cheque? This one! Don't look so innocent; you know what I mean, sir!" and Helene held up the cheque that Von Barwig had found awaiting him at his room the night before, and that he had carefully mailed back to her.

Von Barwig looked pained.

"Herr Von Barwig, let us have a little understanding!" said Helene in a far more serious tone than she usually took with her music master.

"Ah, don't be angry, please don't be angry to-day! Not on such a day as this!" he urged. "To-morrow you may scold me if you like; but to-day, no, please, no!" and he looked at her so pleadingly that Helene was forced to smile. "I wish nothing to happen that shall interfere with the happiness that has come to you," he added.

But Helene was insistent. "It has been on my mind some time to ask you why you take such an interest in me," she said, "and now this," and she looked at the cheque.

Von Barwig was silent. What could he say? He dared not tell her the real reason.

"When I came to your studio with the little boy and asked you to teach him, you refused to accept money. Your reasons were that you were devoted to your art and that you loved to help the children of the poor. Surely I don't come under *that* classification, Herr Von Barwig?"

"Oh, no, no!" faltered poor Von Barwig.

"Then why do you refuse to take my money? Heaven only knows you've worked hard enough for it! Your efforts to instill your ideas into my head deserve far greater recognition than mere money payment."

"No, no! I have not worked. It has been so great a pleasure. No, decidedly there has been no work! I do not feel myself entitled to take, until you show some progress." Von Barwig felt himself on terra firma again.

"All that is begging the question, my dear Maestro! Whether your work affords you pleasure or no, it is still your work. Teaching is your means of livelihood, is it not?"

"Not altogether; I play at--" and then he thought of the Dime Museum and was silent. He looked at her; she was regarding him quite seriously, and he was afraid he had offended her. There was a pause during which he tried to think out a course of action calculated to offset his mistake. Helene broke the silence.

"You left your own country, where I understand you were well known and successful, and you came over here, where, pardon my saying so, you are not known and where you--" Helene hesitated slightly, "where you are not so prosperous. When I bring you a pupil you refuse to take money for his tuition. When I take lessons from you myself, you refuse to take money from me. Now, my dear Herr Von Barwig, I confess that I cannot understand! You must explain." There was a dead silence. "What does it mean?" demanded Helene. Von Barwig looked at her helplessly. He had no explanation, or, rather, he realised that the one he had was insufficient.

"Why do you take so much interest in me?" she asked.

"At first for a likeness, a likeness to some one I knew," replied Von Barwig, in a low voice. "You resemble a memory I have known, a memory that gives me so much happiness. She is gone, and now you--pardon the liberty--you take her place. I take interest because it was she--and it is now--you--you--a fresh young girl that will never grow old! You have taken the place of--of--" Von Barwig could not go on. He knew what he meant, but he could not express it.

"As I said before, Herr Von Barwig," and Helene spoke now with less show of wounded dignity, "I do not understand. It is simply incomprehensible, but it amounts to this--you must not refuse this cheque. If you do, I--I shall be compelled to--to refuse to go on with my lessons," and Helene held out the cheque toward him. Von Barwig looked at her; his sweet melancholy smile deepened as he slowly shook his head.

"If you knew, if you knew, Miss Helene, how I love to teach you, you would realise that I am over-compensated now. I am a foolish old man, I suppose, a foolish, sentimental old man! Perhaps I do not understand the ways of this country. Here there is no what we call *esprit de corps*, no enthusiasm, no love of art for the sake of art, no love of beauty for the mere sake of beauty. All is exchange and barter; so much done, so much to be paid for. Music, bricks, painting, sculpture and sewing machines all in one item--all to be paid for. Here for me is fairyland! It may not be fairyland for others, but for me it is fairyland. When I walk up the steps of this house and ring the bell, I stand there impatiently till your Mr. Joles opens up for me heaven. When I tell you that Mr. Joles is for me an angel, the archangel that unlocks for me paradise, you will realise to what extent I separate this world of love, of joy, of happiness, the world over which you preside, from the outside world, where together come music and bricks and human misery. Here is my heaven, my haven of rest and sweet contentment. Shall I take money for it; shall I be paid for my happiness? Ah, Fraeulein, Fraeulein, I dream, I dream! For sixteen years I have not rested. Don't wake me, please don't wake me!"

Helene tore the cheque into little pieces.

"To-morrow at three, Herr Von Barwig," she said. And when he had gone she burst into tears without in the least knowing why.

Chapter Eighteen

Whatever Andrew Cruger may have thought in his inner consciousness on the subject of his son's engagement to Helene Stanton, he outwardly showed no sign that he was not well pleased. He simply gave the consent that Beverly asked of him, and accepted the new condition as another event in the continuity of life. "Of course there can be no formal engagement until her father returns from Europe," said he.

"Can't we get his consent by cable?" asked his son.

"I don't believe in these irregularities," said the elder Cruger, whose diplomatic training had made him something of a stickler for formality and precedent. "There will be time enough for that when he returns."

Beverly submitted without another word, for he felt that his father had already given way to him a good deal. The young people did not cable to Mr. Stanton for his consent, for all agreed that there would be time enough to acquaint him with the fact when he returned. Whatever Mr. Cruger's mental attitude toward the engagement might have been his manner toward Helene was most cordial. As for Beverly's mother, she was delighted beyond all words.

"The dear, dear girl, how I shall love her!" she said to Beverly, on hearing the news. And after she had showered mother kisses, plentifully mixed with mother tears, on them both, her happiness was well-nigh complete.

That afternoon the Crugers were to make a formal call on Helene. Andrew Cruger had finally yielded to his son's entreaties and consented to call on her, notwithstanding the fact that Mr. Stanton was still in Europe and his formal consent had not been obtained.

"I have been looking forward to the day when I should see my son's wife," said the elder Cruger, somewhat pompously to Helene, as he greeted her with outstretched hand. He could never get over the idea that formalism was the soul of function.

"I have always felt that I would demand a great deal of her," went on Mr. Cruger, in his best after-dinner manner. "I thank you for giving me everything I could desire! You are the daughter of a man whose charity and beneficence we all respect and admire, and--" Here he paused to take breath.

"Thank you," said Helene simply. She was surprised that he did not kiss her instead of making a formal speech.

"I know that father means what he says," remarked Beverly to his mother; "but I do wish he would say it in a less stereotyped manner."

"Hush!" replied his mother, "your father is speaking again."

"I want your married life to begin auspiciously," continued the elder Cruger, as if he had not been interrupted. "So I have made what I consider to be a sacrifice for you. I had hoped to retire from public life, but I have altered my decision. I shall again represent my country in a foreign land."

Helene gratefully acknowledged the sacrifice, although she did not quite see where it came in. She had heard that most American representatives at foreign courts managed rather to enjoy life than otherwise.

"When I go abroad as hostess in the Embassy that Mr. Cruger represents," Mrs. Cruger said, taking up the thread of the conversation, "I want my son's wife to share my honours. A sweet young woman, far younger than I, is almost a--a--"

"A charming necessity," added Mr. Cruger, who made it a habit to finish his wife's sentences.

"Yes, a charming necessity," echoed his wife, and, then she continued:

"The fact that Octavie is engaged suggests a double wedding. They will marry in June, if the weather is good."

"What has the weather to do with Octavie's wedding?" inquired Mr. Cruger.

"Simply that it's an automobile wedding, Andrew," replied his wife.

Mr. Cruger looked almost pained. "Permit me to remark, Mary, that no Cruger was ever married in an automobile and I trust that no Cruger will so far forget himself or herself as to establish so ridiculous a precedent."

"The motor business comes in after the wedding, father; at least so Octavie said," whispered Beverly.

"Your niece is very frivolous," remarked Mr. Cruger to his wife. "I shall take pains to remind her that we Crugers marry quietly in Trinity!"

Helene laughed aloud. The idea of Octavie doing anything quietly appealed to her sense of humour.

"She does not take us very seriously," thought Mr. Cruger. Mrs. Cruger glanced at her husband and noticed a rather injured expression appear upon his face. Evidently he was not highly pleased at Helene's levity.

"You have written to your father?" Mr. Cruger asked her presently.

"No, Mr. Cruger," replied Helene after a pause.

"No, my dear?" echoed Mr. Cruger in surprise.

"I will tell him when he returns," said Helene.

Mr. Cruger was almost dismayed. "You have not written to your father?" he repeated. "My dear Helene, these formalities must be complied with! Your father's consent is of the utmost importance. Not that I anticipate any--er--opposition from that quarter, but it's merely the idea of the thing! Of course, I am somewhat old-fashioned, I admit."

"In France, for instance, it is against the law," interrupted Beverly in a satirical tone.

Helene smiled. Her prospective father-in-law appeared to her somewhat punctilious, but she determined to humour him.

"Your father is quite right, Beverly," she said. "I should have cabled at once."

At this moment Joles entered, apparently somewhat nervous. "Mr. Von Barwig is here, miss," he explained. "I told him you were engaged, but----"

"Ask him to come up, Joles." Joles was surprised, but being a well-trained servant, his face gave no outward indication of his feelings.

"It is my music master, Mrs. Cruger. I think this is a splendid opportunity for you to see him about your niece's music lessons." Mr. Cruger looked almost shocked. A music master invited to take part in a family function! Such conduct savoured of socialism, and socialism did not appeal to him.

"Herr Von Barwig is a most exceptionable person," said Helene, quite unconscious of the thought her words had aroused in her prospective father-in-law.

"Von Barwig? Von Barwig?" repeated Mr. Cruger, apparently interested in the name. "Don't I know that name? It seems quite familiar. A music master, you say?

Yes, it seems to me that I do know it!"

"He's one of the dearest old chaps I ever met," broke in Beverly, "such a gentle creature, a most excellent musician, but rather unfortunate."

"I know the name quite well, but if it's the man I mean it's impossible that it can be the same. He was a fine musician, from Dresden I think. Was it Dresden?" he asked himself, as if annoyed that his memory had played him false. "It must have been Dresden or Leipsic."

"Herr Von Barwig," announced Joles, in his most formal and freezing manner.

Poor old Von Barwig came into the room expecting to see no one but Helene, and was painfully astounded to see so many strangers. He wore his old broadcloth suit; it was well brushed, but more shiny than ever. Poons had carefully brushed it for him that morning and it was more than scrupulously clean. His gloves were old, but Jenny had mended up the holes the night before, so he looked even neater and more genteel than usual this afternoon. He carried the cheap little bunch of violets, wrapped in paper, in one hand and his hat in the other, for Joles had never been able to persuade him to leave it in the hall. He stood by the door, as close as he could get to it, as if afraid to come in, and then bowed low to Helene and the others. There he waited with timid dignity, uncertain as to what he should do next. There was a dead silence for a few moments.

"I'm so glad to see you," said Helene in an affectionate tone, coming to the rescue; and taking him warmly by the hand she led him away from the door into the middle of the room.

"Glad to meet you again, Herr Von Barwig," said Beverly, coming forward, and shaking hands with him far more cordially than the occasion called for. He then introduced Von Barwig to his mother and father. The elder Cruger looked at him very closely.

"It seems to me that we have met before, sir. Your face is very familiar. Yes, yes; Prince Holberg Meckstein introduced me to you at one of your concerts."

"Holberg Meckstein," repeated Von Barwig in a frightened voice. "Yes, I--I knew him; but--but--I--forgive me, I--I do not remember!"

"It was in Leipsic; oh, it must be fifteen years ago!" said Mr. Cruger. "At that time I had the United States Embassy at Berlin. Surely, you must remember! You became nervous that night while conducting your own symphony, and you fainted away right before the audience. Don't you remember?"

"I remember," said Von Barwig, in a low hoarse voice, which he controlled with great difficulty.

"And then a few months later you made some inquiries at the Embassy for me," went on Mr. Cruger, "but I was unfortunately not there at the time, and so was unable to be of service to you. You had some mission, some object in going to America, the Secretary of Legation said. You wanted a list of all the large towns in the United States. I hope you were successful in finding what you were searching for?"

"No, sir, I did not accomplish--my mission," replied Von Barwig, who had gained command of himself to some extent, and could speak without giving evidence of his emotion. "It is extremely kind of you to remember me!" His retiring, bashful manner was somewhat disconcerting, but beneath it there was the unmistakable evidence of birth, breeding and dignity.

"I am glad to find you in the house of such a distinguished citizen of the United States as Mr. Stanton," said Mr. Cruger at parting with Von Barwig.

"Ah, you know him, her father! He is a distinguished citizen?" said Von Barwig, and the last ray of hope died within him. "He is a distinguished citizen," he said to himself, "and he is her father." He sighed deeply, and reproached himself for ever having hoped.

"That old man has a history," thought the elder Cruger, as he went up to Helene, intent on saying good-bye to her. Joles had announced his wife's nieces, and he did not care to stay longer. He had done his duty by Beverly and that was all that was necessary. As he shook hands warmly with Helene, he said to her:

"I should like to see Herr Von Barwig again."

Helene squeezed his hand warmly; it was the first note of affection that had been sounded between them.

"Let me know if I can be of any service to him," he said.

"I will, I promise you I will," replied Helene, and Mr. Cruger took his departure, accompanied by his son.

The girls were introduced to Herr Von Barwig. "And this is Helene's romance," thought Octavie, as she looked at Von Barwig and laughed aloud. Von Barwig thought she was a very pleasant young lady, and smiled back in return.

"I should like Charlotte to study for the next two years, Herr Von Barwig, and

Octavie till about June," said Mrs. Cruger, who was determined to get Herr Von Barwig to teach her nieces, since Helene had recommended him so highly.

"I don't want to study at all," said Octavie. "Who ever heard of an engaged girl studying?"

"And pray, am I not an engaged girl, as you call it?" asked Helene, who was pouring out tea. "And do I not study?"

"Yes, but you're an accomplished musician and----"

"One lump or two, Herr Von Barwig?" broke in Helene, to change the conversation.

"No lumps! Yes, thank you, I take one," said Von Barwig, somewhat confused by the incessant chatter of the young ladies, who smiled at his awkwardness.

"Cake, Herr Von Barwig?" Helene held out the dish to her music master.

"No, thank you," he replied quietly, and then catching an appealing look from her, he took a cake, and then another.

"The idea of waiting on a music master," whispered Octavie to Charlotte; "she'll spoil him."

"She's a socialist," said Charlotte.

"Come, girls, tell Herr Von Barwig what you know. If he can teach such a finished pianist as Helene, I am determined that you shall have the advantage of his tutelage."

"A finished musician?" thought Von Barwig. "Heaven save us! You have had lessons before?" he continued to ask one of the gay young ladies. "You have studied a great deal, yes?"

"We've had lots of lessons," replied Octavie, "but I don't think we've studied; at least I haven't!" she confessed.

"Don't count on me! I know nothing; absolutely nothing!" volunteered Charlotte.

"Well," said Von Barwig sententiously, "that is something at all events! Many musicians take years to discover that."

"I only want to know enough to do a few stunts," said Charlotte to him gaily.

Von Barwig's face fell. "Stunts! they do not love music," he thought, "they want to do tricks." And then the girls talked on the subject of musical comedies, popular songs and dance music, until their aunt interrupted them.

"Come, Charlotte," said the excellent Mrs. Cruger. She thought her nieces had had time to prevail on the eminent professor to take them. "Remember your appointment at the museum."

Von Barwig, in the act of drinking tea, nearly choked. He thought of his Dime Museum. "If they should ever dream of such a thing!"

"My drawing master is meeting me at the Museum of Art," explained Charlotte to Von Barwig.

"Will you play something before you go?" asked Von Barwig. Charlotte went to the piano and banged out a two-step march that was the raging popular tune of the day.

"Ah, that is the stunt! Now, if you will play some music," ventured Von Barwig, "I can just tell you where you are."

"Isn't that music?" asked Charlotte.

"It is rhythm and jingle--a stunt as you call it. Real musicians do not write such things."

"Isn't there a method of learning how to play without practising?" broke in Octavie.

"From nothing comes nothing," said Von Barwig with a sigh.

"Quite true," assented Mrs. Cruger.

"Some day," said Von Barwig prophetically, "some day they will invent a machine that will play itself. All you will have to do is to pump a bellows, or turn a wheel and the music will play itself! You will see; there is so much demand for it, some one will rise to the occasion."

"Splendid!" said Charlotte. "Won't that save lots of hard work!"

"We'll write and make an appointment; Helene will give us the address," said Octavie, as they said good-bye to Von Barwig.

"Thank you so much, Herr Professor, for your patience and courtesy," said Mrs. Cruger at parting.

Herr Von Barwig bowed. The girls accompanied by their aunt took their leave, and he was left alone with Helene. He took the paper from the little bunch of violets he had brought with him, and handed them to her.

"Ah, thank you so much! But why do you always bring me flowers?"

"Why do we love the light?" he asked. "Because it gives us joy."

She took an orchid she was wearing and tried to pin it on his coat. "I am afraid," said Von Barwig, "that it is healed up!" Helene laughed.

"What a curious expression!" she said. Then she walked up to the window and looked out.

"Shall we begin where we left off?" asked Von Barwig as he opened the music. He had been waiting some time for her to come to the piano.

"You like him, don't you?" said Helene in a low voice.

"The young Herr Cruger?" asked Von Barwig. Then without waiting for an answer he went on: "Yes, he has a fine noble heart. He is different to the young men here; quite different."

"I am glad you like him!"

"Why?"

"I don't know. I am glad, that's all!"

At that moment Von Barwig was supremely happy. Neither of them spoke for a few moments.

"Shall we not begin?" he said, breaking the silence.

Helene walked slowly to the piano and sat down.

At that moment Joles entered the room with a message for Miss Stanton.

"Put it down, Joles," she said, striking a note here and there on the piano.

"It's a telegram, miss."

"Oh! bring it to me, then." He obeyed. She opened it and read:

"Left Paris this morning en route to New York.

    FATHER."

A feeling of dread crept over her; the smile on her face gave way to a hardness of expression. Gone was the joy, the happiness, in the girl's face, and in its place was doubt, apprehension, anxiety.

Von Barwig looked at her; the keen eye of love quickly detected the presence of fear. He did not speak, but his look demanded an answer to its question.

"My father is coming home," she said, forcing herself to smile.

"Ah? So? I shall be glad to meet him," said Von Barwig.

Chapter Nineteen

Henry Stanton's return to New York was not marked by any special outburst of joy on the part of the large retinue of dependents that constituted the machinery of his household. He was feared rather than loved by his servants, and this feeling, as has been indicated, was shared by his daughter in common with others. It was not that he did not want to be loved, or that he was indifferent to the feelings and opinion of others concerning him. On the contrary, he, of all men, was most anxious that others should think well of him. But his manner was stern, harsh and repellent, and he did not seem to have the capacity to gain the confidence or sympathy of those around him. Although generous even to extravagance where it gratified his vanity, of broad-minded charity in its higher and nobler sense the man knew nothing. He gave not because he loved, but because his charities reflected lustre on his name; and here was the man's most vulnerable point, his sensitiveness as to name, fame, honour, reputation dignity, public opinion. "What will the world think?" stood out in blazing letters on a glittering signpost pointing to the motive of all he did. And so when Mr. Stanton told his daughter, the day after his arrival, that he approved of her engagement to Beverly Cruger and that it gave him great happiness, the utter absence of genuine fatherly tenderness in his manner showed the girl plainly that his happiness was brought about mainly by the fact that it advanced him several rungs in the social ladder, and not because she was going to marry a man who would make her happy.

"He is a splendid catch," were Mr. Stanton's words on first hearing the news. "He belongs to a fine solid family and you will have *entree* into the first establishments in America and Europe."

Helene was instinctively repelled by the manner of his congratulations. Not one solitary word was uttered as to love, happiness, or the sacred nature of marriage itself, not a regret at parting with her; nothing but an adding up of the advantages that would accrue to him from a social point of view.

"The Van Nesses and the de Morelles can't refuse to meet us now. We can snap our fingers at them! Bravo, my girl, you have achieved a splendid victory. They can't dig up hidden and dead scandals now."

Helene had never known that the Van Nesses and the de Morelles had refused to meet them. She knew that several of the historic New York families did not make it a point to ask them to their functions, but she had always thought it was because her father was personally unpopular with the more exclusive set. His reference to hidden and dead scandals she did not in the least understand, for she had heard nothing.

"At a moment like this," Helene thought, "if he had only opened his heart, if he would only let me love him!" But no, he had not shown the slightest encouragement, not a particle of sentiment.

"With your husband's people and my money back of you," he said, "you ought to become a leader, nothing less than a leader! I'd give half a million to see you take Julia Van Ness's place."

Helene was disappointed. "Oh, father, please don't speak of those things now! It's not a question of social advantage. It's my whole future happiness; my whole life itself is Involved."

"Do you know, Helene, you are rather selfish in your love affair as I suppose you call it," cried Mr. Stanton angrily. "My ambition is for you, not for myself."

"I have no ambition," said Helene, stifling a tendency to burst into tears, "that is, no social ambition. I love my friends and they love me. Indeed, father, I have no desire to extend my circle of acquaintances; I can't do justice to those I know now! If it is for my sake you are trying to----"

At these words Mr. Stanton completely lost his temper. "Of course it is for your sake, don't you believe me when I say so? Please remember that I am your father, and it is your duty to believe me whether my statement convinces you or not. It is your duty to believe me and to love me!"

"God knows I try hard enough," broke from the girl, and now she too lost control of herself. "I hate myself for saying it, but it's true, father, it's true! I don't seem to love you, not as most girls love their fathers, and I want to, I do so want to! You believe that, don't you, father?"

Mr. Stanton was silent, and Helene went on: "I always feel that there is something between us. I think of myself only as one of your possessions. You were so good, so gentle to mother; why aren't you more kind, more loving to me?"

"Is there anything you want that you do not get?" demanded Mr. Stanton.

"Yes," cried Helene, "there is love, love! I do not get it! Your manner is cold, hard, repellent!"

"How dare you!" shouted her father.

"I repeat it!" cried Helene, now utterly regardless of consequences. "Something in you repels me. I came to you this morning with the news of my engagement of marriage. I came to you with earnest longing to have you take me into your arms and kiss me, to have you congratulate me on my happiness. Instead of this you repelled me with cold calculations as to the effect the marriage would have on your own social position. Oh, father, father! is that the way to sympathise with a girl? I have no mother; you should supply her place. All the luxuries in this palace don't make up to me for the lack of love I find in it."

"Is it my fault that your mother died when you were eight years old?" said Mr. Stanton in a milder tone. The reference to his dead wife had had a softening influence upon him.

"No, no, father; no, no! I can't help thinking of her now, that's all! I need her now, so much. I have no one to go to but you, and--" the girl shook her head helplessly. "I can just remember her, so delicate, so beautiful! She was an angel, wasn't she?"

He nodded assent. "I remember that she was always in tears, always afraid to go out in the streets, afraid to be seen," said Helene somewhat irrelevantly. "You did love her, didn't you? I always feel you did! Why, why can't you love me as you did her? Why am I not as near to you as she was? Your own flesh and blood should be very near and very dear to you; especially at such a time as this."

He regarded her more tenderly. "You are near me," he said and kissed her. "Poor little thing," he muttered to himself. "I suppose I am selfish," he said aloud, "but you'll have my money some day. Surely that should give you a great deal of comfort!"

Helene smiled sadly. Her father seemed incapable of understanding her. She could only shake her head and say, "That's nothing, nothing!"

"You'll find it a great deal, my girl," he said.

That afternoon when her music master came he was astonished to find her pensive and downcast instead of joyful and happy, as he expected. "There has been a lovers' quarrel," he said to himself. "Little missie wanted her way and young master wanted his. It is nothing," he decided, as he opened the music books.

"Have you studied your lesson?" he asked.

"No," replied Helene, without thinking.

"Well, do the best you can," he said. To his utter astonishment she played the whole exercise through without looking at the music, without any effort and without playing a single false note.

To say that Von Barwig was astounded is putting it mildly. He simply gasped for breath.

"Gott in Himmel, Fraeulein! Ach, du lieber Gott! what style, what touch, what progress! Ah," and then it came to him all at once, "your father has come back; you want to show him progress, is it not? You have practised on the sly, eh? Ah--" and he shook his finger reproachfully at her.

Helene looked at him and laughed. "If father was only like you," she thought.

"Yes," she said aloud. "I suppose I wanted to show my father the progress I have made, so I practised on the sly."

"Let us continue," said Von Barwig, who was now very anxious to see what new surprise his pupil was going to give him.

"Have you arranged with Mrs. Cruger about giving her nieces lessons?" asked Helene, carelessly striking a few chords on the piano.

"Not yet," replied Von Barwig, "I am to go next week." Then he added with a little laugh, "The young ladies postpone me as long as possible."

Here they were interrupted by the entrance of Denning, the under-butler, who informed Miss Stanton that her father wished to see her in the library. Von Barwig saw a downcast expression on Helene's face as she left the room. "Perhaps he does not approve of the marriage, this Mr. Stanton. Well, I do!" he said with emphasis. "I do, and I am determined that she shall marry the man of her choice. He is a splendid fellow, fully worthy of her. If this father interferes, I shall-- Let me see, what shall I do?"

Von Barwig laughed at his own foolishness in allowing his thoughts to run on unchecked. Somehow they always led him into a ridiculous position from which he could never extricate himself.

"I shall tell this father," he went on in a more compromising vein of thought, "I shall tell him that his daughter's happiness is at stake, and that he must not allow personal considerations to interfere with that happiness. Then he will have me flung out of his house. No, thank you, Barwig, you will not speak; but none the less that is what I think! Her happiness first, last and all the time. Let me tell you a secret, Mr. Stanton," said Von Barwig mentally. His thoughts rushed him along pell-mell now and he followed them, thoroughly enjoying the mental pictures they brought up. "Let me tell you my secret, Mr. Stanton! She is my daughter as well as yours. I have adopted her. She does not know it, nor do you, but I do! She has taken the place of my own little one and I love her, Mr. Stanton. I love her just as much, aye, even more than you do, sir, and this love gives me the right to speak. You shall not interfere with her happiness! Do you hear me, sir?"

Von Barwig had now lashed himself into a whirlwind of imaginary indignation and was pacing up and down the music room; his thoughts completely engrossing him. They were the only realities in life to him now, these thoughts, and he treasured them as philosophers do the truths of existence. All at once his eye caught a pile of music that lay on the table next to Miss Stanton's dolls' cabinet in the corner of the room opposite the piano. He observed the Beethoven Concerto for pianoforte which had Helene Stanton's name on it, also the C Minor and F Minor concertos of Chopin, besides other compositions for pianoforte of an exceedingly difficult character; all this music was marked with her name and the date.

"There must be some mistake," he thought, as he read the names. "She cannot play these difficult compositions, surely! It may be her mother had played them, but no, they are dated within a year or so of the present day!"

Everything was explained to him now. He was no longer surprised at the unaccountable unevenness of her playing. She had deceived him. "Why, why?" he wondered.

Then it came to him. "Of course! Fool, dolt, idiot! she wanted to benefit you, so she pretends she cannot play and takes lessons she does not need. But why should she wish to befriend you, why?"

Von Barwig was silent a long time. "Why, why?" he kept asking himself and his thoughts could get no further. "Am I dreaming?" He looked around. "Is it all a dream? Do I merely believe these things happen, or are they real? Sometimes these people seem like phantoms of the past; phantoms that come and vanish like the thoughts that give them existence. There seems to be no substance in them. But real or phantom, dreaming or waking, my love for her is real. That is God's truth! I feel it, I know it! I love her, I love her! Of that alone I am certain. That is truth, if nothing else is!"

In the meantime, Helene found her father awaiting her in the library. Mr. Stanton was in very excellent spirits.

"Why did you trouble to come down, my dear child? I intended to come up and see you," he said as she entered the door. "I told Denning to find out if you could receive me; servants are so stupid!"

"Oh, it doesn't matter! I was only taking a music lesson."

"Yes, so Denning said. I didn't know you'd taken up your musical studies again," and then before Helene could reply, he went on:

"Sit down, my dear, I want to ask, no, not ask; I want to make a suggestion. I want you to do something for my sake. The spring has fairly set in; in a few weeks it will be summer, and I may want to go abroad again. Can you arrange to have your marriage take place late in June or early in July?"

"No, father!" replied Helene in a somewhat decided tone. "I am sorry," she added quickly, as she saw an expression of disappointment in his face.

"Why not, may I ask?" inquired her father.

"Because Beverly is engaged in Washington at the State Department. The secretary has promised him an under-secretaryship in one of the European embassies if his work there is satisfactory, and our marriage would interrupt his work."

"Not necessarily," said Mr. Stanton. "Besides he doesn't need any career! He will have plenty of money, and----"

"I don't think all the money in the world would be sufficient to support Beverly Cruger in idleness," responded Helene with some spirit. "The Crugers are not well off, and he refuses to accept anything from his father; and as for living on my income, it's out of the question, father! He insists on earning his own living and working out his own career."

"Well, after all, that shows a good spirit," said Mr. Stanton, "but I really don't see how an early marriage would interfere with his resolutions on that point. He could go on working."

"His income is insufficient just at present," said Helene, "and it will be until next year. The marriage cannot take place till then. I am sorry."

"Some time next winter, eh? That's a long time, Helene; so many things may happen," said Mr. Stanton thoughtfully.

"What could happen?" asked Helene in surprise. "What do you mean?"

"I don't know; I'm nervous and apprehensive. I want to see you married and settled," replied her father almost peevishly, as if he didn't want to go into explanations. "I've a curious notion that I want to see you married and settled. It's a--a-- my anxiety for you, Helene," added Mr. Stanton, forcing a smile.

"You're very kind," repeated Helene. She did not understand her father in the least. He seemed to be afraid of something, his manner was distinctly apprehensive. She moved slowly toward the door, deep in thought.

"Are you going?" asked Mr. Stanton.

"My music master is waiting for me," replied Helene.

"Your music master? Oh, yes, you said you'd taken up your studies again."

Helene smiled. "You can hardly call it taking up my studies," she said. "Herr Von Barwig just--so to speak--goes over; I hardly know how to describe it. I think he tries to improve my technique."

Was it imagination or had her father turned ashen pale? He looked at her, barely able to speak; he seemed to have received an awful shock and he was gasping for breath. What had happened? There was a pause during which Helene wondered why she had not noticed before how pale and ill her father looked, and how his hands trembled.

"What did you say was his name?" asked Mr. Stanton, barely able to repress the emotion in his voice.

"Professor Von Barwig. Oh, he's not known here as well as he was in Germany! What's the matter, father?" she cried out as the man almost tottered into his chair. "Father, father! what is it?"

"Nothing, nothing; what should be the matter? I--these attacks come periodically now. A little heart trouble--it will soon pass away. Ring for Joles!"

She obeyed him instantly.

"Good God, good God! Is it possible? Right under my own roof!" muttered Stanton, "and with her! Oh, God!"

"I rang for him, father," said Helene, looking at him anxiously.

"It's Ditson I want to see. Ditson, Ditson! not Joles." Then he added quickly, "No, I don't want to see any one! I'm better now; these attacks pass away quickly. Sit down, my dear child; I want to talk to you. What were you saying?" he asked, anxious to hear and yet not wishing to arouse her suspicion as to the cause of his anxiety.

"Nothing of any importance, father."

"Yes, yes; I insist! Go right on with our conversation where we left off. You were speaking of your--your--musical professor, Anton Von Barwig." Mr. Stanton had almost completely recovered himself now.

"How did you know his first name, father?"

"You mentioned it, you must have done so," said Mr. Stanton quickly. "Yes, I remember you did! When you first mentioned his name, you called him Anton. And he is upstairs," added her father with a curious laugh, "in this house."

Helene thought his manner most strange. He was regarding her now with a curious, searching gaze. "He can have told her nothing," he muttered, "he must be as ignorant of the truth as she is. Good God, what a coincidence!"

Joles came and Ditson was sent for. When the confidential secretary arrived, Mr. Stanton and he went into the private study. Helene followed them.

"Will you need me any more, father?" she asked anxiously.

"No, no!" replied Mr. Stanton.

Helene went out and closed the door. As she reached the stairway she heard the key turn in the lock. "Why does he lock himself in?" she thought. When Helene returned to the music room she found her music master waiting patiently for her.

"Forgive me for keeping you waiting!" she said.

"There is great pleasure even in waiting for those we love; we love to teach, I should say," he added quickly.

Inwardly Helene found herself contrasting her father with this man. "If only he had the tenderness, the lovable qualities of this old musician," she thought, "how

I could love him!" As he was taking his leave, her eye caught the music on top of the cabinet and in a moment she saw it had been disturbed. She looked quickly at Von Barwig, but he gave no sign that he knew of its existence.

"I hope some day to be able to play those compositions for you," she said, pointing to them.

"Yes," replied Von Barwig with a smile. "I hope so."

"I'll surprise you some day," she added.

"Yes," said Von Barwig simply, and he determined to allow her to surprise him. "Good-bye!" he said, bowing. She held out her hand.

"Good-bye!" she replied almost tenderly.

"To-morrow at the same time?" he asked anxiously.

"Yes, of course."

Von Barwig breathed a sigh of relief. "She is not angry," he thought. "And it will very soon be to-morrow!"

Chapter Twenty

As Von Barwig walked down Fifth Avenue on his way home to his lodgings in Houston Street he could not help contrasting his present happy existence with the miserably hopeless state in which he had found himself on his first arrival in New York. "And it is to her, Miss Stanton, that I owe all this blessedness. I am a changed man," he said to himself, almost gaily, "I live, I enjoy, for to-morrow I shall see her again. To live that one hour of restful blessedness," he thought, "is well worth the bare existence of the other twenty-three." His friends felt the change, too. They all knew that something had happened, that something had entered the life of the old professor and changed it, but not one of them attempted to pry into his secret.

"*Ma foi*," said Pinac, "he shall tell himself if he wants to. If not, he shall not!"

Fico's reply was characteristic of that Italian's sunny disposition, and it inverted a familiar saying.

"What the hell we care, so long as he is happy," he said.

Poons loved Von Barwig as a son, but the best of sons are self-centred when they are in love; and Poons saw nothing.

Jenny was silent, she felt that she had lost her dear professor, but with that spirit of sacrifice of which woman alone is capable, she resigned her place in his heart to another. Be it said to her credit there was not a jealous pang, not a moment of envy, nothing but mournful regret and sweet resignation to the inevitable. As a mother gives her son to another woman in marriage, so did Jenny give up Von Barwig; to whom she knew not, nor did she seek to know.

His secret was sacred to all his friends, all, save one, and this solitary exception led to a slight change in the Houston Street establishment. It came about as follows:

"When a man comes home with orchids pinned to his coat," confided Mrs.

Mangenborn to her friend Miss Husted, "it looks as if it was only a question of time when he would move uptown into more elegant apartments. Orchids in winter only goes with blue diamonds and yellowbacks!"

Miss Husted shook her head. "Move upstairs more likely than uptown," replied that lady regretfully. "Why, the poor old gentleman don't even get enough to eat. You mark my word for it, some day he's going to keel over! Only yesterday morning I had to beg him almost on my bended knees to join us at dinner and then he only came in to oblige me. He ate scarcely anything, poor dear!"

"Does he pay regularly?" inquired Mrs. Mangenborn, with a lack of sympathy noted by her friend.

"As regularly as clockwork," snapped Miss Husted. "Half price, but how long will he be able to pay even that? Only three pupils, and only one of them pays him in cash. Oh, how people round here have changed since I first came here; how much they do expect for their money nowadays!"

"He's out every afternoon, regularly. He's out evenings with his fiddle; home at four in the morning, he doesn't do that for nothing. I don't think he tells all he knows," concluded Mrs. Mangenborn with a significant wink of the eye, which brought her fat cheek very close to her eyebrow.

"Well," said Miss Husted with a sigh, "of course it's no business of mine where he goes and what he does, but--whatever it is, it's all right! That you can depend on, it is all right."

This was intended to be a rebuke to Mrs. Mangenborn, but it was entirely lost on that lady, for with the very next breath she said bluntly: "Why don't you ask him?"

Miss Husted set her lips firmly together, and this movement might have warned a less obtuse person.

"Why don't you ask him?" repeated Mrs. Mangenborn.

"Because," replied Miss Husted, with more temper than she had ever exhibited before to her friend, "because, Mrs. Mangenborn, it's none of my business!"

There was a slight pause.

"Not wishing to give you a short answer, my dear," supplemented Miss Husted, sorry that she had been compelled to take extreme measures to stay her friend's curiosity.

To her utter surprise Mrs. Mangenborn still persisted.

"Well, it is your business, in a sense," went on that lady. "This is your house, and it is your duty to see that it is conducted respectably!"

"Respectably? Am I to understand, Mrs. Mangenborn, that you intend to convey a hint that my house is not conducted respectably?" demanded Miss Husted. Her back at this moment could not have been straighter had she been leaning against the wall.

"Why, no!" assented Mrs. Mangenborn, who saw that she had gone a little too far. "I merely said that it was your duty, and so it is! People should always do their duty," she added somewhat vaguely.

"I trust I know my duty, Mrs. Mangenborn," said Miss Husted severely, "nor do I require to be put in the path of my duty by anybody, be it he, or be it she, be it transient, or be it permanent."

This was a direct shot and Mrs. Mangenborn gave signs that it had gone home; for she arose. "I am very sorry," she said with heavy-weight dignity, "I am very sorry."

"There is nothing to be sorry for, only this, Mrs. Mangenborn! I'd like it to be thoroughly understood that no person in this living world can besmirch the character of Professor Von Barwig without besmirching me," and Miss Husted folded her arms somewhat defiantly.

"Oh, Miss Husted, Miss Husted, how can you say such a thing! Did I besmirch even a particle of his character? Just prove your words, please; did I, did I?"

Mrs. Mangenborn now came slightly closer to Miss Husted and for a moment it looked as though there would be a personal altercation between the two ladies.

"You said that his hours were not respectable hours, and that he didn't tell all he knew, and--and--oh, I can't remember all you said, Mrs. Mangenborn, nor does it matter in the least! Pray, why should he tell all he knows? It's no lady's business--what he knows! For that matter, do you tell all you know? No," went on Miss Husted, now thoroughly aroused, "but you tell a great many things that you don't know! Not one of your fortunes has come true, lately, not one!"

The cards had toppled over, there were no more fortunes in them, and Mrs. Mangenborn saw that her reign had come to an end.

"I do not care to discuss the question any further," she said loftily, and giving a wide sweep to her skirts she added somewhat grandiloquently:

"Kindly send my bill to my room, and please consider yourself at perfect liberty to dispose of it to some one else."

"With great pleasure, Mrs. Mangenborn," replied Miss Husted, "with very great pleasure! And I may add I was going to ask you for your room this very evening."

Mrs. Mangenborn's only answer was a loud and prolonged laugh, which she kept up all the way to her room and which only ceased when she had shut her door with a loud bang.

"Good riddance!" thought Miss Husted, "a very good riddance!"

Thus the friendship of years was sundered.

At this precise moment the innocent object of their strife let himself in at the front door.

"Ah, my dear Professor Von Barwig, I was just thinking of you," said Miss Husted, as she followed him into his rooms. "I've got rid of her at last; Mrs. Mangenborn is going."

Von Barwig smiled. "Is she?" he said simply, "I am glad for your sake. Now you will be mistress of your own establishment."

"I was always mistress of my own establishment, professor," replied Miss Husted with dignity. "Always."

"Except sometimes when the cards would direct the policy of the house," said Von Barwig. "Whenever there is a superstition, dear lady," he went on, "there is no freedom! We become slaves of our own beliefs."

"Well, I'm glad she's going, anyway," said Miss Husted, not quite comprehending, but not wishing to dispute with Von Barwig. "Why, professor!" and Miss Husted started. She had just noticed that his clothes and books were packed into bundles, as if ready to be carried away. "Professor, professor!" she gasped, "what is the meaning of that?" and she pointed to a big stack of music tied up, "and that, and that, and that," pointing to various articles.

"It means, dear lady, that I'm going to move," said Von Barwig complacently.

"Move!" almost shrieked Miss Husted.

"Yes, as the top floor will not come down to me, I shall move up to the top floor. You see I am nearly all ready. Pinac and Fico will help me; and up I shall go! It is one way of getting up in the world, eh, Miss Husted?" he said with a little laugh, and he looked at her as if he expected her to laugh, too, but she did not join in his merriment.

"There's no room upstairs," she said at last, as if determined he should not go.

"Oh, yes, in the hallway; a nice little room, large enough for my wants."

"But that is a storeroom," cried Miss Husted.

"When I occupy it, it will be a bedroom," laughed Von Barwig, "and just think," he added, "I shall be nearer my friends! They can visit me without running up and down stairs. I shall have additional advantages, at a less rental."

Miss Husted looked at him sorrowfully. She knew it was useless to argue with him, so she gave her consent, but insisted on taking a very small sum for her room. And so Von Barwig moved from the ground floor to the attic. This floor with its huge atelier window on the roof and its stair running down at the back had been used by an artist on account of the splendid light. Although a hallway, it was fitted up as a room. There was a stove, a sink, a large cupboard, and other conveniences for light housekeeping. There were four bedroom doors opening into this hallway, three of which were occupied by Pinac, Fico and Poons, and the fourth Von Barwig took possession of. They all begged him to take their rooms, but he shook his head and smiled and they knew it was useless to ask him, so the skylight musketeers, as they called themselves, had complete possession of the hall, which served them as a common parlour.

It was roomy and airy in the summer, but draughty and cold in the winter; as it was now warm weather, Von Barwig and his friends did not suffer any inconvenience at this time. The men did not see much of each other in these days. Pinac and Fico had secured engagements on an excursion steamboat that plied its way to Coney Island and back. They were away all day, and when they came back late at night Von Barwig was at the Museum. He saw more of Poons than he did of the others, for that young man had no regular engagement, but played now and then as substitute in one of the downtown theatre orchestras, so he just about managed to eke out an existence on a cash basis, and the three older men were as proud of this fact as if he were their own son. Von Barwig was strangely happy; he took no interest whatever in his physical existence. His immediate surroundings, the people he saw, the food he ate, made no mental impression upon him. Life was a mechanical process, a routine existence to him till midday, when he would, to quote his own words, "begin to live," that is, he would start uptown on his walk to Fifty-seventh Street. Rain or shine he would not ride, for the motion of riding on the bumpy stages interfered with the flow of his thoughts. "Now begins my day," he would say to himself as he started on his journey to his pupil's house, some four or five miles from Miss Husted's establishment. The old man was happy; happy in going, happy when there, happy when thinking that the next day he would see her again. So when, for the third successive time, in as many days, Joles informed him that Miss Stanton was not at home, Von Barwig experienced a feeling of disappointment accompanied by a sense of fear.

"She--Miss Stanton is well?" faltered he to the dignified Mr. Joles, who was regarding him with a haughty expression, not unaccompanied with disdain.

"I beg your pardon!" said Joles in anything but an apologetic manner.

"Miss Stanton is well?" repeated Von Barwig.

"Oh, yes," replied Joles. "Indeed, yes." His answer intended to convey to Von Barwig that such a question was entirely unnecessary, not to say uncalled for.

"It's very strange," Von Barwig mused as he walked home. "She always writes me a little note or leaves a message for me with one of the servants, letting me know when to come for the next lesson."

Then he tried to assure himself that it was all right, that in the stress of her social obligations she had forgotten.

"It's all right, Barwig, you make yourself miserable for nothing. You expect too much. She is a petted, pampered, feted young lady of fortune, the daughter of a Croesus; do you think she can always think of you? Who are you that she should spare you so much time? You overrate yourself; you--you idiot." People stopped in the streets to look at the old man, who was walking so rapidly and gesticulating so excitedly. When Von Barwig saw that he was observed, he calmed down. "It's all right," he said. "To-morrow! I shall see her to-morrow!"

That evening at the Museum the night professor was strangely inattentive. So deeply was he engrossed in his own thoughts that he entirely forgot to play when Bosco was announced. He was rewarded by that young lady with a look that was intended to annihilate him on the spot, but the professor did not happen to be looking that way. "She will be there to-morrow, or she will leave a message," he was saying to himself.

"Bites their heads off; bites their heads off! Holy gee! Don't you hear, profess'? It's her cue," came in thundering tones from the throat of Mr. Al Costello. "What the hell's the matter, profess'? Eats 'em alive, eats 'em alive!" he bawled, glaring at Von Barwig, and then the night professor "found himself."

"Oh, my gracious," he thought as he banged on the piano--the chords intended to depict musically the armless wonder's cannibalistic proclivities. Bosco not only bit their heads off, she bit her lips with vexation. It was too late; not a hand applauded when she came on and the fat lady laughed aloud and fanned herself vigorously. She hated Miss Bosco, who, being a headliner, had lorded it over the rest of the unfortunate freaks in a manner deeply resented by them; so the fat lady was glad to see Bosco's act fall down. The skeleton looked wise and tapped his bony forehead with his bony fingers.

"Dippy," he articulated. "All musicians are dippy," he added.

The midgets looked serious, for they loved the professor. Tears started in the little lady's eyes; she expected a storm, for she was terribly afraid of Bosco.

"I do hope that Mr. Costello won't haul him over the coals," said the albino to the tattooed girl. "He's such a nice old guy!"

After the show Mr. Costello listened to Von Barwig's apology in silence, and silence meant a great deal of self-restraint for him.

"It's all right if she don't raise a holler," he said, taking his diamond ring off his necktie and placing it on his finger for the night. "But you must keep awake, see? It looks like blazes to see the profess' asleep! It not only sets the audience a bad example, but it looks as if we was givin' a bum show." Then he added warningly, "We had one profess' last year who went to sleep on us regular, and snored so that we used his noise instead of the snare drums. Well, we left him sound asleep after the show one night and turned the lights off. When he woke up he thought the wax figures was ghosts, and he threw a fit right on the piano. Holy Mackerel! It took nearly two quarts of whiskey to get him right for the next show; so don't do it again, profess'," he ended solemnly.

Von Barwig promised that he would not--but he made up his mind that just as soon as terms for teaching Mrs. Cruger's nieces were arranged, he would at once give Mr. Costello notice of his determination to resign from the night professorship at the Museum. This thought contributed in no small degree to his peace of mind, for he had begun to loathe the very thought of this place.

When Von Barwig arrived home he found a letter on the hall table. He went up to his little room, lit the candle, sat down on his bed and read the following:

"Mrs. Cruger presents her compliments to Herr Von Barwig, and regrets to inform him that unexpected circumstances have arisen which will obviate the necessity of his calling upon her in regard to her nieces' studies."

"Very well," he said to himself, as he folded up the letter. "I shall have more time to think of her," and he went to bed and slept peacefully.

A week elapsed. Each day he had patiently gone uptown to Miss Stanton's house. He had started out full of hope and returned home in despair. On each occasion he had been informed by Mr. Joles that Miss Stanton was out, that she had left no message for him, and that he did not know when she would return. Finally he wrote to her and waited patiently for an answer; but there was no word. The old man's hope of seeing her again gradually grew smaller and smaller until at last the old feeling of dull despair, the old gnawing pain of unsatisfied affection came back to him again. "I am doomed," he thought; "doomed to live my life alone!" He would sit for hours and hours and try to think out why she did not see him, why she did not answer his letter. Was she away? If so, why did she not let him know? Had she found out that he played in a Bowery museum? Or did she suspect that he knew that she did not need lessons? If so, was that sufficient cause for her neglect? No, he could not reason it out on those lines! Why did Mrs. Cruger send him a note dismissing him after practically promising to engage him as music master to her nieces? Did Mrs. Cruger dismiss him at all, or had circumstances arisen that obviated the necessity of engaging him? Was it merely a coincidence that she should dismiss him at the same time that Helene avoided seeing him? Were these two conditions in any way connected with each other? Was Helene really trying to avoid him? Had she received his letter? Did she really know? This last question gave him much comfort and he persistently dwelt on that phase of the situation. To believe that she knew; it was inconceivable to him. She would surely have written. "Did I address the letters properly? Did I put stamps on?" he asked himself. "There is a mistake somewhere," he concluded; "a mistake that time will surely adjust."

The next day, after going through the usual performance of asking for Miss Stanton and being informed by Mr. Joles of the young lady's absence, Von Barwig ventured to extend the field of his inquiry.

"Is Mr. Stanton in?" he asked in a low voice, scarcely knowing why he should ask for her father, or what he should say if he was fortunate enough to obtain an interview with him.

"Mr. Stanton!" repeated Mr. Joles, almost horrified at the idea of Von Barwig's asking for his master.

"Mr. Stanton?" he repeated. "Have you an appointment with him?"

Von Barwig admitted that he had not.

"Mr. Stanton sees no one without an appointment," said Mr. Joles, slowly recovering from the shock Von Barwig had given him. "Besides which, he is at present at Bar Harbour."

"Are you sure there is no message for me?" pleaded Von Barwig.

"Quite sure," responded Mr. Joles.

"But there must be," pleaded the old man. He was desperate now. "Did she get my note?"

"My advice is for you to go home and wait till Miss Stanton signifies that your presence is required. That's the best thing to do--really." Mr. Joles volunteered this advice, which contained little comfort, but Von Barwig's lip quivered and he nodded his head thankfully. Even the advice to go away and stay away contained more hope than the cold stolid stone-wall indifference he had encountered day after day from Mr. Joles.

"Thank you, Mr. Joles! I will, I will," and Von Barwig plodded his way wearily back to Houston Street. For one whole week he did not go near the Stanton house. He contented himself with hoping. He would sit in his little room and rush out every time he heard the letter-carrier's whistle, but no letter came. One day, when he could no longer restrain himself, he carefully brushed his clothes and prepared to walk uptown again.

"She must be in, she must be in; and she will see me. This time I know she will see me; I am sure of it; sure of it," he kept repeating to himself. "She can't be so cruel!"

He found himself looking into a florist's window and started with a cry of joy.

"That's a good omen, a very good omen! You're all right, Barwig; she will see you."

He had recognised the florist in Union Square that he had bought the violets he presented her with on the day he first called upon her. He went in and bought a bunch of violets.

"We begin all over again," he said to himself. "We forget all this weary waiting, all this stupid fear. Now, Miss Helene, we are prepared for our lesson," he said, as he took the box of flowers and walked uptown with renewed hope. His heart beat very rapidly as he walked up the steps.

"Courage, Barwig," he said to himself; "the tide turns I You will see!"

He rang the bell. There was no answer. Several times he repeated this action; each time he waited several minutes. Finally he rang the bell, and added to it a loud knock. His persistence was rewarded, for Mr. Joles came to the door. He did not wait for Von Barwig to speak, as he usually did, but proceeded to inform the old man that his actions were "simply disgraceful."

"Miss Stanton is not in and what's more she is not liable to be in," he said severely. "Some people cannot take a hint! If Miss Stanton wanted to see you, Miss Stanton would have sent for you," added Mr. Joles, and his manner was quite ruffled. He took it as a personal offence that Mr. Von Barwig should so persist in calling at a house where it was evident he was not wanted.

Von Barwig was speechless; he could make no reply. Insulted, turned away, humiliated by her servants! She must know, he felt sure she knew now and his degradation was complete. The old man turned to go now desiring only to get away, somewhere, anywhere, where he could hide his head, where he could hide his grief from the world. Joles shut the door with a bang. He evidently intended that the music master's dismissal should be final. That door bang put a new idea into Von Barwig's bewildered brain.

"That does not come from her," he cried, "she does not insult, she does not lacerate the heart, she would not purposely humiliate me. No, this last degradation could emanate only from one who has the soul of a servant. This is revenge! He hates me, but why? Good God! Why? I've done nothing to him," and the old man groaned aloud in his misery. "I'll wait and see, perhaps she is at Bar Harbour with her father. How do I know? How do I know?"

After this, Von Barwig did something that he had never done before in his whole life; he hid himself in the shadow of the opposite corner, and watched. "It is a mean action," he said to himself, "but she will forgive, she will forgive!"

For hours he stood there watching and waiting, and the time slipped by almost without his being conscious of it, until the shadows of night began to fall. Once a policeman, seeing him crouched in the corner, stopped and looked at him.

"What are you doing there?" he asked.

Von Barwig turned his pale, tear-stained countenance and looked at the officer; then a gentle smile crept over his face.

"I am waiting," he said simply.

There was such utter pathos in the old man's voice, such gentle dignity in his manner, such a pleading look in his eyes that it seemed to satisfy the guardian of the law, for he walked on without uttering another word.

Von Barwig's weary vigil soon came to an end. A pair of horses and a carriage drove up to the Stanton mansion and stopped at its doors. Von Barwig instantly recognised the Stanton livery, but the carriage was empty.

"It is waiting for some one," he muttered to himself. "Courage, courage! We shall soon see!"

It was now nearly dark, and he could approach nearer to the house without fear of being seen. The carriage stood there quite a time, during which the horses pawed the ground impatiently.

"Patience, patience," said Von Barwig to himself. "You soon see."

His patience was rewarded, for the door opened, and Helene Stanton issued forth, clad in a handsome evening costume. To Von Barwig's fevered mind, she looked more radiantly beautiful, more tranquilly happy than he had ever before seen her. She walked rapidly down the brown stone steps, stepped quickly into the carriage and was whirled away before Von Barwig could realise what had happened. The old man could have shrieked aloud in his agony.

"She knows, she knows, she knows!" he kept saying to himself, as he groped his way toward home. He was dazed, benumbed. The many figures coming and going, this way and that way, seemed like a spectral vision to him. How he got as far as Union Square he never knew, but the first place he recognised was the open square. A large piano organ was playing and quite a number of people were grouped around it. This music recalled him to himself.

"I know the worst now; the sword of hope no longer hangs over my head. At least my suspense is over," he said, "thank God it is over!"

He now realised what had happened.

"No more waiting and watching for the word that never comes!" he thought. "My dream is over! I am awake again, I will think no more of it."

He was walking across the square now. The evening was warm and sultry and all the benches were crowded with people except one on which a woman was seated holding a babe that was crying.

"Either people do not want to disturb her, or they do not want to be disturbed by the crying infant," thought Von Barwig, mechanically taking in the situation. He was now acutely conscious of things going on around him.

"What is the matter with that baby?" he wondered. He stooped and looked at the infant. It was crying piteously, so he looked at the woman and was struck by the fact that she was taking no notice of her child. She seemed to be absolutely unconscious of the fact that it was crying.

"How strange!" thought Von Barwig.

She was a young, girlish woman with rather attractive features, but pale and wan. Von Barwig could not help noticing the look of abject despair on her face. The child cried on, but she seemed oblivious of the fact.

"Can she hear it?" he asked himself. "Is she the mother and yet allows the babe to suffer without trying to help it?" Von Barwig's interest was aroused and he determined to speak to her.

"I beg your pardon," he said gently to the girl. "Can I not do something for you?"

She turned to him and shook her head.

"Can I do something for the child? It--it suffers."

"Yes," responded the girl in a hoarse voice. "I suppose it does--it's hungry!"

Instinctively Von Barwig put his hand in his pocket, but the girl shook her head.

"Not that, not that!" she said quickly. "I have enough to eat, but--" She looked at him more closely, looked into his eyes, and felt rather than saw that it was not mere idle curiosity that was prompting his question.

"It's very kind of you to take an interest in a stranger. I'm feeding the child myself," she said after a pause; "but I can't now, I can't!" The girl tried hard to keep back her tears. "It would poison her if I did! I dare not until I feel different. I'm full of hate and misery and hell, and I dare not feed it to the child. Mother's milk is poison when the mother feels as I do!" she cried, striking her breast in her misery.

The old man took her hand. "Don't, please don't," he said gently; "unless you want the child to die. Compose yourself, my dear girl, and tell me what has happened. I'm a stranger to you, yes, but misery brings us together and makes us old friends." He seated himself beside her. "Tell me; I am old enough to be your father! You have none, eh?"

"Yes," said the girl, "I have, but--" she broke off suddenly. Then she said, "My husband has left me, and the child not eight weeks old. Isn't that hard luck? Left me--for another! Oh, I know it's an old story, but it's new enough to me. God knows it's new enough to me!"

Von Barwig comforted her as well as he could, and when the girl quieted down she told him her story. It was conventional enough. She had run away from home and married a young fellow she met in a Harlem dance hall. She knew nothing of his people or of his early life. She simply married him, and now he had deserted her after the arrival of her child. There was nothing uncommon or strange either in her story or her way of telling it. Von Barwig had heard such stories hundreds of times, but to him the pathos of the situation lay in the inability of the young mother to feed the crying child owing to her distracted mental condition. Further, the fact that she was sufficiently acquainted with the laws of physiology to realise this truth showed Von Barwig that the girl had received a better education than most of her class.

"Have you money?" he asked her.

"A little," the girl replied listlessly. "Oh, God, if the child would only stop crying," she said as she kissed and fondled the babe. Then she sighed. "I feel better now," she said, "much better. Perhaps in a little while I shall be myself again." Von Barwig handed her a five dollar bill.

"You will buy the little fellow something with the compliments of a stranger. What do you call him?" he said quickly, for he saw that his generous action had brought tears to the girl's eyes and he wanted to prevent her crying. "He's a fine little chap," he added.

"It's a girl," she said, the ghost of a smile coming into her face. "Her name is

Annie. I'll take this for her sake. Thank you, sir, thank you!"

"A little girl," he said in his low, gentle voice; "a little girl! I had a little girl once," and he stifled the sob that came into his throat. The girl heard this sob and squeezed his hand gently in sympathy.

"Let me tell you a story, my child, it may help you to bear the burden of life, as your story has helped me!"

Von Barwig reseated himself by the girl's side and recounted to her the whole story of his miserable unhappy existence from beginning to end. This stranger was the only one to whom he had ever told it all. The girl was intensely interested, and it had the desired effect of taking her thoughts off her own misery. When Von Barwig took his leave of her an hour or so later, the colour had come into her waxen cheeks and she was quietly nursing her baby.

"I have been asleep," he said to himself, "but I am awake now. Life is all about me; I must not be blind to it again!"

As Von Barwig turned the corner of Houston Street and the Bowery, he glanced at the clock in the watchmaker's on the corner. It was eleven o'clock. He did not go to the Museum that night.

"Are you quite sure there is no letter for me, Joles?" Helene asked anxiously, as she came in late that night.

"Quite sure, miss."

Helene thought a moment. "It's very strange," she said. "I've written to him so many times."

Joles's face expressed nothing. Helene shook her f head slowly and walked upstairs. Before she went to bed that night she sent the following note:

"MY DEAREST BEVERLY: Come to-morrow morning and take me to lunch. I want you to do a little diplomatic work for me.

"Your loving
"HELENE."

Chapter Twenty-one

Von Barwig now firmly made up his mind that it would never be his good fortune to see his beloved pupil again. "She has gone out of my life as suddenly as she came into it," he said with a deep sigh.

To a man of his mental activity the loss of almost the sole object of his thoughts created an aching void, and yet so hopeful was he in spite of the constant repetition of blasted hopes and unfilled desire that two or three days after the occurrences just narrated he had resolved on a new plan of action.

"Poons and Jenny shall marry at once," said he as he arose that morning and dressed himself to go to the rehearsal of a new songstress at the Museum.

"The son of your old friend and the niece of your good landlady shall mark a new epoch for you, Barwig. You overrated yourself, you loved the daughter of millions, you lived beyond your means, my friend. Now it is time you lived within your income," he said, looking at himself in the glass, as he combed his grey hair. "Love Jenny and Poons; poor little neglected ones, you had forgotten their existence! No more extravagances, no more reaching for the impossible! Here down in Houston Street is your life! It is your own, live it! Don't go after the fleshpots of Fifth Avenue, don't cheapen yourself that servants and lackeys may insult and deride you."

Yet ever as he spoke, a mental image of his beloved pupil came before him, and his heart sank as he thought that he should never see her again.

"Why has a mere thought, a stray idea the power to make us so unhappy?" he asked himself. This question was still unanswered when there came into his mind the memory of the unfortunate young woman he had met on Union Square a few nights before. Her misery, her agony of mind, the crying babe, all came before him in a flash. "My God, when I think of her, I am ashamed of myself! Here I howl and tear my hair and rail at fortune because I lose something that I never had; she was never mine--this girl of millions--I had no right to her. But the sufferings of that poor child-wife are real, deep, heartrending; and there are thousands of others like her in this world. Get up, sluggard, get up! Go out and comfort them; go out into the world and mend broken hearts. It is your trade! You have qualified, for your own is battered to pieces."

This idea gave him peace of mind for a short time, but presently his thoughts ran into the old groove. Try as he would he could not direct them away from the line of easiest mental resistance.

"If I could only see her once again," he thought, "perhaps I could explain away the cause of our separation. Perhaps I--" and he started up suddenly, the idea sweeping him off his feet. "By God, I make one more effort; just one more effort! And if that fails, I give it up; it shall be the last! This time I swear it shall be the last. Yes, I go, I demand an interview. It is my right." He was as full of hope now as he had ever been. As a gambler eagerly stakes his last bet, so Von Barwig hastened to finish dressing and go to her, to make his one last appeal.

As he brushed his coat hurriedly, there came a knock at the door. "Come in," said Von Barwig rather impatiently, thinking that it was Poons. He did not feel in the mood just at that moment for casual conversation. "Come in," he repeated in a louder voice, and to his utter amazement in walked Beverly Cruger.

Von Barwig could only stare at him in speechless astonishment. He was literally dumfounded. Young Cruger evidently saw this, for he seized Von Barwig's hand and shook it warmly.

"How do you do, Herr Von Barwig?" he said.

"Thank you, well! Sit down," the old man managed to gasp out, as he pointed to a chair. "You come from her, from Miss Stanton?" he articulated in a voice just loud enough to be heard by the younger man.

"Yes," said Beverly, taking off his gloves and placing them on the table. "I want to have a little talk with you. May I?"

Von Barwig did not answer his question.

"Did--she--did she send you?" he asked. His eyes glistened; his very life seemed to depend on the answer.

Beverly nodded. "Yes, she wanted me to ask you a few questions. Are you sure you have the time to spare?"

Von Barwig laughed from sheer joy. Time! to some one who came from her! He could only nod in acquiescence and wait for the young man to speak.

"How many letters have you received from Miss Stanton?" asked Beverly.

Von Barwig looked at him. "Not any," he replied, shaking his head sadly.

Beverly made no comment, but he made a mental note. It was not his intention at that moment at least to acquaint Herr Von Barwig with all that had passed between Helene and himself as to the letters that had failed to reach their destination.

"Didn't receive one, eh?"

"No, not one," said Von Barwig, in a low voice. "Has she written?" he asked falteringly.

Beverly made no reply, but thought a moment.

"How many letters have you sent Miss Stanton?" he asked.

Von Barwig hesitated. "Perhaps--perhaps some five or six," he said apologetically.

"Hum!" commented Beverly, "five or six, eh? How many times have you called during, say, the past month?"

Von Barwig shook his head; he could not remember. "Perhaps twenty, perhaps thirty times."

"And she was always out?" queried Beverly.

"Yes," said Von Barwig sorrowfully, "always!"

"Whom did you see?"

"Mr. Joles," came the ready reply.

"Every time you called?"

"Yes, I--I think so!"

Beverly Cruger looked at Von Barwig a few moments and knitted his brows thoughtfully. "It's damn queer," he said, after a pause.

"Has she written any letter to me? It did not reach me, that I am sure," began the old man.

"That's all right. Now let me give you Miss Stanton's message! She would like you to be at her home at four o'clock this afternoon. Can you manage it?"

Von Barwig did not trust himself to reply. He could only nod his head affirmatively.

"I'm glad I came up; awfully glad!"

Beverly arose from his seat and held out his hand to Von Barwig.

"Good-bye! Be on time, won't you?" he said.

Von Barwig smiled. "Yes, I'll be on time," he said joyfully.

The look in the old man's face went to Beverly Cruger's heart and he showed his sympathy as he shook hands with him again. He hurriedly passed through the group of children who had gathered to look at the not too familiar spectacle of a hansom cab waiting at the door of Miss Husted's establishment.

Von Barwig will always remember how wearily the hours dragged along until the time of his appointment uptown came. Finally they did pass, and though it lacked several minutes of the hour of four, Von Barwig walked up the stone steps of Mr. Henry Stanton's house on Fifth Avenue and Fifty-seventh Street.

There was no change in the expression of Mr. Joles's face to denote that he had received imperative instructions from Miss Stanton to admit Herr Von Barwig the moment he called. Nor did Mr. Joles appear to think it at all curious that young Mr. Cruger should happen to be in the hallway just as the music master came in at the door. His face displayed no emotion whatever when that young gentleman came forward and led the old man upstairs to Miss Stanton's room. Neither Mr. Cruger nor the music master saw the pale face of Mr. Stanton's secretary, Ditson, peering over the staircase at them. But a moment later a telegram was sent to Mr. Stanton, telling him that there was an urgent necessity for him to come home at once. Curiously enough at about the same time Mr. Stanton received this telegram, he also received a letter from his daughter begging him to come home as soon as he could, as her mail had been tampered with and she strongly suspected Joles of acting in a most deceitful manner for reasons she could not fathom. It was because she expected her father that she acted under Beverly's advice and did not mention the subject to Joles, nor even to Herr Von Barwig until her father had instituted an inquiry.

The meeting between Von Barwig and his pupil was marked by no special display of emotion or even more than ordinary interest; for Von Barwig had steeled himself for the occasion. They greeted each other cordially, but it was only with the greatest self-control that he managed to conceal his delight at seeing her once more. Again occurred the formal presentation of the little bunch of violets; again the casual remarks about the weather.

"You are not angry?" asked Helene tenderly.

Von Barwig dared not reply; he could only smile and look at her in silence. After a pause he ventured to say:

"I have offended Mr. Joles's feelings. I am sorry!" Helene held up a warning finger, indicating her desire to keep silence on that subject, at least for the present.

"Later on!" she said. "I intend to take up the subject with my father when he returns."

Von Barwig watched himself closely. He was determined to make no more mistakes, nor to yield to any temptation to give way to his feelings in the slightest degree.

"You have practised since I--during my absence?" he asked, assuming a sternness he by no means felt, and that she saw through at once.

"Yes, *maestro*," she replied meekly. "I have practised every day. I've really made great progress, *caro maestro*!" and she laughed softly.

"We shall see," said Von Barwig, with a critical frown on his face. He was a little self-conscious. He knew his own weakness, his temptation to become sentimental, and he had to watch himself continually to prevent his emotional nature from getting uppermost. This self-restraint made him slightly ill at ease, and Helene noticed it.

"You are strangely quiet this afternoon," she said. "I should have thought you would have had a great deal to tell me." Von Barwig merely looked at her.

"Come," said he, "we must get to work!"

"You did not receive a single line from me?" she asked as they neared the end of the lesson. "What must you have thought?"

"What right have I to think?" replied Von Barwig. "I am only a teacher! There are so many. I thought perhaps you had replaced me."

"Don't talk like that, please," said Helene quickly, and shutting the piano up with a bang, she arose. "You know that I esteem you very highly," and she stopped suddenly. "I am going to find out all about these stolen letters and father will punish the culprit. He is very strict in these matters; he always punishes the guilty."

"But it is over and done now, so why punish any one?" began Von Barwig. Helene shook her head.

"It hasn't begun yet," she said, ringing the bell. Denning answered it. "Send Joles please," she said.

Denning bowed and a little later Joles appeared.

"Herr Von Barwig, my music master, will be here at three o'clock to-morrow afternoon. You will please admit him at once."

"Yes, madam," and Joles bowed his head rather lower than usual.

Von Barwig took leave of his pupil, appearing not to notice her outstretched hand, but merely bowing to her as he said good-bye. Joles opened the front door for him and Von Barwig looked at him pityingly. His triumph over the servant was so complete that he felt sorry for him.

"Perhaps you did not mean to keep back the letters," said Von Barwig to him in a low, sympathetic voice.

Joles looked at him in blank astonishment.

"You have perhaps a family to support," went on Von Barwig. "I will ask Mr. Stanton to forgive you."

"Sir!" said Mr. Joles, with some slight show of indignation, "I do not understand you."

Von Barwig looked at the man a moment, and seeing that it was useless to discuss the matter with him he walked slowly down the stone steps, wondering what it all meant.

On the following morning Mr. Stanton arrived home. He appeared to be in very high spirits. Helene could not remember when her father had been so light-hearted and gay. She wanted to tell him about the suppression of her letters, of Joles's contempt for her orders, and his lies about Von Barwig, but these were matters that evidently did not interest Mr. Stanton, for he paid very little attention to her complaints.

"It is your birthday," he said, "let no unpleasant features mar the day! See, I have not forgotten!" and Mr. Stanton produced a box that came from the most fashionable and most expensive jewelry establishment in America. "A trifle," he said. "Put it with your other gifts and show it to your friends when they come this afternoon."

Helene opened the box. Accustomed as she was to beautiful jewels, she could only gasp. Within it was a magnificent pearl necklace, beautifully graded, with colour matching to perfection.

"A trifle!" she repeated. "Father, it's beautiful!" She wanted to throw her arms around his neck, to kiss him for his bountiful gift, but something in his manner checked her, so she stifled the impulse and contented herself with holding up her face. Mr. Stanton kissed her coldly and Helene drew back. It was an instinctive repulsion and she could not help showing it; he, on his part, appeared not to notice it.

"I will inquire into the matter of your letters being tampered with," he said, "although I am confident that you will find that you are labouring under some mistake. Joles is as honest as the day. What could be his motive?"

Helene was silent. Her father did not pursue the subject.

"The Crugers are coming to-day," he said finally.

"Indeed?" said Helene, somewhat surprised. "Beverly is coming, I believe; but I did not know his father and mother were."

"I informed the Crugers that I had returned to town, and that I should be very pleased to see them this afternoon. I told them it was your birthday and--" He paused, saying in a more decided tone:

"It is my intention to urge an immediate marriage, Helene." He spoke with an effort. "I may be called away at any moment, and----"

Helene noticed that her father looked pale and worried and decidedly ill at ease.

"I shall esteem it a great favour if you will not interpose any objection to my project for this marriage. I have asked several of our friends here to-day, and I have given them to understand that the date of the marriage would be announced. It is your birthday, so it will be a double event, as it were." He paused and looked at her.

"Do as you think best!" she said finally. She felt it was useless to contend with him. For some reason or other he wanted an early marriage; so be it!

"You have asked several friends," she said. "Have you asked any of my mother's people?"

"No," replied Mr. Stanton abruptly.

"Mrs. Cruger said she hoped some day to meet some of my mother's relations. Father, how is it I know nothing of her or her people? What is the mystery about her? Every time cards are sent out from this house for any function I am always reminded that there is not one of her family to come to this house. On an occasion like this I should have thought----"

"She had no relatives," interrupted Mr. Stanton, "or I should have asked them. Please discontinue the subject; it is by no means a pleasant one. Good God, what a girl you are! I come to you with a gift fit for a princess; and you, you ungrateful----"

Mr. Stanton looked at her with a look of intense anger, almost of hatred; then turned on his heel and walked out of the room.

Helene returned to her room. She was quite thoughtful. "An early marriage! Yes, the sooner the better!" She almost threw the necklace among the many gifts that had been sent her. She wished her father had not given it to her. It was evidently not in her to express the gratitude he deserved and she was angry with herself that she was not more grateful to him.

That afternoon when Von Barwig was admitted to her presence he saw a pile of boxes, flowers, jewelry--gifts of all sorts on the piano. He noticed also that the dolls were on the outside of the cabinet, instead of inside, where she usually kept them.

"It's my birthday," she said in explanation. "I've been having a good time with my dolls." She smiled as she saw that he was holding out a little bunch of violets.

"For you!" he said.

"You must really stop this sort of thing, sir, or I shall be very angry!" But she took them and pressed them to her face.

"They look very meagre among all this great horticultural display," said Von Barwig regretfully.

"They came from the heart and I love them," she said as she fastened them in her corsage.

"Well, now we begin," he said as he took out the lead pencil that he always used as a baton. "There must be progress to-day."

He opened the piano and she sat down and looked at the music he placed there for her. He had chosen a well-known exercise, a Czerny; not a difficult one, but requiring some technique to play with precision.

"Come, begin!" and she rattled off at a 6-8 allegretto, the music which was intended to be played in three-quarter andante.

"Very pretty," commented Von Barwig, "very pretty indeed, but you finish before you commence!"

"That's the rate at which I'm thinking," said Helene. "When I think rapidly I play rapidly. My thoughts can only be described as ***presto***."

"That's rather hard on the composer, Miss Stanton. Come, I count for you! One, two, three. One, two, three; One, two, three. The fingers should be little hammers, so! One, two, three. Dear young lady, this is not a thumb exercise; it is for the fingers."

"Am I playing with my thumbs?" she asked.

"Come; please, please!" he entreated.

"I can't refuse when you plead so hard," she said.

"One, two, three; one, two, three," he counted monotonously.

"You like me, don't you?" she asked irrelevantly, a mischievous smile on her face. Von Barwig tried to look stern but failed ignominiously. "Please attend," he said. "One, two, three; one, two, three. Ah, you play so unevenly! Sometimes you have the touch of an artist, at another you make bungles."

"Bungles?" repeated Helene, laughing. "What are they?"

"One, two, three; not six-eighth, dear lady, not six-eighth! So! One, two, three! one, two, three."

"Did I show you my new necklace?" she asked as she played on.

Von Barwig shook his head. "One, two, three," was all she could elicit from him.

"Father gave it to me; to-day is my birthday."

"Your birthday; so?" said Von Barwig, still marking time. "Your birthday?" he repeated.

"Yes, mio maestro; I am nineteen to-day."

"Nineteen! One, two, three; one, two, three," he counted. Then after a pause, "nineteen?"

She looked up, he was still counting and beating time with the lead pencil as a baton. But there was a far-away look in his eyes, as if he were trying to recall something. "Nineteen to-day; nineteen to-day!" he repeated, as if he had not quite realised what she said.

"One, two, three; one, two, three." Was there a break in his voice?

"Nineteen to-day!" Then he looked at her as she played.

"Where were you born?" he asked suddenly.

"In Leipsic," she replied carelessly.

Von Barwig stopped counting, his baton poised in the air.

"In Leipsic!" he repeated hoarsely. "In Leipsic? She--would have been nine-teen to-day. Ach Gott, Gott!"

Helene turned and looked at him.

"One, two, three; one, two, three," chanted the music master. He dared not let her see his agitation. "What does it mean? How can it be? Good God, how can it be?" His brain was in a whirl; the possibilities came to him in an overwhelming flood.

"You really must see that pearl necklace," said Helene, "and some of the other presents are very beautiful. Do look at them!"

"One, two, three; one, two, three," came in monotonous tones from the old man. Completely gone was his sense of rhythm now. "One, two, three; one, two, three," he continued, trying to collect his scattered thoughts. "Does it mean that she is my--my-- Oh, God! I must be mad, crazy! Barwig, Barwig, pull yourself together, for God's sake; or you lose her again." One, two, three; one, two, three seemed to be the only safe ground for him to tread on!

Helene felt that he was not following the music, for her fingers strayed idly over the keys, playing snatches of different melodies, a fact which he apparently did not notice.

"The necklace is over there," she said.

"Yes, yes," he gasped, going in the direction she pointed. "One, two, three; one, two, three. It is beautiful; beautiful!" He scarcely looked at it.

"Did you ever see my dolls? I don't think I ever showed them to you. They're over there in the cabinet."

"Your dolls? Yes, I look at them!" he said. He was glad of an opportunity to escape observation. After a while his mind became calm enough for him to be able to realise what he was thinking, and the urgent necessity for him to conceal from her his mad folly. Nineteen to-day, born in Leipsic, the daughter of the rich mil-lionaire; yet, on the other hand, the image of his own lost Helene, born on the same day, at the same place and bearing the same name. It was all so consistent and yet so contradictory! What could it mean? Was it a phantasy of his brain, a dream? It seemed to him that he had once witnessed just such a scene as was taking place at that moment. Surely it had occurred before! He was now picking up first one doll, then another, but he did not see them----

"One, two, three; one, two, three;" he said pathetically, trying to control his thoughts. He realised that he was counting "up in the air," so to speak, but he was afraid of betraying himself. "If she suspected that I dared to think that she was my own Helene, she'd turn me from the house," he thought.

"I've kept all these old dolls since I was a little baby; even my little German doll is there," said Helene as she played on.

Von Barwig took up the dolls, one by one. "Your German doll?" he repeated.

"Yes, the one I had in Leipsic. It's a queer little sawdust affair, but I love it to pieces. It always reminds me of my mother. Do you know what I am playing?" but Von Barwig did not hear her.

"The little German doll," he repeated. "The one she had in Leipsic."

"I heard this at your house the night we first met," went on Helene, playing dreamily. "It's a beautiful melody; it has so much sentiment in it, so much pathos, but oh, isn't it sad," and she sighed deeply.

Was it illusion, too, that the ghost of his long-forgotten symphony should be played by the girl at the piano there, who so resembled his own lost loved one? Was it illusion that he should recognise that little doll, her doll, as the doll with which his own child, his own Helene, had played so long ago?

Von Barwig did not start as he picked up this mute evidence of the truth; he was almost prepared for it. It was as if he knew she was his own, and yet did not know it.

"That eye was never mended after all," he said in a pathetic, broken voice, and as he spoke the whole scene of years gone by came back to him. He saw once more his little girl pleading with him to mend the doll with the broken eye.

Von Barwig was quite calm now. He had grasped a certainty at last; he knew now that he did not dream. He looked over at the piano. The girl felt deeply the music that she was playing, for it responded to something in her own nature; and so interested was she at this moment that she almost forgot his presence. Tears filled his eyes as he gazed at her longingly, lovingly.

"Little heart! Ach, lieber Gott, my little Helene; my little baby! How long, how long!" he murmured, smothering his emotion, but looking now at her, now at the little German doll clutched tightly in his hand.

After a while a feeling of great peace came upon him. His mission was ended; he had found her at last. His longing heart had reached its haven.

"That's the doll my mother loved best," said Helene, without pausing in her playing. "She loved to play with that doll and me."

He, too, was thinking of her mother. Was it telepathy that she should think the very thought that was uppermost in his mind?

"There's a portrait of her in the next room," and she pointed to the door off the main room. "It was painted by an artist here in New York three years before she died."

Von Barwig dared not trust himself to speak. He silently opened the door and looked. "Elene, Elene!" he murmured in a low voice. He stood there some time gazing at the portrait of his dead wife, and his eyes were swimming with tears. "Yes, there she is," he said, his low, sad voice scarcely audible through the music. "Elene! Ach, Gott! dead, dead! Better so; better--so----"

He closed the door gently. As he did so a tear ran down his cheek and dropped on the little German doll. "I baptise it," he said with a smile, and then he sighed deeply.

The feeling of deep, unsatisfied longing died out of his heart and from that moment a sense of great freedom took possession of him. He looked over at his beloved Helene. She was still rhapsodising on the piano, utterly unconscious of the great struggle going on in the heart of her music master. What could he offer her? Should he ruin all her prospects? Had he a home fit for her to come to?

These thoughts surged through his mind as he looked at her. His first great impulse was to tell her who he was and take her to his heart, but with a supreme effort he controlled himself. He had so often pictured the scene of his first meeting with his child that it seemed almost as if he had been through this crisis before, but he had never dreamed that she would be occupying such a high station in life, never dreamed that to make his relationship known would ruin her prospects, and perhaps her happiness. This realisation gave him a perspective of the situation and he resolved for the sake of her future not to betray himself. He walked slowly to the piano, and stood behind her a few moments, then suddenly he lost control of himself and took her hands in his.

"What is it?" she said, in some surprise, but with no tinge of anger in her voice.

"You slurred," he faltered, not daring to look her in the face, for fear his great love would show itself.

"You mustn't slur--please," he murmured apologetically.

"Did I slur?" she asked. "Well, I assure you, it was unconscious. I didn't mean to do it."

"You are very happy here?" he asked.

"Yes," she answered, surprised at the irrelevancy of the question.

He was now stroking her hair with his gentle, loving hand.

"You have everything in the world, everything?" he asked.

"Yes," she replied, scarcely conscious of his meaning.

"And you are happy?" he repeated.

"Why shouldn't I be?" she said. "I suppose I have everything to make me."

She stopped playing. This seemed to bring Von Barwig to a sense of his surroundings.

"Come," he said. "We must work! To the lesson! One, two, three; one, two, three."

He could not resist the impulse. He leaned over and again grasped her hands in his. She looked up at him, this time in utter surprise.

"You were slurring again, slurring again," he said, frightened at his lack of self-control.

"Was I, indeed?" said Helene. "Well, you'll have to punish me severely if this goes on."

"One, two, three; one, two, three," he counted. His voice was choked with emotion, and he could barely see for his tears.

"No, no; I could not punish you. I could not put one straw in your way--only--I want to meet your father. Yes," he said in a more decided tone, "I want to meet your father! One, two, three; one, two, three." Whenever Von Barwig wanted to conceal his real feelings he counted.

"I've gone into the 4-4 exercise," commented Helene.

"Yes, yes! One, two, three, four," counted Von Barwig timidly. "One, two, three, four; yes, I want to meet him." Then he added almost savagely, "I must meet him!"

The lesson was interrupted by Denning.

"If you please, miss, will you come down in the library?"

"What is it, Denning?"

"Mr. Stanton wishes to see you at once, miss," said Denning in a low voice, so that Von Barwig could not hear.

"My father?" repeated Helene. "Please don't go till I return, Herr Von Barwig," and Helene left the music master alone.

Chapter Twenty-two

Helene found her father awaiting her in the library. His manner was excessively nervous. He seemed to be labouring under a strain.

"Sit down," he said briefly. His voice was harsh, his manner commanding. Helene sat down. In front of Mr. Stanton lay a pile of letters. He pointed to them.

"Here are your letters to this man, and his letters to you. They were withheld by my orders."

"Then Joles," began Helene.

"I am responsible, not Joles," he interrupted.

Helene arose; the blood mounted to her face.

"Why have you done this?" she demanded.

"I wished to bring your association with this man to an end. I ordered him to be turned from the house, his letters kept from you and yours from him."

"But, father, why did you not come to me?" cried Helene.

"Please don't interrupt me!" thundered Stanton. "I won't have that man in this house! Please understand that. Send for him, tell him you do not wish to continue your lessons, and dismiss him definitely, finally."

"Father, I cannot." Helene could scarcely go on.

"You must, Helene; you must," insisted Mr. Stanton.

"I cannot!" she repeated.

"You can say you have changed your mind."

"Impossible!"

"But I tell you you must! I won't have this man in my house again."

"What has he done? Tell me, what has he done?" demanded Helene.

Stanton paused. "He--he is a scoundrel, a disgrace to society--to--to--" Then in sudden fury he went on: "When a man gets down to playing for a mere pittance, as he does, in a disreputable theatre, and dwelling in a squalid neighbourhood, with low companions----"

"Can he help his poverty?" interrupted Helene, now thoroughly aroused. "The man has pride, he refuses to take money; he is a gentleman! You have no right to insult him because he is poor."

"There are other reasons," said Stanton quickly.

"What are they?"

Stanton was silent.

"What are they?" again demanded Helene.

"It is enough that I know," replied Stanton. "It is enough for you to know that I know."

Helene shook her head. "It is not enough," she said.

"If you don't tell him to go at once, you will force me to have him ordered from the house!"

"Father," Helene was almost calm now. "Tell me, for God's sake, tell me what has he done?"

Stanton bit his lip with anger. The obstinacy of the girl was fast driving him to extremes. "He is not fit to be in this house," he almost shouted, "or to associate with gentlefolk."

"But he is so good, so gentle! How can I suddenly tell him to go? Father, I cannot believe that."

"You don't believe me? Has it come to a question of my word--your father's word against a stranger, a beggar! Do you know I can have the man put in prison?"

Helene stopped suddenly; she was very quiet now. "Is it as bad as that?" she asked almost in a whisper. Stanton was silent. "Father, can you--put--him--in prison?"

Stanton felt that it was necessary to convince her.

"I think the situation speaks for itself," he said. He, too, was calm now, for he felt that he had to resort to extreme measures. "The man leaves his own country, where he is successful, and comes here, and lives with the lowest of the low. Would a man do that if he were not--afraid--or in danger?"

Helene's heart sank.

"Don't say any more, don't please!" She felt that her father had good reasons for speaking as he did.

"If you had only told me before," she said plaintively; "if you had only confided in me it would have saved so much suffering. Why didn't you speak before, father?"

Stanton shook his head.

"Very well, you--you shall be obeyed, father." she said in a low voice. "I'll tell him that you----"

"No," he interrupted quickly. "No! I don't wish him to know that I'm in any way cognisant of his presence here. Simply dismiss him and let him go. Above all, make him understand that he is never to come here again."

Helene nodded. "If his coming here is likely to endanger his liberty, he must not come," she thought Stanton thanked her, but she did not hear his words. Silently, sorrowfully, she returned to the music room, where she found Von Barwig awaiting her.

The old man looked up as she entered the room. She came toward him and looked at him a few moments in silence. The same tender, gentle smile that had so endeared him to her from the first was on his face. She could not bear to look at him, so she turned her gaze away and spoke without seeing him.

"Herr Von Barwig," she said, and then she paused. It was so hard, so very hard, to say what she had to say. He stood there expectantly, waiting for her to continue, as a little child looks up at the sound of its mother's voice.

"I'm very sorry," she said in a deep, low voice. "I--don't," still she hesitated, then finally, with much effort she said: "I cannot take any more lessons from you."

Von Barwig looked at her as if he did not comprehend her meaning.

"Not to-day, no, but to-morrow?"

Helene shook her head.

"Ah, the next day!"

Again Helene shook her head. "No," she said in an almost inaudible voice. Von Barwig noted that her face was sad, that her tone was low and mournful and his voice faltered as he asked, with his usual smile, "The day after that, perhaps?"

"No, Herr Von Barwig. I cannot take any more lessons from you."

"Cannot take any more lessons," he repeated mechanically; then as he realised her meaning he tried to speak, but his tongue clove to the roof of his mouth. There was a long pause, during which neither of them spoke.

"You wish me no more at all?" he asked finally.

"I am very sorry, I am very grateful; believe me I am, Herr Von Barwig, but--" she shook her head rapidly. She could not trust herself to speak.

"I--do--not--understand," he said, and his voice was almost inaudible, for his heart was beating so furiously that he could feel its palpitation. She could only shake her head in reply. Von Barwig suddenly found his voice, for he was desperate now.

"A moment ago we were here, good friends, and--" suddenly an idea occurred to him. "Some one has told you that I played at the Museum, the Dime Museum. Ah, is that Indeed so terrible? I do not play there from choice, believe me, dear-- dear *Fraeulein*! It is poverty."

"Yes, yes; I know, I know!" cried Helene. She was nearly frantic now. "It is not your fault, but please, please, dear Herr Von Barwig, let us say no more! Good-bye," and she held out her hand, "good-bye! I hope better fortune may come to you."

"No better fortune can come if you--if you are not there," wailed Von Barwig. "You don't know--what I know; if you did you would realise that--" he paused. "I cannot stay away! It is simply impossible--I cannot!"

"You must," said Helene firmly. "Please go! Don't you understand that it is as hard for me as it is for you?"

"Why do you so punish me?" pleaded Von Barwig. "For what? What have I done?"

"I am not punishing you, Herr Von Barwig. I-- Don't ask me to explain! You must not call again. Please go; go! There, I've said it; I've said it!" cried Helene in despair, and she walked to the window to hide her emotion.

Von Barwig looked at her in silence.

"Very well," he said after a few moments and then he looked around for his hat, which he always brought into the room with him.

He realised that it was useless to try and move her and he turned to go. He reached the door and had partly opened it when he felt impelled to make one more effort.

"I leave the Museum," he said at the door. "I go there no more."

Helene shook her head. The old man came toward her.

"You must forgive me, Miss Helene, I must speak," he said in a low voice choked with emotion; his English was very broken now. "A moment ago I was thinking what shall be best for you, for your future, your happiness; and I said to myself: 'Don't say that which will perhaps hurt her prospects, her future, her marriage with Herr Beverly Cruger!'"

"I don't understand," said Helene in surprise. "What can you say, Herr Von Barwig, that will hurt my prospects or in any way affect my marriage with Mr. Cruger?"

"Ah, I don't know what I say," pleaded Von Barwig, who felt at that moment that for her sake he must not tell her who he was. "I don't know what I say! I am struck down; I cannot rise, I cannot think! Ah, don't discharge me, please don't discharge me!" wailed the old man pitifully. "Let me come here as I always do; don't send me away!"

Helene was silent; she felt that she could say no more.

"It is the first time in my life I have ever begged of a living soul," pleaded Von Barwig, "and now I beg, I beg that you will not send me away! You have made me so happy, so happy, and now--please don't discharge me, don't discharge me!" It was all he seemed able to say.

Helene was looking at him now, looking him full in the face while a great storm was surging in her mind. "I can't obey my father," she was saying to herself, I can't! It's too hard--too hard! The old man mistook her silence for the rejection of his prayer and slowly turned to go. The shrinking figure, the concentrated misery, the hopeless expression on his face, the tears in his eyes, the pathetic woebegone listlessness in his walk were too much for her; she could resist no longer.

"Herr Von Barwig," she cried, her voice ringing out in clear strong tones, "I don't believe it, I don't believe it!" He turned with a slight look of inquiry on his face and gazed at her through his tear-bedimmed eyes. "I don't believe that you ever did a dishonourable action in all your life," she cried. "My father is mistaken, mistaken! I'm sure of it."

"Your father?" There was no hesitation in his voice now. "Your father," he repeated, his voice rising higher. "Ah!" and a flood of light came in upon him. "When you left me a few moments ago, you went to him, and then, on your return--you--you sent me away; is it not so? Tell me," he demanded, "is it not so?"

Gone was the hopeless misery, gone were the shambling gait, the pathetic smile, the helplessness of resignation to overwhelming conditions. Gone, too, were the tears, the pleading look, and in their place stood Anton Von Barwig, erect and strong, his eyes glittering with fire, the fire of righteous indignation, his voice strong and clear. Helene looked at him in amazement. She could not understand the transformation.

"Your father!" repeated Von Barwig in a loud, stern voice. "So! the time has come! I think perhaps I see your father. It is time we met; a little explanation is due. Miss Stanton, I shall see--your--father."

"Yes, you shall see him!" said the girl. "I'll--I'll speak to him for you; I am sure you can explain."

"Yes, I can explain," said Von Barwig with a low, hard laugh. "Where is he?"

"In the library," replied Helene.

"Ah? Then I go there and see him," said Von Barwig in a decided tone. This new mental attitude of the music master amazed her. The little low, shambling figure was transformed into an overwhelming force.

"Perhaps I had better see him first," suggested Helene.

"No," said Von Barwig. "I see him." His tone was almost commanding. Helene looked at him in astonishment. She was pleased; at least these were not signs of guilt on his part. She no longer hesitated.

"Perhaps you're right," she said. "Come, we'll see him together."

Von Barwig followed Helene through the corridors that led to the library. She paused a moment as she stood at the door and looked around at Von Barwig. There was a stern, cold, hard look in his face which was new to her. "He feels the injustice as I do," thought Helene, "and he is angry. Thank God, he will be able to clear himself!" She turned the handle of the door and went in. Von Barwig followed her. Stanton was sitting at a desk table, writing, as they entered.

"There has been a mistake, father," she said.

Stanton looked up and started as if he had been struck. He saw his daughter, and he saw the man he had wronged standing there in the doorway like an avenging Nemesis. He tried to speak, but could not.

"What's the matter, father?" cried Helene in alarm.

"Nothing--nothing!" replied Stanton incoherently. He was trembling in every limb.

"Helene," he said, forcing himself to speak, "I will have a word with Herr Von Barwig alone."

"I beg your pardon for coming in unannounced, but we wanted to see you, father," began Helene.

"Yes, yes; please excuse us now, Helene. I'll see him alone," said Stanton, speaking with great difficulty. "Alone!" he repeated sharply.

Helene turned and looked at Von Barwig. He stood there in silence, his slight figure seeming to tower above everything in the room. Even Stanton, tall as he was, seemed dwarfed by the strong personality of the music master. At this moment Joles made his appearance. "A number of ladies have arrived, miss," he said to Helene, his quick eye catching sight of Von Barwig without looking at him. "They are in the reception-room."

"I must go at once," said Helene. "I forgot all about my birthday reception."

"Young Mr. Cruger and his father are asking for you, sir," Joles said quietly to Mr. Stanton.

"Ask them to wait--I must see this gentleman," said Stanton, indicating Von Barwig. Joles bowed himself out. Helene was pleased that her father acceded so readily to her wishes. She went to him and placing her hand on his arm said in a low voice:

"Let him explain, father! I want him to come back to me. It will make me very happy--please--this is my birthday."

Stanton nodded, but made no reply. Helene gave Von Barwig an encouraging smile and went out of the room, quietly closing the door after her.

Von Barwig had been studying the man before him. There was quite a silence.

"Well, Henry?" he said after a few moments.

"Anton," murmured Stanton in a low tone as if ashamed to speak. Von Barwig's eyes glittered as he heard his name familiarly pronounced by the man he was regarding with deadly enmity.

"The world has revolved a few times since I last saw you--but I am here," he said, repressing his anger; and this repression gave a curiously hard and guttural effect to his voice.

"I have been expecting this moment for a long time," said Stanton in a conciliating tone. "I've tried to forget."

"You have been very successful," replied Von Barwig. "You have forgotten your own name for sixteen years. A prosperous friend has a poor memory, Henry."

"I have not prospered," said Stanton quickly; "that is, not in the real sense of the word. I am rich, yes; but I am not prosperous."

"You have changed your name?" said Von Barwig.

"Yes; my uncle Stanton died in California. I took his name when he left me his great fortune."

"That is why I could not find a trace of you," said Von Barwig thoughtfully.

Stanton thought he detected signs of relenting in Von Barwig's voice.

"I suppose there's no use my telling you how sorry I am for----"

"Sorry, sorry!" almost screamed Von Barwig. "Does that bring back anything? Does that put sixteen years in my hands? Damn the empty phrase 'I am sorry' when there is no use in being sorry!"

"I have repented, Anton! Before God I have repented!" said Stanton huskily. "She made me repent, and God knows she repented. She never had one happy hour since she left you!"

Von Barwig was silent.

"This is the only blot on my life--the one blot on my life," cried Stanton.

"And that one blot was my wife and child," said Von Barwig. "While you were at it you accomplished a great deal. Mein Gott, you were colossal! You always were a damned successful fellow, Ahlmann," he added vindictively.

"Before God, Anton," cried Stanton with a show of emotion, "I didn't mean to do it; I swear I didn't. It was a mad impulse! It's not in my real nature."

"Nature never makes a blunder. When she makes a scoundrel she means it," said Von Barwig.

Stanton started and then looked through the library window. His sharp ear had detected the sound of carriage wheels stopping in front of the house.

"What are you going to do?" he asked quickly. The fear of exposure was doubly increased by knowledge of the fact that his guests were arriving. Von Barwig made no reply.

"Barwig, for God's sake don't ruin me! At least, I've given the child everything. She knows nothing, and the world respects----"

"The world always respects a successful rascal," interrupted Von Barwig with a harsh laugh. "Of all people he is the most respected. Why, if I had not found you, I have no doubt you would live on a church window-pane after you died! But now I anticipate that everybody shall know your virtues while you are alive. I cut off that window-pane! I am going to baptise you, Ahlmann; I give you back your name."

"Anton, Anton! Why not sit down calmly and talk it over?" pleaded Stanton.

"Ah, you were always a polite man, the kind women like; a man born with kid gloves and no soul. Now we take off the gloves; we show you as you are," and Von Barwig shook his finger at the man opposite him.

There were echoes of laughter out in the hallway; Stanton heard them and trembled. He recognised the voices of Mrs. Cruger's nieces. If these gossips, ever found out the truth, he thought, not a family in New York but would be acquainted with the facts in twenty-four hours.

"Anton, be calm," he pleaded. "Give me a few days to think it over."

"No!" declared Von Barwig.

"A few hours," pleaded Stanton.

"No!" repeated Von Barwig; "not even a few minutes."

Stanton moved toward the door.

"Stay here!" commanded Von Barwig. He was plainly master of the situation now, for Stanton instinctively obeyed him. "If I let you go into the next room it might be sixteen years before you got back again! Sit down."

Stanton obeyed him and there was a slight pause.

"You know what a scandal this will make," he pleaded.

"I know," replied Von Barwig in a quiet tone. "I know!"

"The whole country will ring with it," said Stanton.

"You shouldn't have prayed so loud, Ahlmann," replied Von Barwig with a sardonic smile. "You laid too many cornerstones; your charities are too well known. You should have kept them a secret and not blazoned your generosity to the whole world. When you fed an orphan or a widow you shouldn't have advertised it in the newspapers."

Stanton looked at him and saw no hope.

"You're going to ruin me?" he asked.

Von Barwig made no reply.

"You're going to tell her?" demanded Stanton.

"Yes," replied Von Barwig in a quiet tone; "I'm going to tell her."

"You'd better think first."

"I have thought."

"How will you explain her mother's shame?"

"Ah!" Von Barwig glared at him in silence. "You will shield yourself behind the mother, eh?" he asked.

"How will you explain her mother's shame?" again asked Stanton.

"I don't explain it! You talked her mother's name away--now talk it back! You're a clever man with words. You'll find a way out of it, Ahlmann."

Stanton was now almost beside himself with fear and anger.

"What can you do for the girl after you have disgraced her? Think what I have done for her," pleaded Stanton. "She is honoured, respected, cultured, refined, a lady of social distinction. Are you going to drag her down to Houston Street, to the Bowery, to the Dime Museum?"

Von Barwig felt the force of this argument, and he knew there was no reply to be made. His anger was gone--he was thoughtful now.

Stanton saw that he was gaining ground. "For her sake, Von Barwig," he pleaded; "for her sake! Just think!"

Von Barwig interrupted him with a gesture, motioning him to silence.

"Look here, Ahlmann," his voice was strangely quiet now. "I knew! I knew an hour ago who you were, whose house I was in. As she sat at the piano near me I could have touched her with my hand. My heart cried out, 'I am her father; I am her father!' For sixteen years I wait for that moment and then I get it; I get it! It's mine; but I pass it! I put it aside; I would not tell her."

"You knew," interrupted Stanton, "and you did not speak!"

"I would have come here, to this house," went on Von Barwig, his voice quivering with excitement and emotion; "I would have come and gone as a friend, an old friend, if you had kept silent. But no, two fathers cannot live so with a child between them. One of them is bound to speak out and that one is you, you! You spoke. 'Twas you who said to your servants, 'Take this man and throw him into the streets like a dog.' 'Twas you who destroyed my letters; 'twas you who destroyed my child's letters--letters to me. 'Twas you who told my own flesh and blood to treat me as a dog--a dog! You made me plead and beg; you made me suffer for six-teen long and weary years. Now I take what is mine," screamed Von Barwig. "You hear! I take what is mine!" and he strode over to the bell and deliberately rang it.

"Don't, don't for heaven's sake!" shouted Stanton, trying to restrain him. It was too late and Stanton almost fell back into his chair.

"Come, stand up! To your feet, Ahlmann!" shouted Von Barwig in a loud voice. "I cannot throw you from your house as you would me; but I can empty it for you. Come! I want to introduce you to your friends." He threw the door wide open. Stanton came forward as if to close it, but Von Barwig waved him back. "Stay where you are," he cried. "I introduce yon to your friends as you are. She shall choose between us. Against your money and respectability I put my life. Your friends shall choose; she shall choose; the young man she is to marry--he shall choose." The old man was now almost incoherent. "I have her back! she is mine, she is mine!" At this juncture Joles entered.

"Speak; tell him!" shouted Von Barwig. "If you don't, I do!"

"Call Miss Stanton," said Mr. Stanton.

"And her friends," commanded Von Barwig.

Stanton nodded acquiescence; and Joles left the room.

"You've ruined me; and you'll ruin her," said Stanton in despair.

"I get her back, I get her back!" repeated Von Barwig over and over again. "She is mine."

"Very well! she is yours, then," replied Stanton in desperation. "Yours with this disgraceful scandal over her head."

"I don't care! She is mine--I get her back," was all Von Barwig could say.

"Yours with her engagement at an end, her heart broken! Yes, her heart bro-ken! Do you think they'll take her into that family, do you think they will receive your daughter, the daughter of a----"

Von Barwig was now almost hysterical. "If they don't take her, I take her! If they don't want her, I want her. She's mine, I'm going to have her! I want my own flesh and blood. Do you hear, Ahlmann? I'm tired of waiting, tired of starving for the love of my own. I'm selfish, I'm selfish!" in his excitement the old man banged his clenched fist several times on the table. "I'm selfish! I want her, and by God I'm going to have her!" At this juncture Helene came into the room. There was a dead silence. Von Barwig saw her and his clenched fist dropped harmlessly by his side. He stood there silently waiting. Helene looked at Mr. Stanton; his head was bowed low and he uttered not a word. She looked inquiringly at Von Barwig. He seemed incapable of speaking.

"Father," she said in a low, gentle voice. Neither man answered. Stanton dared not, and Von Barwig steeled himself against telling her the truth. Stanton's words had had their effect; Von Barwig was unwilling to ruin the girl's chances for his own selfish interests.

"You have explained?" she asked Von Barwig. He nodded, but did not speak. The sound of approaching voices caught their ears. Joles threw open both doors and Mr. Cruger came into the room with his son and Mrs. Cruger, followed by many others. They greeted Mr. Stanton, who welcomed them as well as he could. In a few moments the conversation became general. Von Barwig stood apart from them. Mr. Stanton, nervous and anxious, watched him closely. Mrs. Cruger fastened a beautiful diamond pendant on Helene's neck. Mr. Cruger kissed her.

"We cannot give you the wealth of your father, my dear child," said he; "but we can give you a name against which there has never been a breath; an honoured name, a name with which we are very proud to entrust you!"

Von Barwig heard this, and groaned aloud in his misery.

"I'm very happy, very happy!" said Helene.

Others gathered around the happy pair and showered congratulations on them. After a short while Beverly saw Von Barwig in the corner of the room and went over and greeted him. Helene joined them.

"Is it all arranged between you and father?" she asked.

Von Barwig nodded.

"I knew you could explain," said Helene.

"Yes, he has let me explain!" said Von Barwig with a deep sigh. He was quite calm now. "Pardon the liberty I take--I--forgive me--" he placed Beverly's and Helene's hands one in the other. "Pardon the liberty I take; I am an old man," he said in a low voice. "I wish you both--long life--much prosperity--much happiness--much joy to you both. God bless you, children; excuse me, I speak as a father. God bless you!" and the old man picked his hat up from the table on which he had deposited it and wiped away the tears that were coursing down his cheeks. Stanton, who had been watching him closely, uttered a cry of joy. Von Barwig went out of the room slowly, shutting the door behind him.

Chapter Twenty-three

It was midwinter nearly a year later. The cold was the severest in the memory of any inmate of the Houston Street establishment, including Miss Husted herself. Everything was frozen solid. It was nearly as cold inside the house as it was outside, greatly to Miss Husted's dismay, for added to the increased expenditure for coal, the services of the plumber to thaw out frozen water and gas pipes were in constant requisition. Houston Mansion was a corner house with an open space next door, and the biting north winds on three sides of the unprotected old walls added greatly to the discomfort and suffering of the "guests" within. In every sense it was a record breaker. There had already been three blizzards in the past month and a fourth was now in progress. It was on the top floor, however, that the extreme severity of the winter was felt. The cold biting winds howled and wailed over the roof, circling around the skylight and forcing their way through the cracked and broken panes of glass. It was impossible to keep the draughty old hallway warm with the one small stove intended for that purpose. Pinac, Fico and Poons, huddled together around the fire bundled up in their overcoats, had to place their feet on the stove to keep them warm or blow on their fingers and walk about the room to keep their blood in circulation.

At this time Pinac and Fico were playing at Galazatti's for their dinners, being unable to obtain more profitable engagements, and Poons was playing in an uptown theatre. Poons was trying to save enough money to get married, and neither Pinac nor Fico would touch a penny of his earnings, although the boy generously offered them all or any part of his savings to help them tide over until the Spring, when they were reasonably sure of obtaining lucrative engagements. The men had just finished their breakfast and Jenny was washing the dishes for them.

"I shall lay a cloth for the breakfast of Von Barwig when he shall wake up," said

Pinac, suiting the action to the word and spreading a red tablecloth on the rickety wooden table. "His work at the Museum keeps him so late he must sleep late."

"Sacoroto, the rotten museum he play at, I wish it was dead," growled Fico.

They knew now that Von Barwig played at a cheap amusement resort on the Bowery, and that it kept him out till early morning; and they loved him for it all the more. They knew that necessity, not choice, had driven him to it. Besides, it made them more akin to him, for it brought him nearer their own artistic standard, and yet they did not lose one atom of respect for the old man. Gone was his commanding spirit, and in its place was a quiet, gentle dignity which called forth respect as well as love; but above all--love.

"He is sleeping later than usual," said Jenny as she restored the crockery to its proper place in the cupboard.

"All the strength of the coffee will boil away," murmured Fico.

"Parbleu! we make new coffee for him," replied Pinac.

"He have sleep long enough. I call him," said Fico, tapping lightly on the door of the lumber room that served Von Barwig as a bedroom. Receiving no reply, Fico knocked louder. Finally he pushed open the door. It had no lock on it and the catch was broken. Fico looked into the room, shook his head and then turned and stared at his friends. "He have gone up," he said with an anxious look. "You mean he have get up," suggested Pinac. "Got up!" corrected Jenny. "Yes," replied Fico. "He is got up and out."

Poons, who had not quite followed the intricacies of the conversation, went into Von Barwig's room and satisfied himself that his beloved friend was not there. The three men stared at each other. They said nothing, but the expression on their faces denoted anxiety. "Where has he gone?" seemed to be the question each asked silently of the other.

Von Barwig had been very quiet in the past year, so quiet that his actions seemed to his friends to be almost mysterious. Not that he was more reserved than usual, but there was a calmness, a resignation to existing conditions, a listlessness that seemed to them to amount to almost a lack of interest in life, and this mental attitude on Von Barwig's part caused them no little anxiety.

"It's such an awful day," said Pinac as he looked out of the window.

"By God, yes!" assented Fico. "Another bliz."

The wind was howling up and down the streets and flurries of snow were being driven against the windows, banging the shutters to and fro as the great gusts of wind caught them in their grasp. The iron catch that held the shutter had long since been torn out by the winter blizzards, and the constant banging sound grated harshly on the sensitive ears of the musicians. Poons suffered more than the rest, and swore roundly in German every time the shutter struck against the window jamb.

"Jenny," came the shrill voice of Miss Husted up the stairway at the back of the hall. That lady was more than ever set against her niece's "taking up with a musician," as she called the love match between Poons and Jenny. Whenever Miss Husted missed Jenny on the floors below she invariably found her upstairs talking to young August.

"We were looking for the professor," said Jenny, as her aunt's head came up into view from the staircase below.

"Looking for the professor! Why, where is he?" asked Miss Husted. "Surely he hasn't gone out on a day like this! Why, it's not fit for a dog; not fit for a dog! Oh dear, dear! I'll be worried to death till he comes back," and Miss Husted pressed Skippy more closely to her and went down stairs again; not, however, without first sending Jenny to the floor below, out of the reach of Poons's love-making eyes.

"It is true; he has gone out," said Pinac dolefully, as he looked out of the window at the blizzard.

Von Barwig had risen very early that morning and dressed himself with more than his usual care. He had much to do, for on the morrow he was to depart from the shores of America and return to his old home. He was going back to Leipsic, and the steamship sailed very early the next morning. The real cause of his absence at that moment was the fact that his daughter Helene was to be married that day, and he desired to witness the ceremony. Altogether, there was much to be done and little time to do it in. He had told Mr. Costello the night before that he was not going to return to the Museum; so that was ended, and his few clothes were packed in his little portmanteau with the assistance of Jenny, who was the only one who knew his secret. He also had to go downtown and buy his steamship ticket and make arrangements with an expressman to take his trunk, and he felt he must say good-bye to a few acquaintances before he went away forever. So, in order to complete all these arrangements in time to get to the church where the wedding was to take place, he had to get up quite early.

Von Barwig did not mind the cold weather at all. He trudged along the streets and stamped his feet to keep them warm while he brushed the snow off his face as it blew under his umbrella. His heart was light, for he rejoiced that his darling Helene was going to marry the man she loved. Her happiness was assured, he thought; besides, he himself was going to do something. He had a plan of action and he was going to carry it out. During the last few months he had had a great yearning to see his old home again, to hear his native language spoken, to hear the folk songs and familiar German airs sung once more and to look upon the faces of his fellow-countrymen again. Now that he knew his child was happy, he felt that he would be content simply to sit placidly in an obscure corner of the market-place in Leipsic, and watch the ebb and flow of life as it is lived over there in the beloved Fatherland. He did not ask to take part in it or to be one with his countrymen; all he asked was the privilege of watching their life for the few remaining years of his earthly existence. His pride had completely gone now, and it caused him not one pang to feel that he had left his native land in the flush and prime of success and was going to return an old, broken-down failure. On the contrary, the thought of again walking the streets of his native land, breathing the atmosphere, and hearing the voices of his beloved countrymen so lightened his heart that his steps were almost elastic. He kicked the snow aside with vigour, and jumped on the street car as if he were a boy. He saluted the conductor with such a hearty good-morning, that the man looked at him in astonishment.

"You must be feeling pretty good to call this a good morning," said that functionary, as he collected his fare.

"Back of this awful blizzard is the beautiful sunshine," said Von Barwig, with a smile.

"Yes, if you can see it!" replied the man, compelled to smile when he looked into Von Barwig's beaming face. "How far are you going downtown?" asked the conductor to prolong the conversation. The car was empty, and Von Barwig's cheery smile encouraged him to talk.

"Fowling Green," replied Von Barwig. "I buy my ticket back to Germany," he added lightly.

"Ah!" said the man, as if that explained everything. "You're glad to go back, eh? Most of 'em would never have come if they knew what they were going to get over here."

Von Barwig shrugged his shoulders and laughed a little.

"If you don't strike it right," went on the car conductor, "it's worse here than anywhere in the world!" Von Barwig nodded. "There's no room in America for the man who fails," he added, ringing up a fare with an angry jerk and then relapsing into moody silence.

After many delays, owing to the packing of the snow on the car tracks, Von Barwig arrived at the steamship office, bought his ticket, and commenced his weary journey uptown.

"I shall see her to-day," he thought. "I shall see her. How beautiful she will look in her white dress and her orange blossoms! He--he--will give her to her husband. That scoundrel!" Von Barwig's heart sank. "But she is happy, she is happy!" and this thought sustained him.

He had not seen her since the memorable moment in which he had placed the hand of his beloved pupil in that of her affianced husband and wished them joy and happiness. He had written to her and told her that her father, Mr. Stanton, was right; that it would be better that he did not resume his teaching. He had done this, that her happiness might not be destroyed by the coming to light of the scandal that had been dead and buried so many years. He felt it would not be right in the highest sense for him to expose Stanton merely to gratify his own sense of revenge. He believed that his child had learned to love Stanton as her own father; that it would be a cruelty to her to expose him; that it would rob her of her social position and perhaps of the man she loved. The girl might even turn on him and hate him for his selfish indulgence of revenge at the expense of her happiness. At the very best, he had nothing to offer her, and he knew she would refuse Stanton's bounty when she learned the truth. Von Barwig had reasoned it out on these lines, and at every fresh pang of suffering he found comfort in the false logic that seemed so like truth. It never occurred to him that Helene disliked Stanton; that she felt in her heart that the man was not her father; and that young Cruger would have married her in spite of a dozen scandals. Furthermore, he did not even dream that his pupil loved him and grieved for him to such an extent, that Stanton felt it absolutely necessary to separate them completely by telling her that her old music master had gone back to Germany and had died there. The car windows rattled noisily and the bells jangled monotonously, as the horses tramped through the snow on their way uptown, but Von Barwig heard them not, for his brain was thronged with thoughts of his darling Helene and his impending departure to his own country. How could he leave those kind hearts in Houston Street--Jenny, Poons, Miss Husted, Fico, Pinac! What would they all say?

Von Barwig bought a morning paper and in it he read that his daughter's marriage was to be attended by a very large and fashionable audience; that admission to the church was only by personal invitation. Von Barwig started. How was he to get into the church? He had no card of invitation. He almost laughed aloud as he thought of his position; her own father would not see her married because he had no invitation. He must invent some story to get in, but he must attract no attention. No one who knew of his association with the family must see him. He dare not risk a public *expose* at the eleventh hour. No, her happiness must not be clouded even for a moment! But he must get in; he made up his mind to that.

When Von Barwig arrived at the church there were quite a number of people gathered there in spite of the inclemency of the weather, for news of the wedding had been largely heralded forth by the New York daily papers, owing to the great wealth of Mr. Stanton and the high social position of the Crugers, and it was looked upon as one of the great fashionable events of the year.

Thanks to Mr. Stanton's love of display and lavish outlay of money, the presents had been enumerated, the trousseau described, the names of the guests published in all the fashionable papers, greatly to Helene's annoyance. She would have preferred a quiet little wedding unattended save by those directly interested in the marriage, but Mr. Stanton wanted to spend money, and he did, most lavishly. A special orchestra and tons of flowers were ordered, notwithstanding that it was midwinter, and every prominent social and political person available had been invited to attend. In consequence, a platoon of police was needed to keep the crowds back, and when Von Barwig arrived, a long line of carriages had already formed at the church door.

A policeman barred his way when he attempted to enter without a ticket. "Sorry, sir; but we must obey orders," said the man in uniform. It was the same at all the doors, and Von Barwig soon saw that it was useless to attempt to get in without a ticket. He stood there for a few moments trying to think what he should do, when he saw several men carrying violins and other musical instruments going through a small side door on the side street, off Fifth Avenue, that led into the vestry situated at the end of the great church. "I am a musician; I go in with the musicians," said Von Barwig, and he followed the men, unchallenged and unquestioned through the passage leading to the vestry and from thence into the body of the great church. "For the first time in my life," thought Von Barwig, "my profession is of service to me!"

The great church was beautifully decorated with flowers, and the guests were now beginning to arrive. Von Barwig, unobserved, crept silently to the darkest and farthest end of the church. He seated himself in a great pew on the centre aisle, where he could see without being seen. The church was now filling up; it was a splendid sight. The orchestra and the organ played some selections; finally the wedding march from Lohengrin sounded, and every one arose to get a peep at what was happening in the centre aisle. Von Barwig craned his neck to see. The bride had entered the church and was coming up the aisle on the arm of Mr. Stanton, her supposed father, preceded by the ushers. The bridegroom and his best man awaited them at the chancel steps. At the sight of Stanton Von Barwig felt his heart beat thickly. This man had broken up his home, robbed him of his wife and child, and now posed as the girl's father. What a splendid revenge he could take by publicly denouncing him in the midst of his friends. Von Barwig quickly stifled any impulse in that direction. He had come to witness his daughter's happiness, not to mar it by the demonstration of publicly unmasking a villain. He sat back in his seat and watched the proceedings with breathless interest. The marriage ceremony proceeded. The old clergyman who read the service, unlike most of his class, read it with feeling, as if he understood the meaning of the words he was uttering. So clear, so natural was his utterance that Von Barwig followed every word of it, scarcely realising that the man was reading and not merely speaking. When he came to the question, "Who giveth this woman to be married to this man?" the clergyman looked around the church as if expecting some one in the vast congregation to rise and say, "I do." There was no answer. It seemed to Von Barwig that the minister was looking directly at him, and not only looking at him, but tacitly asking a reply.

Once more in compelling tones came the momentous question, "Who giveth this woman to be married to this man?" Von Barwig was now quite positive that the clergyman was addressing himself directly to him, and he felt that the moment had come to declare the truth to the whole world.

As in a dream one makes no effort to connect the present with the past or future or to account in any way for the logic of events, so did Von Barwig make no effort to understand how or why his secret was known to the clergyman. He simply accepted the fact as it appeared to him and made no effort to resist the impulse to rise and declare himself. So when Henry Stanton uttered the words, "I do," almost at the same moment from the back of the church came the loud, deep voice of Von Barwig quivering with emotion, "I do, I do!" Everybody arose and looked around. For a moment there was great consternation in the church. Cries of "Hush, hush!" came from every quarter and several of the ushers came over to the pew in which Von Barwig sat. At the sound of Von Barwig's voice, Helene started as if she had received an electric shock. Beverly thought she was going to faint and supported her with his arm.

Helene recognised in a moment that it was the voice of her old music master, the man she had been told was dead and buried months ago. She looked quickly at Mr. Stanton for an explanation. "He is not dead; what does it mean?" she asked. "Go on with the ceremony," was all the reply she could get from Mr. Stanton. The clergyman went on quietly with the marriage service. Von Barwig, as soon as the usher tapped him on the arm, realised that he had made a dreadful mistake, and sank back into his seat, trembling with excitement and shame. He had not intended to do such a thing and could not explain even to himself how it had happened. The wedding ceremony was now over, the process of signing and witnessing gone over in the vestry, and in a short while the bride and bridegroom came down the aisle to the sound of Mendelssohn's inspiring wedding march. As they passed by the pew in which Von Barwig crouched to avoid recognition, some of the roses in the bride's bouquet fell to the ground almost at his feet. He picked them up and tenderly kissed them. Apparently unconscious of his presence, Helene, surrounded by her friends, passed down the aisle, down the steps and out into her carriage escorted by Beverly. They were both radiantly happy.

"It's a happy marriage," said society with an approving nod.

"It's a happy marriage," alike said friends and relations.

"It's a happy marriage," said the stranger outside as the blushing bride stepped into her carriage and the smiling bridegroom closed the door shutting them out from view.

"It's a happy marriage," echoed Von Barwig as he trudged through the snow on his way home. "It's a happy marriage. Thank God for that!"

Chapter Twenty-four

As Von Barwig walked wearily up the stairway leading from the third floor to the top floor (or *atelier* as Miss Husted preferred to call it), he heard the sounds of music. It was Fico playing a waltz, "The Artist's Life," on the mandolin, while Poons extemporised a *pizzicato* accompaniment on the 'cello.

"Ah, my boys, they are in," he said to himself. "I hope they didn't wait breakfast for me."

"Professor, professor!" came the cheery voice of Miss Husted, as she greeted him warmly. "I'm so glad to see you!"

The music stopped.

"Hello, Anton, old friend," cried Fico as he grasped Von Barwig by the hand.

"Go on playing, don't stop for me!" said Von Barwig, taking off his rubbers and brushing the snow off his hat and coat.

Poons hurriedly put away his 'cello. He was ashamed of playing ordinary waltz music in the presence of Von Barwig. With him tradition was strong; the old man was still Herr Von Barwig, the great Leipsic Gewandhaus Concert conductor, with whom his father had had the honour of playing first horn.

The boy's mother had instilled this into his very soul.

"Why, Great Scott! Look at him! Where have you been? *Ma foi*, you look like a wedding; oh, Fico?" and Pinac pointed to Von Barwig.

"That's so, professor, you look just as handsome as a bridegroom," burst out Miss Husted.

Von Barwig wore a grey satin tie, a flower was pinned in the lapel of his old Prince Albert coat, and his spotlessly clean cuffs and kid gloves gave him an appearance of festivity that was most unusual. "A wedding? You are right, all of you!" said

Von Barwig, with a deep breath. Then he added, "I have been to a wedding, yes, a wedding! Ah, Jenny, how is my little girl?" Von Barwig took the flower he had in his coat and placed it in her hand. "Wear it, Jenny, wear it! Perhaps it will bring you good fortune! There should be two weddings, not one," he added, looking at Poons.

"Two, indeed!" ejaculated Miss Husted, with a toss of her curls. "One is too many sometimes!" Then she asked suddenly, "Have you had your breakfast yet?"

Von Barwig shook his head.

"Then, professor, you won't say no to a bite of hot breakfast with me," and Miss Husted smiled sweetly. Von Barwig still shook his head.

"Ah, do," pleaded Jenny.

"Dear, good, kind hearts, no! Many thousand thanks, no! I have much to do. Early to-morrow morning, my--" He was going to tell them that the steamship on which he had taken passage was going to sail early next morning. He looked at them all and did not complete his sentence. "How can I tell them I am going to leave them forever," he thought.

"I am not at all hungry; I have had breakfast, I assure you," he added quickly, partly to change the subject, and partly to avoid breakfasting alone with Miss Husted. He was in no mood to listen to imaginary troubles.

"I'm sorry, very sorry!" sighed that lady, and she went downstairs, disappointed, taking Jenny with her.

Von Barwig put on his little velvet house coat. "What have you for lunch, boys?" he asked. "I am a bit hungry."

"I thought so," said Pinac, quickly jumping up and opening the cupboard which housed their slender stock of provisions. "Some sausage, some loaf, some cold potato," he said, as he surveyed the contents of the shelf on which reposed the articles mentioned.

"Good; splendid!" said Von Barwig.

Fico laid the cloth while Poons set the knives and forks.

"And here's a 'arf bottle of wine," said Pinac.

"The same wine as yesterday?" asked Von Barwig.

"The very same wine," replied Pinac, handing him the bottle.

The old man pulled out the cork and smelled the contents of the bottle. "It *was* wine; it *is* vinegar," he remarked tersely as he handed Pinac back the bottle. "I prefer coffee!"

Pinac rushed to get it. Poons put on a few coals and some more wood into the little stove, and the process of coffee-making began.

"There's nothing like hot coffee to cheer you up on a cold day," said Von Barwig, rubbing his hands. "Not that I need cheering up, boys," he added quickly; "but hot coffee, the smell alone is enough to--to--whoever invented hot coffee was a genius! The chord of the ninth and the diminished seventh were ordinary discoveries; any musician was bound to stumble across them sooner or later. But this," and he poured the ground coffee into the pot, "is a positive invention of genius!"

Pinac noticed that Von Barwig was thinking of something else than what he was saying, for his eyes were glistening, and he was obviously labouring under some great excitement.

"We could have waited for you, Anton, but we were cold," said Pinac. "And hungry," added Fico.

"You were right; quite right!" said Von Barwig.

"Whose wedding did you attend, Anton?" asked Pinac.

"A pupil's wedding," answered Von Barwig quickly; as if he expected the question and was prepared to answer it. "Gott in Himmel, it's cold! Ha, of course," and he looked up; "that skylight isn't mended! Dear Miss Husted, she always forgets it. I must fix it myself. Yes," he went on thoughtfully, "a pupil of mine was married; a young lady. She is very happy, very happy; and I am happy that she is happy--I must always remember that."

"Remember what?" inquired Fico after a pause.

"Always remember that this is a happy moment and that I must live on it. This moment is my future; it is all I have to live on. The wedding day of my pupil is the sum and end of all for me."

"Was it a fine wedding, Anton?" asked Pinac gently. He could see that the old man was much moved and he wanted to bring him out of the world of abstract ideas into the world of tangible, concrete thought.

"Very fine," replied Von Barwig. There was silence for a moment, then he went on reminiscently: "The father and mother of the bridegroom sat in church. The mother of my little pupil is dead, or she--she would have been there. When the minister said, 'Who giveth this woman to be married to this man?' perhaps you think I did not envy that father who answered 'I--I do!' Ah, he was a fine looking man, indeed yes, a fine looking man! After the wedding was over--I--I walked home. What is in my heart I cannot tell you; but she is happy, happy! What more can I ask? What more dare I ask?" he broke off suddenly.

"What is it, Anton?" asked Fico gently, "you are worried, anxious!"

"You are in trouble, Anton," said Pinac, taking Von Barwig's hand. "Come confide in your friends; they help you."

Von Barwig forced a laugh. "I troubled? Why, no, no! I have been to a wedding; a happy wedding, a smiling bride, a fine fellow of a bridegroom. A few tears, yes; but happy, happy tears! Come, come, long faces! Cheer up," cried Von Barwig hysterically, and he slapped Poons on the back to conceal his emotion.

"Mazette! Do you smell something?" inquired Pinac, sniffing the air. "Something is burning!"

Von Barwig started and hastily looked into the coffee pot. "Ach Gott, boys," he said, "it's the coffee!" and he laughed.

"Is it boiling?" asked Pinac.

"Boiling! No, it's burning! I--forgot to put the water in it," and he laughed aloud.

"Let me make the coffee this time," said Pinac, busying himself at that occupation without further delay.

"Yes, and I mend that skylight," said Von Barwig, climbing up the steps that led to the skylight window. But Von Barwig was not successful. The wind was so strong that it blew away everything that he tried to substitute for the missing pane of glass. Finally he determined, as he could not mend it, to stuff it up temporarily and to that end he asked Pinac to hand him up a cloak, which was lying on a chair, and which he thought was his own. His effort to stuff it into the broken skylight was only too successful, for, as it went through to the other side, the wind caught it, tore it out of his hands and blew it completely away. There was a great outcry as the men realised that Pinac's overcoat had blown away and was lost. It was only when Jenny brought up the missing article, which had fallen into the street below, that their excitement was allayed. Von Barwig made no further effort to mend the skylight.

A little later, after the men had gone out to their respective engagements, Jenny found Von Barwig busily engaged in packing his last few remaining possessions into the little old-fashioned portmanteau which he had brought over from Leipsic with him. He had pulled it out into the hallway, as his room was too small for him to pack comfortably.

"I've packed all your other things away. Everything is ready now," said Jenny in a low voice.

The old man nodded and patted her hand as if to thank her for all her goodness.

"Have you told them?" she asked.

"No," replied Von Barwig sadly; "I can't, I haven't the courage. I can't stand parting; I shall write them."

Jenny was so filled with emotion that she could hardly speak. "You told *me*," she said after a while.

"Yes, you are the only one that could understand. I had to tell you, Jenny! I can't go like a thief in the night without letting some one know. You will tell them that I had to go, that there was nothing else to do. Explain for me; you will do that, won't you? Don't let them think that I--I didn't care."

Jenny nodded. Tears were running down her cheeks. "And you never found the baby, the lost little girl you came over to find; the baby that is now a young lady?"

"Ja, I go back without her," said Von Barwig, avoiding the question. "That is our secret, eh, little friend? You will never speak of it, never tell a soul, eh? And you write to me, you tell me all the news of the neighbourhood. Let me know how the poor pupils get on without their old music master. Here, Jenny! here is money for stamps."

The girl shook her head. "No, no!" she cried, "not that!"

"Hush! Money for stamps for the little letters, about the little pupils," and Von Barwig pressed a bill into her hand.

"Any one on these woiks?" bellowed a loud, deep bass voice from below.

Von Barwig started as he recognised the voice of Mr. Al Costello. "I see you again before I go, Jenny," he said quickly as the portly person of the Museum manager emerged up the stairway. He carried a large newspaper parcel in his hands. Jenny looked in amazement at the fat, florid face of the big man. The incongruity of this great big, noisy individual calling on the dear, quiet little professor was too much for her and she went away wondering.

"Say, profess'!" bawled he of the large diamond; "if the freak that runs this joint don't put some one on the door, one of these days she'll get her props pinched."

Von Barwig bowed. He had not the slightest idea what Mr. Costello was talking about, but he knew it was advice of some sort and that he must appear to be grateful.

After shaking hands with Von Barwig and making a few passing inquiries as to the night professor's health Mr. Costello came to the direct object of his visit.

"The members of my bloomin', blink house," began Mr. Costello in his most ponderous manner, "want me to present you with this--er--token, as a memento and a souvenir and a memorial of the occasion, in which our night professor gave us the grand shake, or words to that effect. I can't remember the exact hinkey dink they gave me; but, professor, it amounts to this," and Mr. Costello unwrapped the parcel he had so carefully brought upstairs with him. "This loving cup is a token of the regard and esteem in which you are held by us in general, and me and my wife in particular. And I can tell you my wife is particular, very particular," added Mr. Costello sententiously. "Here, take it!" and the Bowery Museum proprietor thrust a large pewter water pitcher into Von Barwig's hands.

The old man was quite surprised and not a little affected. This new proof of the affection of the poor, unfortunate creatures who made their afflictions the means of earning their livelihood touched him to the very heart, and for a moment he was unable to find words to express his feelings.

Mr. Costello lit a cigar.

Von Barwig looked at the water pitcher and then at Costello and began: "Mr. Costello, and--and--" he paused.

"Freaks," prompted Costello.

"No, no!" interposed Von Barwig quickly. "No, not freaks! Ladies and gentlemen of the Curio Salon."

"Very neatly put, but they'd get a swelled head if they heard it," broke in Costello, puffing on his cigar.

"I accept your gift with--with great--great pleasure," went on Von Barwig; "with more pleasure than I can say!"

"Drink hearty and often," said Costello loudly. "May it never be empty! Say, profess', the fat woman's all broke up; honest, she liked you!" and the big man roared with laughter at the bare idea of the stout lady's sorrow.

"The midgets," inquired Von Barwig. "How is their health?"

"You couldn't kill 'em with an axe!" replied Costello.

"And 'eat 'em alive!' She is still eating 'em, eh?" inquired Von Barwig with a slight smile.

"She does nothing *but* eat! Ah! she gives me a pain; she's a four-flush!" growled the Museum proprietor. "She don't make good!"

"Tell them, I have grown fond of them all, and I--part from them with regret, deep regret! They have kind hearts. Ah, there are many kind hearts in this world," and Von Barwig sighed deeply.

Costello looked at him and shook his head slowly: the man was touched. That any one could express anything like affection or sentiment for the poor creatures in his curiously assorted collection was a marvel to him.

"Put it there, profess'," he said, and held out his hand to Von Barwig. "You're all right, profess'; you're all right, and your job is always open for you, rain or shine, summer or winter! You can always come back--good or bad biz--the job is yours for the askin'. There ain't nobody that can touch you in your line; and you're all to the good at that! Good-bye, profess'," and shaking Von Barwig's hand heartily the big man went away, leaving the object of his praises standing alone, deep in thought.

His reverie was interrupted by the sound of a slight scream. It was Miss Husted. She had met Mr. Costello on the stairway, and that gentleman had frightened her by playfully poking her in the ribs and bursting into a loud laugh.

Von Barwig hastily put the water pitcher into his trunk.

"What a rude man!" declared Miss Husted, as she came into the room, holding Skippy in one hand and a dish of hot steak and potatoes in the other. "Well, professor--" she said with her sweetest smile, "if Mahomet won't come to the breakfast, the breakfast must come to Mahomet! There's some hot coffee downstairs, oh, I see you have some," she said, as she looked at the coffee pot on the stove; "come now, sit down and eat!"

Von Barwig meekly obeyed her. In his excitement he had forgotten that he had not tasted a mouthful that day. He did not know how hungry he was until he sat down to the steaming hot coffee and the excellent little steak and potatoes furnished by Miss Husted. If she furnished the professor with food for the body, she also furnished him with food for the mind, for the dear good lady talked, and talked, and talked. Fortunately Von Barwig was a good listener; that is, he had the faculty of thinking of something else than what was being said. He had always been the repository for all her troubles, but until to-day she had never gone so far as to confess to him the reasons why she had never married, and would never marry, not if the last man in the world asked her. She told him of her first engagement and how it had resulted disastrously, how she had loaned the object of her affections large sums of money, until finally he ran away, leaving her penniless, and she had been compelled to work for a living. Von Barwig was very sympathetic that morning and it was this sympathy which drew her out.

"We live too much in the past, you and I," said Von Barwig. Then, after a pause, he added: "I, too, have had a loss. You live in your loss, I in mine. We remember what we should forget and we forget what we should remember. We must turn to the present, the here, and the now; the living claims our attention, not the dead. What is gone before is over and done with. Have done with it. The memory of the past kills the present and the future. It never cures it. Ah, dear lady, live in the present; it's your only chance of happiness. Jenny, August Poons, they are the present! Live in them, don't discount their happiness, your own happiness, by waiting for some impossible future for your niece. It is in them, my dear friend, you will find happiness. It is in them you will find affection and love. It is in their joy you will find joy; their children shall be your children. Don't deny yourself that happiness!"

Miss Husted was silent for a long while. Von Barwig took her hand in his, speaking in a low, gentle voice. "It is the last request I make before I go to-morrow!"

"Before you go!" cried Miss Husted. "Why, where are you going?"

Von Barwig still held her hand tenderly clasped in his. He looked at her sadly, but made no answer.

"Professor!" she gasped, and then for the first time she noticed that his trunk was outside his room; packed, ready to go.

"You're going away?" she wailed pathetically. "You're going away?" The tears came to her eyes. "Where, where are you going?" she asked in a tone of entreaty.

"Where? Where?"

"Home," he replied simply.

"Home?" she repeated tearfully.

"Home, back to Leipsic. My life here is over. I should have gone months ago, but I waited to see a dear, dear pupil married. What I have come for is accomplished, and now I go back; my mission is ended. See, I have bought my ticket," and Von Barwig brought out his ticket to show her.

Miss Husted was fairly stunned. She could only look at him in silence.

"Look! see my ticket," repeated Von Barwig, handing it to her to look at.

"First-class?" she asked plaintively. She always thought for her dear professor's comfort.

"Yes, first-class steamer," he replied.

"Why it's a steerage ticket!" she said, looking closely at it.

"Yes, first-class steerage! Ach, what does it matter? I get there all right," said Von Barwig. "Here is what I owe you, all reckoned up to the penny! Here," and he thrust a small roll of bills in her hand.

"Oh, professor!" wailed Miss Husted. It was all she could say. She did not even realise that he had given her money.

"I shall not tell the others until the very last moment. I'll wake them up before daylight and say good-bye to them. Ah, it is not easy to see these old friends go out; one by one, like lamps in the dark!"

Miss Husted could only gaze at him through her tear-bedimmed eyes and shake her head mournfully. Von Barwig tried to cheer her.

"Come, think of Jenny, of Poons! New thoughts, new life, a new family! Now I say good-bye to one or two good neighbours, to Galazatti and the grocer, and the poor old Schneider. I'll be back, I'll be back," and Von Barwig put on his cloak and rushed off.

How long Miss Husted sat there at the table she never knew; she was too stunned to think. Going, her dear professor, going! It could not be true, she would not believe it! But she had seen his steamship ticket and there was his trunk. She went over to the little portmanteau and saw that the key was in the lock. She opened it to see if it was packed properly. She then noticed the little roll of bills in her hand and for the first time realised that it was his money she had taken. "Perhaps it is his last few dollars," she mourned. She stooped down and secreted the money in one of the pockets of his Prince Albert coat; then she closed the lid of the portmanteau. As she did so she burst into a flood of tears, and giving way completely to her feelings, she knelt by the little trunk and fairly sobbed as if her heart would break. When Pinac, Fico and Poons returned to their respective rooms they found her kneeling by the trunk. When they spoke to her she pretended to be singing a worn-out ditty of years gone by. It struck the men as being most tearful for a comic song.

It was some time before Miss Husted had sufficiently recovered herself to knock at Poons's door and inform him that she had withdrawn her opposition to his marriage with her niece. How she made herself understood is one of the mysteries and must remain so, but Poons understood and felt that she was now his friend. With a boyish shout he seized her around the neck and hugged her so tightly and kissed her so fervently that her principal curl came near severing its connection with the portion of her hair that really and truly belonged to her. It was not until she had slapped his face several times, and told him she was to be his aunt and not his sweetheart, that he released her, and even then he insisted on holding her hand and telling her how much he loved Jenny. So much noise did the boy make that Pinac and Fico rushed out of their room to find out what was the matter.

Poons's explanation to them was nearly as lucid as his previous effort to enlighten Miss Husted. He threw his arms around their necks and kissed them on both cheeks and danced them around the room. He pointed to Miss Husted and tried to kiss her again, just to show his friends the relationship between them, but that good lady had had enough of Poons's osculatory manifestations and indignantly threatened to slap him again if he tried to carry on with her! Jenny joined them and there was more explaining and still more kissing. When Von Barwig came back he found them all in an uproar congratulating each other in mixed American and Continental fashion. His presence added to the general joy. He kissed Jenny tenderly and formally gave her to Poons. He squeezed Miss Husted's hand in silence as he realised that his efforts on behalf of the young couple had been successful and he shook hands with his friends.

"It is a day of rejoicing, so let us rejoice!" said Von Barwig, as he emerged from his little room with a violin bow and some music in his hand. He then took a ring off his finger. "Poons, here! This ring was given me by your father twenty-five years ago. Wear it for my sake! For you, Pinac, my Mendelssohn Concerto. See, here is Mendelssohn's own signature! Fico, here is my Tuart bow. It is broken in two places, but it is a fine bow."

"What is all this?" asked Pinac.

"It is my birthday!" replied Von Barwig, slightly at a loss for an answer.

"Your birthday is next month, Anton," said Fico.

"Well, I celebrate it now! It is my birthday, I celebrate it when I please. Come, no more questions, let us make this a day of rejoicing! Come, wish me luck! Your hands in mine, boys, and wish me luck and God-speed!"

They did not understand, but did as he asked them. Miss Husted and Jenny understood, and they were sad and silent as they watched the men wish Von Barwig good luck. As they stood there, clasping each other by the hands and singing one of their glees, Thurza rushed up stairs and shouted: "Some one to see Miss Husted." The good lady invited them all downstairs to her room to have a glass of wine in honour of the occasion, and disappeared below stairs, followed by the men. Von Barwig promised to join them later, but now he wanted to be alone.

After they had gone he seated himself by the stove.

"All is finished," he thought. "Helene is married; a happy marriage. Jenny and Poons are provided for, so my work is done. To-morrow I shall be here no longer! Leipsic, once more Leipsic. Heimweh, Heimweh!"

Although he spoke habitually in English, he thought in the German language. How strange it all seemed! The music of his last symphony had been running through his head all morning. He could hear it plainly.

"I pick up the pieces of my life where I left off," he mused. "Back to Leipsic I go. How strange it will seem after all these years?" Home, home; the thought soothed him. He was tired out, for he had been awake since early dawn and the food he had eaten and the warm glow of the fire on his face made him drowsy. With the music of his last symphony echoing in his mind, the old man fell asleep.

Chapter Twenty-five

Without doubt it was one of the largest and most fashionable weddings ever given in New York's social history. Society attended *en masse*, not so much because it was the fashionable thing to do, as that the young people were great favourites in their world.

The wedding breakfast was a crowded affair, and both Helene and her husband were glad when that function was finished, and the business of receiving congratulations and saying good-byes was over and done with.

The steamer on which they were going to Europe was to sail in three hours.

"Let us go early, and escape from our friends," whispered Beverly to his bride.

"I must have an interview with my father before I go. I must!" said Helen. Then she added in a voice that sounded strangely harsh, "He has avoided me ever since the ceremony!"

Beverly Cruger had noticed that Helene was nervous and emotional, and he attributed it to the excitement of the moment. But the deep-drawn lines of her mouth and the stern look in her eye indicated anger and deep-seated determination, rather than mere excitement.

"What is it, darling?" he asked tenderly. "Can't you trust me?"

"My father has purposely avoided me," she replied. "He knows it is necessary that I should see him," and Helene then told her husband of her recognition of Von Barwig in church. "I have mourned for him as one dead and gone, and when I saw him to-day rising up like a spectre, as if reproaching me for my neglect, I was terribly overcome. Oh, Beverly, I can't explain, I don't understand why, but I think of him constantly, and my heart goes out to him! Even at this moment I am haunted by the thought of his dear, sweet, gentle smile. Why did my father tell me he was dead? There is some mystery connected with Herr Von Barwig that I am determined to find out! You'll help me, won't you? I mean, you'll be patient with my--my unaccountable anxiety?" Beverly nodded.

"Of course I will," he said. "Aren't you my wife?"

"Somehow or other," Helene went on, almost unconscious of Beverly's presence, "I feel sure that he is in some way connected with my mother. I know you'll think I'm foolish, but whenever I look at her portrait I think of him. Why **should** I think of him, unless--" Helene paused. "I shall never forget that day, the day I dismissed him. He stood at the door gazing at her portrait, the tears running down his cheeks, and oh, such a sad, sad, longing expression on his face! Why should the sight of my mother's portrait make him cry? What is he to her, Beverly?"

Beverly shook his head. "I wish to God I hadn't sent him away," moaned Helene. "What is this man to me that even the memory of his face makes me suffer! To-day of all days I should be happy, but I'm miserable, miserable, miserable!"

"If Mr. Stanton knows, he must tell us," declared Beverly emphatically.

"Yes, he shall tell us!" echoed Helene. "Let's go to him and demand the truth."

"You stay here, Helene! I'll bring him to you."

Three minutes later Beverly had found his father-in-law surrounded by friends, and had taken him by the arm and led him to Helene's room. It was the room in which the old music master had given her lessons on the piano. Helene now confronted him; and Beverly going up to her stood beside her as if to protect his wife.

"Why did you tell me he was dead?" demanded Helene. Stanton was silent.

"You must tell her, sir," said Beverly. "It is necessary for her peace of mind!"

"It is necessary for her peace of mind that I remain silent," said Stanton.

"But she is suffering!" cried Beverly.

"She'll suffer more if I tell her the truth," and Stanton turned to go.

"One moment, sir," and Beverly laid his hand gently on Mr. Stanton's arm; "you must answer, this uncertainty and suspense must come to an end."

"What is he to me? Tell me!" entreated Helene. "Father, father, won't you tell me? for God's sake tell me!" and Helene clasped him by the arm.

"Tell her, sir," said Beverly in a commanding voice.

"I--I cannot," faltered Stanton; "it's impossible!"

"Then I'll find out from him," cried Helene. Stanton realised that he was cornered.

"Find out what you please, from whom you please," he said harshly.

"We'll go to him; he'll tell us. We should have done that at first," and Helene turned to Beverly.

"I warn you, you'll bring untold misery on your head!" shouted Stanton. He was infuriated at the idea of his authority being ignored.

"We want the truth, the truth!" cried Helene.

Stanton was now beside himself with rage. "Then have it; have it!" The words came in short gasps. "And pay the price for it! The man is your father! Now you know the truth; you can get the details from him!" and Stanton went out slamming the door behind him, the same door through which Von Barwig had gone out in despair the day that Helene dismissed him.

"Herr Von Barwig my father! My father!" Helene sank on her knees and clasped her hands. She was trembling with joy. "Thank God! Thank God! Thank God!"

*   *   *   *   *

As Von Barwig partially awoke from his sleep he became dimly conscious that he was not alone. Without opening his eyes he realised where he was, and that he was still sitting by the stove, for he felt the glare of the fire on his face, and his immediate surroundings were familiar. The snow on the glass roof above, the portmanteau outside his bedroom door, packed and ready to go; the broken balustrade at the back of the hallway, the sink in the corner, the shelf with the lamps on it; all these familiar objects seemed to be present without his looking directly at them. But there was something else, for a dim figure hovered over him like an angel beckoning him to a fairer, happier land; and the perfume of flowers seemed to fill the room.

"I sleep," said Von Barwig to himself, "but I shall soon wake, and then--it will go." Soon the figure began to take form and to his half-conscious mind it seemed to assume the shape of his dead wife. It was her face, her figure as he had known her many, many years ago.

"Elene, Elene!" he murmured, "you have come to take me away from this place. Oh, God, I hope I never wake up!"

The figure now stretched out its arms, and seemed to be handing Von Barwig a bunch of flowers. The old man's eyes were fully opened now, and, as he gazed up, he recognised the face of his beloved pupil. Then he knew that he was not sleeping. The dreaming and waking process had probably occupied but a few seconds of time, but it seemed to Von Barwig to have lasted many hours. Helene was looking down at him now as he sat there, her great blue eyes suffused with tears. She beamed tenderness and love upon him and her outstretched hand held a bunch of orange blossoms.

"You didn't seek me out to-day, so I came to you," she said in a low, tender voice. "I have brought you my orange blossoms!"

Von Barwig did not speak. Another figure now outlined itself to his vision and became flesh and blood--the figure of Beverly Cruger.

It seemed to Von Barwig that young Mr. Cruger looked pale and anxious.

"What does he know?" the old man asked himself. "Is he here to find out?" and in that moment he determined to keep his secret.

Helene waited for Von Barwig to speak, but he remained silent.

"You must think it strange that I should call upon you to-day of all days," she said, shaking her head sadly, "and that I should bring my--my husband with me." She looked around at Beverly and he smiled approvingly. "But I am going away, Herr Von Barwig, and it would be very sad if we never met again; wouldn't it?"

Von Barwig still looked at her sadly, smilingly, but did not speak.

"I feel," she went on sadly, "I always have felt that you never meant to see me again." Von Barwig nodded; he dared not trust himself to speak now.

"What does she know? What does she know?" he asked himself. "Shall her mother's disgrace fall on her young shoulders as a wedding gift from me? No, no, no!"

Again the girl spoke: "I am beginning life all over again; from to-day," she said.

"Ah, that is right!" murmured Von Barwig.

"We were going to spend our honeymoon in Paris," said Helene in a curiously strained voice, for it was all she could do to keep back her tears; "but now we have changed our plans! We are going to the little town where I was born."

Von Barwig drew a deep breath and nodded. "So?"

"We are going to Leipsic," and Helene Cruger looked closely, anxiously, into the old man's face. No sign of recognition was there.

"Shall we go?" she asked after a pause. He shook his head.

"Don't go!" he said simply.

"Why not?" asked Helene, as if his answer meant a great deal to her.

"Leipsic is not a--a pleasant place for honeymoons," he replied evasively.

"That's just what--my--my father said." She was watching him closely now.
The expression on Von Barwig's face was unchanged.

"Your father is--right," he said finally.

"I told him to-day after the service," said Helene, "that we were going to Leipsic,
and he tried to make me promise not to go. When I refused, he forbade me to go,
but he can't forbid me any more; he is beginning to understand that for the first
time to-day." She spoke now with a deep-rooted sense of injury Von Barwig could
only nod. He knew now that she had made some discovery.

"It's so easy to deceive a child," continued Helene in a voice that must have
betrayed the great depth of her feelings. "A child believes everything you tell it.
It will grow up on lies, but when that child is older and a woman, then the truth
comes out! Herr Von Barwig, the truth comes out!" She looked him full in the face,
but still there was no sign.

"What truth?" faltered the old man. He realised now that she knew; but exactly what did she know?

"You ask me that?" she said sadly. "You, my--my--old music master!"

"A music master who taught you nothing," he said evasively.

"Shall I go to Leipsic?" asked Helene.

The old man shook his head. "No!" he articulated faintly.

"Why not?" demanded Helene. There was no reply. "And you won't tell me
why?"

"I have told you," faltered Von Barwig.

"What have I done, what have I done!" cried Helene, "that you won't claim
me?" Her voice was now choked with sobs and she no longer made any effort to
restrain them. "*He* wouldn't tell me either; he referred me to you. What have I
done? I have waited and waited and waited, but you won't speak! You knew me
from the first. You must have known me from the likeness. I was under your roof,
you were under mine; but you wouldn't claim me. There is some disgrace!" The

old man nodded. "Ah, then it's my mother!" cried Helene.

"Your mother? No! No!" cried Von Barwig. "No! she was an angel; an angel of goodness, of purity."

"Then what are you concealing?" cried Helene; "of what are you ashamed? Of what is he ashamed?"

Von Barwig rocked himself in agony, but at last he forced himself to speak.

"It's a little story of life, of love--foolishness; of--of folly. Ah, it is ended, ended!" wailed the old man. "It is over and done with. Why should we bring it out into the daylight when it has slept so long over there in Leipsic. Surely it has slept itself into silence. No! no! The secret is buried there in Leipsic. I--I put these orange blossoms on its grave!" and Von Barwig gently took the flowers from her. "I take them back to Leipsic; a little token of silence she would love."

"Now I know why she cried so constantly," sobbed Helene. "She was thinking of you!" She grasped his hand and looked pleadingly into his face. "Who giveth this woman to be married to this man?"

Von Barwig shook his head. "Silence is best! The marriage is over; I have the orange blossoms," and the old man kissed them tenderly.

"Who giveth this woman to be married to this man?" entreated Helene.

"Your husband, what does he say?" said Von Barwig, in a low voice. He felt he could not restrain himself much longer.

Beverly came forward. "He says: 'Who giveth this woman to be married to this man?'"

Von Barwig shook his head. The tears were running down his cheeks, and when he tried to withdraw his hand from hers Helene refused to let it go.

"Who giveth this woman to be married to this man?" she said entreatingly.

Von Barwig could restrain himself no longer. "Well, perhaps I do," he said in a voice trembling with emotion; "perhaps I do!" Taking her in his arms, he kissed her again and again.

"At last, at last! My little Elene! My little baby--my little baby!"

"Father, father!" was all Helene could say. Beverly looked out of the window.

"Now we mend that doll with the broken eye," said the old man, gulping down a sob and smiling through his tears.

"Yes, father," and Helene took his face between her two hands.

"Say it again!" he murmured. "It is the sound I have listened for these sixteen years."

"Father!" repeated Helene. Beverly looked at his watch. "The steamer leaves in less than an hour," he said. "How long will it take you to pack?" he asked. "You are going with us now, father," he added, patting the old man on the back and shaking him by the hand. Von Barwig seemed dazed.

"Come, father," pleaded Helene, "no foolish pride! My home is your home after this. Now don't hesitate!"

"Hesitate? I, hesitate?" and rushing to the stairway the old man shouted loudly for Miss Husted. Poons was just coming up the stairs to find out why Von Barwig didn't come down to drink Jenny's health. Von Barwig gave him a message which brought them all up in breathless haste.

Mr. and Mrs. Cruger had gone below, and Von Barwig had finished packing and was locking his portmanteau as his friends stood around begging him to tell them why he was going and where.

"I go on a honeymoon," he said, and they all laughed. "I go home," he added. "No cruel farewells, no sad partings! Jenny will tell you. I am called away. Sit down, all of you, where you always sit. Fico, your mandolin; Pinac, your violin! Poons, your 'cello!" They did as he asked them, "So, now! Play, sing, be happy, just as always! Come, the old dinner song we always sang; let it ring in my ears as I go!" Though their hearts were heavy, they burst into their oft-sung glee, Miss Husted and Jenny joining in the chorus.

"So, so!" murmured the old man, beating time and smiling approval. "I want to go away seeing you all happy, as happy as I am, smiling, happy faces!"

"You will come back?" whispered Jenny as the old man kissed her tenderly.

"I come back," he said gently, "I come back! Good-bye, good-bye all of you! Yes, I come back, I come back," and Anton Von Barwig disappeared down the stairs and out of their lives. His eyes were still wet with tears as he took his seat in the carriage. Helene dried them with a beautiful Duchesse lace handkerchief.

"Don't cry, father," she pleaded.

"Ach, I don't cry!" said the old man as he patted her hand. "I--I--" he hesitated. "When I think of the many, many kind hearts in this world--I--I just feel happy, that's all!"

The Codes Of Hammurabi And Moses
W. W. Davies

QTY

The discovery of the Hammurabi Code is one of the greatest achievements of archaeology, and is of paramount interest, not only to the student of the Bible, but also to all those interested in ancient history...

Religion   **ISBN:** *1-59462-338-4*   **Pages:132**

MSRP $12.95

The Theory of Moral Sentiments
Adam Smith

QTY

This work from 1749. contains original theories of conscience amd moral judgment and it is the foundation for systemof morals.

Philosophy   **ISBN:** *1-59462-777-0*   **Pages:536**

MSRP $19.95

Jessica's First Prayer
Hesba Stretton

QTY

In a screened and secluded corner of one of the many railway-bridges which span the streets of London there could be seen a few years ago, from five o'clock every morning until half past eight, a tidily set-out coffee-stall, consisting of a trestle and board, upon which stood two large tin cans, with a small fire of charcoal burning under each so as to keep the coffee boiling during the early hours of the morning when the work-people were thronging into the city on their way to their daily toil...

Childrens   **ISBN:** *1-59462-373-2*

Pages:84

MSRP $9.95

My Life and Work
Henry Ford

QTY

Henry Ford revolutionized the world with his implementation of mass production for the Model T automobile. Gain valuable business insight into his life and work with his own auto-biography... "We have only started on our development of our country we have not as yet, with all our talk of wonderful progress, done more than scratch the surface. The progress has been wonderful enough but..."

Biographies/   **ISBN:** *1-59462-198-5*

Pages:300

MSRP $21.95

The Art of Cross-Examination
Francis Wellman

QTY

I presume it is the experience of every author, after his first book is published upon an important subject, to be almost overwhelmed with a wealth of ideas and illustrations which could readily have been included in his book, and which to his own mind, at least, seem to make a second edition inevitable. Such certainly was the case with me; and when the first edition had reached its sixth impression in five months, I rejoiced to learn that it seemed to my publishers that the book had met with a sufficiently favorable reception to justify a second and considerably enlarged edition. ..

Pages:412

Reference   **ISBN:** *1-59462-647-2*   *MSRP $19.95*

On the Duty of Civil Disobedience
Henry David Thoreau

QTY

Thoreau wrote his famous essay, On the Duty of Civil Disobedience, as a protest against an unjust but popular war and the immoral but popular institution of slave-owning. He did more than write—he declined to pay his taxes, and was hauled off to gaol in consequence. Who can say how much this refusal of his hastened the end of the war and of slavery ?

Law   **ISBN:** *1-59462-747-9*   **Pages:48**

MSRP $7.45

Dream Psychology Psychoanalysis for Beginners
Sigmund Freud

QTY

Sigmund Freud, born Sigismund Schlomo Freud (May 6, 1856 - September 23, 1939), was a Jewish-Austrian neurologist and psychiatrist who co-founded the psychoanalytic school of psychology. Freud is best known for his theories of the unconscious mind, especially involving the mechanism of repression; his redefinition of sexual desire as mobile and directed towards a wide variety of objects; and his therapeutic techniques, especially his understanding of transference in the therapeutic relationship and the presumed value of dreams as sources of insight into unconscious desires.

Pages:196

Psychology   **ISBN:** *1-59462-905-6*   *MSRP $15.45*

The Miracle of Right Thought
Orison Swett Marden

QTY

Believe with all of your heart that you will do what you were made to do. When the mind has once formed the habit of holding cheerful, happy, prosperous pictures, it will not be easy to form the opposite habit. It does not matter how improbable or how far away this realization may see, or how dark the prospects may be, if we visualize them as best we can, as vividly as possible, hold tenaciously to them and vigorously struggle to attain them, they will gradually become actualized, realized in the life. But a desire, a longing without endeavor, a yearning abandoned or held indifferently will vanish without realization.

Pages:360

Self Help   **ISBN:** *1-59462-644-8*   *MSRP $25.45*

The Rosicrucian Cosmo-Conception Mystic Christianity *by Max Heindel*   ISBN: *1-59462-188-8*   **$38.95**
The Rosicrucian Cosmo-conception is not dogmatic, neither does it appeal to any other authority than the reason of the student. It is: not controversial, but is: sent forth in the, hope that it may help to clear...   New Age/Religion Pages 646

Abandonment To Divine Providence *by Jean-Pierre de Caussade*   ISBN: *1-59462-228-0*   **$25.95**
"The Rev. Jean Pierre de Caussade was one of the most remarkable spiritual writers of the Society of Jesus in France in the 18th Century. His death took place at Toulouse in 1751. His works have gone through many editions and have been republished...   Inspirational/Religion Pages 400

Mental Chemistry *by Charles Haanel*   ISBN: *1-59462-192-6*   **$23.95**
Mental Chemistry allows the change of material conditions by combining and appropriately utilizing the power of the mind. Much like applied chemistry creates something new and unique out of careful combinations of chemicals the mastery of mental chemistry...   New Age Pages 354

The Letters of Robert Browning and Elizabeth Barret Barrett 1845-1846 vol II   ISBN: *1-59462-193-4*   **$35.95**
by Robert Browning and Elizabeth Barrett   Biographies Pages 596

Gleanings In Genesis (volume I) *by Arthur W. Pink*   ISBN: *1-59462-130-6*   **$27.45**
Appropriately has Genesis been termed "the seed plot of the Bible" for in it we have, in germ form, almost all of the great doctrines which are afterwards fully developed in the books of Scripture which follow...   Religion/Inspirational Pages 420

The Master Key *by L. W. de Laurence*   ISBN: *1-59462-001-6*   **$30.95**
In no branch of human knowledge has there been a more lively increase of the spirit of research during the past few years than in the study of Psychology, Concentration and Mental Discipline. The requests for authentic lessons in Thought Control, Mental Discipline and...   New Age/Business Pages 422

The Lesser Key Of Solomon Goetia *by L. W. de Laurence*   ISBN: *1-59462-092-X*   **$9.95**
This translation of the first book of the "Lernegton" which is now for the first time made accessible to students of Talismanic Magic was done, after careful collation and edition, from numerous Ancient Manuscripts in Hebrew, Latin, and French...   New Age/Occult Pages 92

Rubaiyat Of Omar Khayyam *by Edward Fitzgerald*   ISBN:*1-59462-332-5*   **$13.95**
Edward Fitzgerald, whom the world has already learned, in spite of his own efforts to remain within the shadow of anonymity, to look upon as one of the rarest poets of the century, was born at Bredfield, in Suffolk, on the 31st of March, 1809. He was the third son of John Purcell...   Music Pages 172

Ancient Law *by Henry Maine*   ISBN: *1-59462-128-4*   **$29.95**
The chief object of the following pages is to indicate some of the earliest ideas of mankind, as they are reflected in Ancient Law, and to point out the relation of those ideas to modern thought.   Religion/History Pages 452

Far-Away Stories *by William J. Locke*   ISBN: *1-59462-129-2*   **$19.45**
"Good wine needs no bush, but a collection of mixed vintages does. And this book is just such a collection. Some of the stories I do not want to remain buried for ever in the museum files of dead magazine-numbers an author's not unpardonable vanity..."   Fiction Pages 272

Life of David Crockett *by David Crockett*   ISBN: *1-59462-250-7*   **$27.45**
"Colonel David Crockett was one of the most remarkable men of the times in which he lived. Born in humble life, but gifted with a strong will, an indomitable courage, and unremitting perseverance...   Biographies/New Age Pages 424

Lip-Reading *by Edward Nitchie*   ISBN: *1-59462-206-X*   **$25.95**
Edward B. Nitchie, founder of the New York School for the Hard of Hearing, now the Nitchie School of Lip-Reading, Inc, wrote "LIP-READING Principles and Practice". The development and perfecting of this meritorious work on lip-reading was an undertaking...   How-to Pages 400

A Handbook of Suggestive Therapeutics, Applied Hypnotism, Psychic Science   ISBN: *1-59462-214-0*   **$24.95**
by Henry Munro   Health/New Age/Health/Self-help Pages 376

A Doll's House: and Two Other Plays *by Henrik Ibsen*   ISBN: *1-59462-112-8*   **$19.95**
Henrik Ibsen created this classic when in revolutionary 1848 Rome. Introducing some striking concepts in playwriting for the realist genre, this play has been studied the world over.   Fiction/Classics/Plays 308

The Light of Asia *by sir Edwin Arnold*   ISBN: *1-59462-204-3*   **$13.95**
In this poetic masterpiece, Edwin Arnold describes the life and teachings of Buddha. The man who was to become known as Buddha to the world was born as Prince Gautama of India but he rejected the worldly riches and abandoned the reigns of power when... Religion/History/Biographies Pages 170

The Complete Works of Guy de Maupassant *by Guy de Maupassant*   ISBN: *1-59462-157-8*   **$16.95**
"For days and days, nights and nights, I had dreamed of that first kiss which was to consecrate our engagement, and I knew not on what spot I should put my lips..."   Fiction/Classics Pages 240

The Art of Cross-Examination *by Francis L. Wellman*   ISBN: *1-59462-309-0*   **$26.95**
Written by a renowned trial lawyer, Wellman imparts his experience and uses case studies to explain how to use psychology to extract desired information through questioning.   How-to/Science/Reference Pages 408

Answered or Unanswered? *by Louisa Vaughan*   ISBN: *1-59462-248-5*   **$10.95**
Miracles of Faith in China   Religion Pages 112

The Edinburgh Lectures on Mental Science (1909) *by Thomas*   ISBN: *1-59462-008-3*   **$11.95**
This book contains the substance of a course of lectures recently given by the writer in the Queen Street Hall, Edinburgh. Its purpose is to indicate the Natural Principles governing the relation between Mental Action and Material Conditions...   New Age/Psychology Pages 148

Ayesha *by H. Rider Haggard*   ISBN: *1-59462-301-5*   **$24.95**
Verily and indeed it is the unexpected that happens! Probably if there was one person upon the earth from whom the Editor of this, and of a certain previous history, did not expect to hear again...   Classics Pages 380

Ayala's Angel *by Anthony Trollope*   ISBN: *1-59462-352-X*   **$29.95**
The two girls were both pretty, but Lucy who was twenty-one who supposed to be simple and comparatively unattractive, whereas Ayala was credited, as her Bombwhat romantic name might show, with poetic charm and a taste for romance. Ayala when her father died was nineteen...   Fiction Pages 484

The American Commonwealth *by James Bryce*   ISBN: *1-59462-286-8*   **$34.45**
An interpretation of American democratic political theory. It examines political mechanics and society from the perspective of Scotsman James Bryce   Politics Pages 572

Stories of the Pilgrims *by Margaret P. Pumphrey*   ISBN: *1-59462-116-0*   **$17.95**
This book explores pilgrims religious oppression in England as well as their escape to Holland and eventual crossing to America on the Mayflower, and their early days in New England...   History Pages 268

QTY

The Fasting Cure *by Sinclair Upton*   ISBN: *1-59462-222-1*   **$13.95**

In the Cosmopolitan Magazine for May, 1910, and in the Contemporary Review (London) for April, 1910, I published an article dealing with my experiences in fasting. I have written a great many magazine articles, but never one which attracted so much attention... New Age/Self Help/Health Pages 164

Hebrew Astrology *by Sepharial*   ISBN: *1-59462-308-2*   **$13.45**

In these days of advanced thinking it is a matter of common observation that we have left many of the old landmarks behind and that we are now pressing forward to greater heights and to a wider horizon than that which represented the mind-content of our progenitors... Astrology Pages 144

Thought Vibration or The Law of Attraction in the Thought World   ISBN: *1-59462-127-6*   **$12.95**

by William Walker Atkinson   Psychology/Religion Pages 144

Optimism *by Helen Keller*   ISBN: *1-59462-108-X*   **$15.95**

Helen Keller was blind, deaf, and mute since 19 months old, yet famously learned how to overcome these handicaps, communicate with the world, and spread her lectures promoting optimism. An inspiring read for everyone... Biographies/Inspirational Pages 84

Sara Crewe *by Frances Burnett*   ISBN: *1-59462-360-0*   **$9.45**

In the first place, Miss Minchin lived in London. Her home was a large, dull, tall one, in a large, dull square, where all the houses were alike, and all the sparrows were alike, and where all the door-knockers made the same heavy sound... Childrens/Classic Pages 88

The Autobiography of Benjamin Franklin *by Benjamin Franklin*   ISBN: *1-59462-135-7*   **$24.95**

The Autobiography of Benjamin Franklin has probably been more extensively read than any other American historical work, and no other book of its kind has had such ups and downs of fortune. Franklin lived for many years in England, where he was agent... Biographies/History Pages 332

Name	
Email	
Telephone	
Address	
City, State ZIP	

☐ **Credit Card**   ☐ **Check / Money Order**

Credit Card Number	
Expiration Date	
Signature	

Please Mail to: Book Jungle
PO Box 2226
Champaign, IL 61825
or Fax to: 630-214-0564

ORDERING INFORMATION

web: *www.bookjungle.com*
email: *sales@bookjungle.com*
fax: *630-214-0564*
mail: *Book Jungle PO Box 2226 Champaign, IL 61825*
or PayPal *to sales@bookjungle.com*

Please contact us for bulk discounts

DIRECT-ORDER TERMS

**20% Discount if You Order
Two or More Books**
Free Domestic Shipping!
Accepted: Master Card, Visa,
Discover, American Express